For Tomorrow

Wellbrook High
Yearbook 1993

First published in Great Britain in 2024 by
Black Shuck Books
Kent, UK

Set in Caslon & BN Chester by WHITEspace
www.white-space.uk

Cover design and interior layout © WHITEspace, 2024

978-1-913038-85-4

Editor's Note

I found the original yearbook for Wellbrook High's infamous Class of '93 in a poky second-hand bookshop off the Charing Cross Road. The cover attracted my attention – almost every detail had been blacked out with a permanent marker. When I opened it, the pages were similarly defaced. Some were drawn over, others torn or gouged with something sharp. Maybe half the text was still legible. Just enough to make out what it was, and where it came from.

Naturally, I bought it without hesitation.

What follows is a reconstruction of that yearbook, a chronicle of one of the strangest episodes in the history of British schools – and, more importantly, what came after. I've been aided in this project by some of the finest writers of weird and uncanny fiction. Without their insights and imagination, the story of the Wellbrook survivors might have stayed buried forever.

The rest of this book is part fiction, part truth. Make of it what you will.

Dan Coxon
July 2023

From the Headmaster

As many of you know, writing these little introductions to the yearbooks is usually one of my favourite tasks. Watching you begin your own lives in the world… it's surprisingly emotional, and catches me every time. I've been known to shed a few tears into my tea (no sugar, thank you!) as I pen them.

Unfortunately, like all of you, I've had other reasons to cry this year.

After the summer holidays, it was a joy to see the energy and enthusiasm with which you threw yourselves into your final three terms. There was the success of the county athletics trials to celebrate, and that glorious production of *Oh! What a Lovely War* to brighten the winter months. I speak for all the teaching staff when I say we were optimistic that we might have our strongest year yet. The work you were all putting in was, and still is, a credit to you.

Looking back, that feels like a different lifetime. I'm sure it's the same for you. The people we were then appear naïve and childish in hindsight. Our eyes have been opened in ways none of us could have anticipated. Like you, every day I wish they hadn't.

On behalf of the school and the governors, I can only apologise again for everything you've been through these past months. Yes, all our paperwork was filed correctly, and from a legal standpoint we did everything we could to ensure your safety and wellbeing. The fact of the matter is that none of us could have anticipated what would unfold in the spring of '93, or the fallout that all of you have endured. While many of you have now been officially discharged from hospital, I know the mental and psychic trauma is ongoing. What we experienced… I cannot put it down in words. Nor should I: it's bad enough that we should have suffered it, but I fear that writing it here, on the page, can only propagate its strange cancer.

Instead, let us look back, if we can, at the good times before 'The Event', and take comfort in the fact that we have not gone through this alone. No matter how strange and unsettling this year has been, at least you have each other. And I write from the heart when I say that I sincerely hope you'll be able to put what we experienced behind you, and live happy, productive lives.

All of which is a way of saying: enjoy this yearbook! It's been a pleasure to serve as your Headmaster, and you've all shown fortitude and resilience beyond your years. One day, I know, you'll be able to sleep through the night again; and when you do, maybe you'll forget what happened here, and remember only the friendships formed and the things you achieved.

Here begins the rest of your life. It may not be the life you thought you'd have… but it's yours nonetheless, the only one you get. Not all your class were so lucky.

Make the most of it, won't you?

John D. Maitland
Headmaster

Carrion

by

Lucie McKnight Hardy

You park your Corsa carefully in the driveway, nudging it up to the rear bumper of Jackie's car so that it doesn't obstruct the road. Not that there's much traffic to worry about around here; you have barely passed another car in the last hour or so, and for a short time you'd thought you were lost. Even though you remember this place from your childhood, it seems changed in a way you can't quite put your finger on. The lanes seem narrower and the hedges which flank them higher. The woodlands you glimpse briefly are, perhaps, denser.

It had been Jackie's idea that you meet up at her house. In the past you have always met somewhere halfway – a country hotel with a spa and a fancy restaurant, or a city break, with parks, art galleries, and museums to explore. It was silly, really, reuniting to commemorate the anniversary of The Event each year. It was a silent nod to a life-changing experience, you supposed, an acknowledgement that something profound had happened which had changed your lives forever. An event about which you have never spoken and never will.

You open the driver's door and ease your feet out onto the tarmacked drive. Rolling your shoulders, you feel the muscles complain about so many hours in the car, and then brace yourself to stand. After years of physiotherapy, you are more mobile now than ever, but still the pain in your legs and lower back persists, and you move slowly and awkwardly as you step away from the car and turn to survey the cottage.

It's smaller than you remember, and stands further away from any of its neighbours. In fact, you only passed a couple of houses while driving along the lane, and they'd had an air of abandonment about them. The curtains in one were half-drawn, as though someone had been on holiday and never returned, and another had a broken window at the front, the inside of which had been boarded over haphazardly with plywood.

Jackie's house displays a similar level of decay, not changed much from when her mum and dad owned it. You'd been surprised when she'd phoned with news of her parents' deaths – within a month of each other – and even more so when she'd announced she was moving back to their house. She'd explained that she'd come to terms with what had happened all those years ago, and thought she might be able to find peace there now. She had grand plans, she said, plans to renovate and turn the house into something new. Blow away the cobwebs. You'd felt apprehensive at the thought of returning after all these years, but the house is far away from where it happened, bordering the copse on the other side of town, the woodland where you made your den when you were teenagers forging a protective shield. That is what you tell yourself.

A glimpse of hair, black, a shriek of pale skin. Blurred eyes dark-ringed with kohl. Behind, in sharp focus, the oak tree, ancient, gnarled. Branches reach for the sky.

The cottage is a detached, shabby red-brick structure, like the others you've passed. It doesn't look as though the doors and windows have seen much attention since you were last here, thirty years ago – the paint is flaking and feathering. The curtains at the windows look tatty and unwashed, and the glass is grimy and smeared.

The front door has both an electric doorbell and a rusty iron door knocker. You select the doorbell first, and push it a couple of times. You hear the chime ring out somewhere at the back of the house, and wait for thirty seconds, preparing a smile for when Jackie's pale face and lank black hair appear from the other side. When she does not materialise, you lift the door knocker and rap harshly three times, but this still fails to elicit a response. You rummage in your handbag and pull out the photo album, which you hold awkwardly in the crook of your arm while fishing out your phone, but when you call Jackie's number, it just rings and rings until it goes to voicemail. Sighing, you look at your watch, feeling the first stab of irritation. Jackie is always so unreliable. You have been driving for more than four hours now, and she knew when you were due to arrive – it's not as though you've been held up. Not much, anyway.

You'd left home early that morning and come off the motorway where the satnav had instructed you. Over the next couple of hours the A-roads had given way to B-roads, which had eventually become a tree-lined track that ran between fields. When the object first appeared in front of you, your first thought was that perhaps it was a pile of leaves in the middle of the lane, or a branch that had been blown off one of the trees. You slowed the car, then came to a complete standstill six feet in front of the brown heap, and peered at it through the windscreen. What was it?

With a sudden shock of realisation you saw that it was fur, not leaves, that you were looking at. It was blocking your path; if you were to carry on the journey, you would have to either get out and move it, or mount the verge to drive around it, and you didn't think your ancient car's suspension would thank you for that. What was it? Badger? It was about the right size, but not the right colour. The fur was matted and wet in places, and a reddish brown. You could make out faint dirty-white blotches here and there. A dog.

You sat very still, silently pondering what to do, aware of the snow shovel still in the boot from last winter until, gradually, you became aware of a high-pitched, bubbling laughter. In a raucous clatter of black wings, a band of jackdaws appeared and landed on the animal.

There were half a dozen of them, and you watched in morbid fascination as they pecked hungrily at the flesh of the dead creature. Now and then, they would pause and look at you, glassy stares from dead eyes, and then, as if deciding you not to be of interest, they would casually return to stripping the meat from the carcass.

With no idea what to do, you considered getting out of the car and shooing them away, but something about the blank, arrogant way they looked at you made you uneasy. You beeped your horn a couple of times, and swished the windscreen wipers, but the jackdaws ignored you and continued to rip at the animal's flesh. You turned off the engine and sat, both repulsed and captivated, alert to the clock on the dashboard ticking through the minutes.

Suddenly, as though alerted by some unheard signal, the jackdaws took off, their glossy wings flapping untidily, taking them away and out of sight over the hedgerow. You started the engine, let off the handbrake, and eased the car up onto the verge, conscious of the scrape of its underbelly against a rock. Determinedly you kept your eyes straight in front of you.

Sitting on the broad bough of a tree, a cigarette just faintly visible between two fingers. Nails bitten, chipped Rimmel polish – Devil's Plum. Broad, drunken, dark purple smile against pale flesh.

You feel foolish, standing there on the doorstep, and when the rain starts – a passing shower that will soon flush itself out – you run back to the car. You try calling Jackie again, but have to resort to leaving a sternly worded voicemail, so then you sit for a while in the driver's seat, scrolling through your phone. Nothing on any of your social media feeds is of particular interest, but then you remember about the photo album, and remove it once again from your bag. It's an ancient thing, the blue vinyl cracked at the spine, and the plastic pockets inside are smeared and smudged with fingerprints. You'd been pleased when you'd found it last week, though. Clearing out boxes from the spare bedroom to make way for the decorators, it had seemed serendipitous to find the last one from your childhood, the one labelled *1993*. You'd sat for a while, sifting through the contents: a ball of scrunchies in various lurid leopard-print shades; a VHS of *Candyman* you'd pretended had been lost so you wouldn't have to return it to Blockbuster; the Swiss Army knife you'd stolen from someone at school, with which you and Jackie had cut your thumbs to swear eternal allegiance as blood sisters. And the photo album. Each page contained two photos, back to back, the colours faded now. Still, it had been more than thirty years since you'd taken the roll of film into Boots, the prints collected a week later, so what could you expect?

An arm cushioning a shoulder, giggling behind hands that barely conceal the grey yawn of a filling. Hair like tar mingles with blonde. A silver hooped earring catches the last of the sunlight.

The key is still in the same place after all these years. When you used to skip school and go to the woods, you'd sneak back to Jackie's house to collect her CD player and grab a couple of cans of Coke, topping them up from the vodka bottle in the sideboard. You'd collect the spare key from under the plant pot by the back door, and as long as you replaced it afterwards, Jackie's parents were none the wiser. The garden was long and narrow, Jackie's dad's pride and joy. The path to the woods lay between flower beds that would bloom in a succession of garish colours, and these gave way to raised beds in which grew vegetables and herbs. At the very bottom of the garden, in between two compost heaps, there was a stile over which you could climb to get to the copse where you'd made your den.

You didn't actually call it a den – such conceits were the things of childhood, and you were both teenagers, on the brink of adulthood. Long hours would be spent there, leaning against the trunk of the massive oak tree, smoking and sometimes drinking, listening to Sisters of Mercy and The Cure, inwardly smug at your adult taste in music. You had both rather self-consciously styled yourselves as indie kids at the end of year ten. Not the stupid flare-wearing, floor-gazing Manchester-obsessed James fans like half your year; instead you'd assumed a much darker identity. Jackie had embraced the look more than you had. You both wore your Doc Martens religiously, along with cut-off denim shorts over thick tights or black satin slip dresses, with second-hand black leather jackets or oversized cardigans to hide your burgeoning femininity. But it was Jackie who had dyed her long blonde hair raven black, and wore lengthy intricate necklaces and too much eyeliner, and lipstick the colour of chopped liver, a look she maintained to this day. You, however, had clung on to your perm and highlights. That was the essence of your relationship: Jackie the devil-may-care risk-taker, keen to try anything once, while you always held back, afraid to do anything too extreme, always egged on by your friend.

Caught in profile, hiding behind a Coke can. Obsidian hair nesting on shoulder. Silver chains adorn pale skin of neck. Faint smile for something out of shot.

You suspect the spare key hasn't been used in years: it is rusted and grimy, and it enters the keyhole reluctantly, yet still it turns under pressure. You push the door open cautiously, not wanting to alarm Jackie, even though you're pretty sure your friend must be out. She can't have ventured far – her car is still in the driveway – so she must have gone for a walk. To the woods, probably.

'Hello?' You know from horror films that this is what people always say in this situation, when they're entering a house and they're not sure if there's anybody there. There's no answer. 'Hello?' you repeat, this time a little louder, but still no reply. You step into the small hallway.

You pause, inhaling, and take in the woodchip wallpaper, the threadbare green carpet, and the brass wall lights. All unchanged after thirty years. There, along the walls, the watercolours of birds' eggs that Jackie painted all those years ago for her GCSE project, framed by her proud parents, even if she never did sit the exam. The startling blue of a robin's egg, its vivid hue preserved behind glass; the goldfinch egg, with its greeny-blue, brown-mottled surface; the perfect porcelain smoothness of the woodpigeon's egg. The paintings are all lifelike and detailed, faithful reproductions of the eggs you and Jackie collected from the nests you happened upon in the woods.

Standing in the apex of the tree, grinning, pointing at the bird's nest above her head. Inky hair stark against parchment skin. Eyes rendered red by the flash of the camera.

You remember that the kitchen is along the hallway, at the back of the house, and you snick the door shut behind you. Surely Jackie won't mind if you make yourself a cup of tea after your journey, especially as she can't be bothered to be here to meet you. You haven't had a cup since this morning and you're parched. You'd woken early, struggling to rise from a dream that had also felt like a premonition, just as the first light was starting to filter around the edges of the curtains. Even though you can't remember the dream now, it had clung to you for minutes after waking. While you lay there and sifted through the details, it had disappeared moments later, like smoke shifting on the wind. You were left only with a weariness and a mild sense of unease, which had dissipated slightly when the dawn chorus had begun. Earlier and earlier every day it comes now that spring is here, and it lifts your spirits every time.

You'd climbed carefully out of bed, and pulled on a dressing gown over your nightshirt. The pain in your legs was enough to necessitate you taking one step down the stairs at a time, while clutching at the bannisters. Once downstairs, you'd swallowed your painkillers and put the kettle on and looked out at the little back garden. Despite its position in one of the dullest parts on the outskirts of this bland northern town, you've managed to make it an oasis for wildlife – birds in particular – and you're rigorous in making sure the bird feeders are full and the bird table swept clean every day. While the kettle boiled, you'd selected a cup from the cupboard above the sink. Your favourite – an elegant porcelain thing, delicate and with the transparency of an eggshell.

Once your tea was brewed, you'd stepped out through the patio doors and closed them behind you. The sun was peering weakly over the horizon, partially obscured by a thick bank of cloud, the air damp. If today was like the last few days, that cloud would disappear by mid-morning, and it would turn out to be bright and lucid, if chilly. A fine coating of dew on the grass gleamed softly in the pale light. You clutched your cardigan around you, grateful for the warmth from the teacup.

You've positioned the bird table at the bottom of the garden – far enough from the house so that any human presence would not scare the birds away, but close enough to allow you to be able to identify each one, and to enjoy the idiosyncrasies of their behaviour. The first bird to alight on the table was a robin, one of your favourites. It was still pecking at the seed when a blackbird landed on the table, and the robin regarded it quizzically before relinquishing its space and darting away to the rowan tree at next door's boundary, where the berries hung, early-swollen, red and bloated like clots of blood. It was a male blackbird, bright-beaked and curious, and you liked to think it was the same one you had heard as you lay in bed that morning, its lilting song soothing you after the bad dreams. You tried once again to catch the memory of whatever it was that had visited you in the night, but it had slipped from your grasp completely.

A couple of sparrows visited next, and were joined by a wren. You were considering whether to go back into the kitchen and retrieve the birdseed from on top of the fridge, and whether the trek down to the bird table to replenish the food would be worth the inevitable sodden slippers, when the angry prattle of the magpies alerted you to their arrival. Sure enough, a few seconds later, there was a clatter of feathers and two black-and-white shapes appeared, talons already spread, and landed on the edge of the bird table, causing the smaller birds to flee in alarm.

A harsh anger rose in you. What right did those brutes have to that food? Bullies, using their size and power to overwhelm the smaller birds. Arrogant and menacing, the magpies had devoured what was left of the seed, and you'd watched, helpless, as they waited on the wooden rim of the bird table, regarding you haughtily. You'd held a vigil then, determined to wait them out, despite being cold in your thin nightshirt and dressing gown. In the end you'd grown impatient, and had run towards them, one arm windmilling, shouting incomprehensible noises, the now lukewarm tea sloshing against your chest. The birds had regarded you lazily, before flapping, unperturbed, to sit in the conifer at the bottom border of the garden and gaze at you. The porcelain cup had fallen from your fingers and smashed on the flagstones. You didn't know why, but you'd broken down then, and cried, all the while feeling the dew seeping through your ruined slippers.

A nest, broken, ragged on the ground. Eggs, four of them, cracked now, destroyed. And chicks, beaks agape, gasping. Black hair surrounds white face. Mouth open wide in horrified delight.

After The Event, pretty much everyone had flunked their GCSEs. You'd spent a year recovering from the worst of your injuries at the seaside town to which your parents had relocated the family, and resat your exams the following year. Your results were adequate and allowed you to study business at the town's sixth-form college, and you'd gone on to a long and unfulfilling career in admin at the county council.

Most of your classmates' families had moved away after The Event – in truth, very few of those who'd been affected wanted to remain after what had happened – but Jackie's family had stayed, shutting themselves away from the world in their little cottage on the edge of the woods. Instead of resitting her exams, Jackie had spent her days in her bedroom, drawing and painting and fine-tuning her ability as an artist. A short-lived and childless marriage – much like your own – had taken her away to a market town in the next county, where she'd established a successful studio and gallery, displaying her intricate paintings of birds and their eggs. Her parents' death had obviously hit her harder than she'd let on, you think, as you sit at her kitchen table, the room barely changed in thirty years.

You sip your tea and riffle through a stack of newspapers and magazines, trying to find something to read while you wait for her to return. You'd sent a couple of text messages after leaving the voicemail, your tone becoming increasingly abrupt as your annoyance at Jackie increased, telling her that you'd let yourself in and would help yourself to tea.

The sketchbook is at the bottom of the pile, hidden under a six-month-old *Countryfile* magazine and the dog-eared TV supplement from last week's *Daily Mail*. It is more of a journal, really – a plain, thick-papered A5 book, the pages of which each have a date written on them in Jackie's characteristic scrawl. Under each date is a drawing – a sketch of a different bird, some painted with watercolours, others coloured with pencils. The pictures are in Jackie's usual style – intricately detailed, the colours of the feathers bright and realistic, highlighted areas lifting the gloss of plumage or the flash of an eye. She really is very good, you think; you yourself have a couple of Jackie's paintings framed in your living room. As well as the drawings in the journal, there is text: sometimes full sentences – 'jays are shy woodland birds, and difficult to spot. They will sometimes announce their presence with a screeching call' and 'cuckoos are summer visitors and well-known brood parasites'. There are also bullet-pointed lists of what each bird would eat: 'insects, seeds and nuts' or 'slugs, snails, beetles and earthworms'.

As you turn the pages, you become aware of a changing pattern. Whereas the earlier pages, dated the previous month, contain delicately drawn, painstakingly coloured illustrations with detailed descriptions of the birds depicted, as the entries continue the text becomes sparser, the sketches more haphazard and ill-defined. The colours, too, change. They are darker in the later pages, and you realise they are all either monochrome or black. Magpies at first, then jackdaws and crows and, finally, on the last page, a raven.

This last journal entry makes you wince. The drawing has been scratched deep into the paper with a sharp pen – a fountain pen by the look of it, that has pressed too deep and rendered the image through the paper and into the pages beneath. Ink spatters sully the top page, and the strokes of the pen possess a savage energy that suggests they have been made by someone consumed with rage or hatred. Before you throw the journal back onto the table, you note that the date on the last page is today's.

Scratches in the dust form the lines and curves of letters on a makeshift Ouija board. An upturned Coke can serves as an improvised planchette. Silver rings adorn long fingers.

There is a muffled *flump*, and you look up to catch a glimpse of dark feathers and the faint imprint of a powdery residue on the outside of the window. You think you know what it is before you stand and go to the back door. You brace yourself, open it, and step out into the damp air.

It is a crow. Its neck is bent at an impossible angle, and as you bend over it, you can see a smear of something wet around its nostrils which you assume to be blood. The one eye that you can see is blinking rapidly, the pupil expanding and contracting in the cold blue iris. Glossy black feathers are ruffled by the breeze and the bird's legs and feet are jutting out, the claws curling and uncurling. You know you should put it out of its misery and your stomach roils, recalling the dead creature you came across on your journey earlier. An unexpected anger rises in your chest, but this time it is not directed at the bird. You shouldn't have to be the one to deal with this. This is Jackie's house, and this should be Jackie's problem.

You don't bother to lock the back door behind you as you set off down the garden, such is your rage. The ground is soggy beneath your feet. You feel the dampness edging into your trainers and think of your ruined slippers back home. Of course, the weather would be different down here compared to there. It is certainly more overcast here than it was when you set off that morning, and despite it only being late afternoon, there is a sallowness to the sky that suggests another rainstorm may not be far off.

You enter the woods by climbing over the stile at the bottom of the garden, the timber worn smooth through regular use, and you picture Jackie walking in the woods, photographing and sketching the birds that inhabit it. Your hand absentmindedly strokes the photograph album in your coat pocket. As you walk, the trees grow thicker, and the path narrower, and you start to doubt your ability to find the oak tree again. It's been thirty years. The tree might have been chopped down, or damaged in the storms a few years back. But it is as though an internal map is switched on and your body moves instinctively in the direction of the den, an automaton programmed by history.

As you move you become aware of a noise that is increasing in volume. It exists on many layers; like an orchestra, the sounds are distinct yet come together as one, but not like the uplifting melody of the dawn chorus. This is the scream of the jays, the machine-gun chatter of the magpies, the hoarse croak of the crows. And aligned with that is the insistent caw of the raven. Corvids, all. The racket is all around you, a clamour of sound that engulfs you and draws you onwards.

So intent are you on your journey that you don't notice the sketchbook trodden into the ground, the loose pages mud-spattered and torn. You don't notice the pencils, scattered in an arc around you, their bright colours at odds with the shadows and the leaf mould. You don't notice the mobile phone, partially obscured by the sharp twigs and mossy curves of a fallen nest.

You don't notice them because your eyes are entirely focused on Jackie, sitting propped against the broad trunk of the oak tree, its branches soaring above her in a victory salute. Her long necklaces have been pulled tight around her neck, a garotte. A flash of white, a tangle of black. And red. So much red.

You try to run, but the pain in your legs and your lower back forces you to the ground, the touch of dampness through your clothes incongruous in your terror. And then the stabbing. Your neck, the soft flesh of your throat, your chin and cheeks. White fire of pain. Dark feathers clatter.

Blind, now. Your eyes, plucked like berries and taken, leaving you clawing at the spaces where they had once been.

Corvids, all. We don't forget.

Lucie McKnight Hardy's stories have featured in a variety of publications, including Best British Short Stories 2019, The Lonely Crowd, Uncertainties IV, The New Abject, Black Static *and as a limited edition chapbook from Nightjar Press. Her debut novel,* Water Shall Refuse Them, *was published by Dead Ink Books in 2019. Of her second book,* Dead Relatives, The Guardian *said, 'This short story collection confirms the author's reputation in the field of literary horror.'*

Finger and Palm

by

Malcom Devlin & Helen Marshall

In the years that followed, he saw her everywhere. She was in the street, in the park; she was a face in every crowd. He saw her dressed as she had been the last time he'd seen her: jean shorts, sneakers and his own olive-green hooded sweater, its arms long enough to cover her fists. Later, he remembered she told him she'd wear blue when they met again, and from then on the hoodie he saw her in was navy, periwinkle, teal, aquamarine.

She was at his wedding, standing at the back of the church, behind the congregation. He was certain he saw her while he made his vows and it had felt like a weight had been lifted from his shoulders. Afterwards, when he noticed the royal blue velvet curtains of the confessional bunched in a slim hourglass, the realisation she might not have been there troubled him more.

In the taxi from the airport, it occurred to him he might no longer recognise her. The Valerie he saw each day was still sixteen years old. The thirty-four-year-old Valerie and the thirty-four-year-old Barney were strangers. The only metric he had to recognise her was the colour she'd promised, and he'd spent the years fixating on so many shades and variations he wasn't certain it would be enough. Again, he felt a well opening inside him. It had been there since they'd parted that day, growing deeper as the years had passed, yawning wider as the date approached. He'd felt it hollow him out as he'd kissed Marta goodbye. *A work trip*, he'd told her, his tone artful in its carelessness. From the look she gave him, touching her belly gently as she did these days, the lie had seared them both – and no wonder, the one falsehood had already swollen to encompass others.

Marta had family around Jiříž and over the last months she'd talked often about returning, seeing old friends, her vast network of great aunts and second cousins. If he'd told her where he was going, of course she'd have wanted to come. It was for the best, he thought as he closed the door between them. Whatever that meant.

The traffic snarled around the taxi. Six lanes going nowhere. It was hard to make out the shape of the city from the bypass, but there was a cool clear pearlescence to the morning haze which reminded him of the Mediterranean. The buildings the taxi crawled past were pale grey and sandy coloured, the fringe landscape of warehouses and industrial yards felt dusty and raw.

His driver leaned on the horn and muttered something under his breath.

'Is the traffic normally this bad?' Barney said.

'I'm sorry?' the driver said.

'The traffic.'

A fraction of the driver's face appeared in the rear-view and regarded Barney sitting in the back seat. The face in the driver's licence glared at him in tandem from the lanyard hanging from the mirror. Alek Kocur: a young man, gaunt, his tracksuit top zipped to his chin.

He said something in the local dialect. 'Festival,' he added in English. A hand appeared then returned to the wheel, a stunted, frustrated gesture. 'Everyone wants to see. Everyone wants to run.'

The eye met him in the mirror again.

'You're here for the festival.'

Barney shook his head. 'No.'

The driver held him a moment longer. Behind them, horns blared.

'You're here for the chase, then.'

'The chase?'

'Sanctuary chase. Break your nose.'

'I'm just meeting a friend.'

The driver nodded.

'Traffic normally fine.' He returned his attention to the road. 'Fine. First time in Jiříž, is it?'

'First time.'

'Jiříž is also fine. A place for lovers, they say.' Then he laughed, an angry sound.

The taxi driver said he was from the countryside, but that meant little to Barney. The city took up so much of the tiny principality there didn't seem to be much room for anything else. It occupied the banks of the sprawling delta of the River Spišta, nestled in a tangled knot of shifting borders. Barney had seen it referred to – with varying degrees of qualified romanticism – as both Venice-in-the-Marshes and Prague-in-the-Shadows. From the guidebooks he'd found, the walled medieval town centre was still pristine. A web of inhabited bridges criss-crossing the river's streams, each cobbled and cluttered with narrow shops and houses stacked like shoeboxes. The eccentricity of the old town had been diluted by surrounding development, where the aesthetic was more prosaic. A sprawl of grimly practical concrete and steel building blocks from the Communist planning playbook, familiar to other parts of Eastern Europe.

Barney had chosen a hotel in the old town. A small place nestled between a bakery and a glass-blowing gallery only a few hundred yards from Union Bridge. The owner, an elderly woman in a bright red housecoat and matching spectacles, greeted him as though he were a lost son, stepping out from behind the reception desk to envelop him in a small but fierce hug.

His room, she assured him, was the best in the house. She drew back the curtains and demonstrated how, if one stood by the window *just so*, the arch of the bridge itself could be seen in the very periphery.

'You're here for the festival.' Again, it didn't feel like a question.

'No.' Barney smiled as though an apology was in order. 'I'm meeting someone.'

'An old friend.'

He nodded. 'I hope so.'

The Union Bridge was the only bridge in Jiříž to cross the main tributary of the river. It divided the city into roughly two halves, wasp-waisted across the rushing water. It was a handsome enough structure: eight broad arches and wrought-iron balustrades. Statues of saints occupying the podiums spaced along its northern flank.

The real bridge felt subdued compared to the print on the wall of Mrs Reisland's cramped office. The unsparing daylight was unflattering and diffuse against the crisp, dreamy Kodachrome of the photograph. Even then, he had barely seen the picture until Valerie had invoked it.

They'd been waiting to be picked up. Taken home. Told everything was all going to be alright despite everything that had happened.

He hadn't wanted to be taken home without her. He'd wanted to stay with her; wanted nothing more than to look at her, but she couldn't meet his eyes. The sense that something had broken inside of them was overwhelming but he didn't want to speak of it in case he made it true. He remembered trying to take her hand – still balled in the sleeve of the hoodie he'd given her to wear. She'd moved away. A small shake of the head.

She read the room as though she were reading tarot cards. When she spoke, her voice was so quiet, so measured, it barely sounded like her at all. If they were serious, she said, if what they had was *true*, then they need to understand two things. First, that it was over. Second, that it wouldn't be forever.

Before he could ask what she meant, she rushed ahead. She already had a plan. If he loved her, and if she loved him, then they should meet once they were both older, once they'd both lived enough to shake off what had happened.

They should meet at the Union Bridge (in the photograph behind Mrs Reisland's desk), on this day in eighteen years' time (the number on the football shirt, folded and framed on the wall to the right) and she would be wearing blue (the colour of the door to the left).

He knew what she was doing. Counteracting the madness of the day with a spell of chance. She smiled at him and the door opened and their parents bustled in and the moment broke like a thread of spider silk.

Barney called Marta during the night. He told her he'd arrived but had to remember where he had told her he was. A siren passed by on the street outside.

'Sleep well,' Marta said, and another siren passed at her end of the phone back home and he was oddly moved. It felt like a connective thread between them. The sense of doom grew. He told her he loved her before he hung up and he meant it. Was it possible to love two people? Did one love need to eclipse another?

He'd always imagined that love was a river he'd dipped his toes into but had never been brave enough to cross. Listening to the empty phone, he felt a sense of disorientation, as though he'd been on the opposite riverbank all along.

He swore he saw Valerie at the hotel reception the next morning. Her back was to him as the old cage elevator cranked him downwards. Her hair still shoulder-length and dirty blonde, the dress she wore was blue. She seemed to be exchanging some heated words with the hotel's owner and had left before the elevator doors had fully opened.

The owner was also wearing blue: a new housecoat and matching glasses. She stopped him before he could follow; her hand rested on his forearm with insistence.

'Your friend,' she said. 'Choose with care and be well.' Her smile was cautious, impatient. He was half-convinced she was close to tears.

He went out into the street and, searching, saw Valerie again, or thought he did. The currents of people carried him bodily towards the bridge. It was still early, but the day was already ripe, thick with murmurs and music, children sat on parents' shoulders so they could better see, coloured bunting spilled from windows and hung in trees. A flotilla of fishing boats threaded the river.

The street opened out once they reached the bridge. A racetrack cordoned off in the middle of the road, ropes on either side. A bandstand near the entrance, a small quintet, all brass and accordions accentuating the tempo of the crowd.

It was only when he got to the bridge that he realised he felt less carried by the crowd than guided by it. He felt eyes on him and there was something invasive about the attention now they'd reached their destination. He felt gentle hands on the small of his back, *pushes* urging him onwards. A runner passed him, close enough to touch: a mad, free-wheeling grin, a flash of teeth.

He tried to turn but another body passed him, blood streaming down his face. Barney staggered away but there was a handprint on his jacket, five fingers of crimson, like a gory lapel flower.

Going back felt impossible. The shifting crowd was dense, the currents too strong, the growing slaughterhouse scent both sweet and repellent.

Ahead of him, he saw Valerie, and he lunged towards her as though she might save him. But his certainty faltered and he saw he was mistaken. There were so many women wearing blue on the Union Bridge. So many women with shoulder-length blonde hair. And they each turned to see him as he came close, they each smiled at him as though they'd been expecting him.

'Marta,' he said, but Marta wasn't there.

Around him the sheer colour of clothes and costumes coalesced and he saw Valerie. He saw Valerie and knew he had been right, that he had loved her, that he had not been wrong to come.

He saw her everywhere and something inside him grew dark and vast, threatening to eclipse him entirely – for he was wrong, too, as he had always been wrong. He wanted to turn away, hail a taxi, go home.

He heard music; he heard a distant cry. Blackness enveloped him and he felt as though he was somehow *falling in size*: diminishing into something tiny and insignificant and unseen, cast adrift like a mote of dust. Blind, he raised a hand – desperate, half-hearted – and hoped someone might see him before he drowned.

2

Verdigris was the kind of person you fell in love to: like a power ballad from the eighties, a song that unknitted all that shy awkwardness, half-bravado and uncertainness.

She went by the name Verdigris now. She told herself it was because she was a performer and it was the kind of eccentric name a performer might have. She didn't want to admit it had something to do with the sweater she had taken. Olive green. It had matched the shade of the patinaed domes of the Basilica in Mrs Reisland's picture. She had worn that sweater when she left for university, a little afraid, a little relieved. She hadn't told Barney where she had been accepted. Hadn't wanted him to write. She knew it wasn't real love between them.

After all, Barney hadn't been the first, had he?

The first had been two years earlier, a chubby-faced boy named Philip who was good at maths and never afraid to raise his hand. At fourteen neither of them had known what they were supposed to do. They had shared a tub of popcorn at the movies and afterwards his tentative kiss had tasted of salt and cheese flavouring. He had said he loved her that night and she had wanted to believe him. But then a month later he had pulled her aside in rush between classes and told her that he really loved another girl, her name was Sarah.

The love between Sarah and Philip had been genuine, hers counterfeit. She heard they were still together now, Philip sticking by Sarah, visiting her in the hospital even though it had been close to twenty years since the accident.

After Philip had been Gary and then Sayeed and each of them had said they had loved her, then each had the same awkward conversation after, sometimes two weeks later, sometimes as many as six. They were all happy now, even Philip. She had seen Philip the day before her thirtieth birthday, a chance meeting when she had gone into the same hospital after her mum had a fall. He had looked good. He had looked happy. He had said as much as they shared a coffee and bad café fish fingers – that he was happy now, and Verdigris had seen the glint in his eyes and known he wasn't lying.

She had asked about Barney then. She hadn't meant to but of course she did and of course Barney was married now too. To whom? Philip hadn't known. Maybe it had been someone from his new school. Maybe it had been Mrs Reisland's daughter. The timing would have been right.

In university her friends set her up on blind dates and without fail the man or woman who bought her drink or paid for her dinner would get that same glint in their eye. The phone calls would stop soon after, the offers of a second, a third date.

It was how she had started singing at the club. One of her dates – Jacob, a little sweaty, but with a freshly ironed shirt at least – had offered her the gig in consolation after he confessed that he had finally had the nerve to tell Emmanuel, the taciturn bartender, why he insisted on helping with closing up each night.

Jacob and Emmanuel were practically delirious now. They had named a cocktail after her: gin, triple sec and blue curacao – with a dash of bitters.

Verdigris sang at the club most nights and most nights there was a spontaneous proposal. Jacob often rolled his eyes and made gagging sounds but then she had sung those lines about sitting alongside someone like finger and palm and he had been climbing up onto a table to offer Emmanuel a ring. She wished them well. She knew she'd get an invitation to the wedding. She had a stack of such invitations and a closet full of dresses to match.

Finger and palm.

It was an old folk song from Jiříž. She sang it the way she imagined Alison Krauss might, with a bluegrass edge.

She had been thinking of Barney when she sang it. How he'd wanted to take her hand. She hadn't let him do it. She was trying to be gentle. He'd said he loved her and she'd known he didn't so she wanted to be kind to him, let him off the hook, stop him from making a fool of himself.

She was thirty-four now.

She asked Jacob for a few weeks off. He scrunched up his lips, he mopped the sweat from his head and pleaded with her to wait a couple of months, the club was doing great and he needed the receipts, he still had to pay off the honeymoon they were planning. But she hadn't taken a week off in five years and they both knew it. She found a cover. The cover was fine but the cover wasn't her. It felt good to be wanted.

She packed the dresses from her closet. There were seventeen of them, all of them various shades of blue, but when she arrived at the airport it turned out her luggage hadn't made it onto the plane.

'Is festival,' said the woman at the airline customer service desk. A spark of anger in her eye, a hint of violence. She was wearing blue.

Then at the market Verdigris leafed her way through a rack of summer dresses but none of them were blue either. The old woman minding the stall shrugged apologetically. She was also wearing blue.

Fuck it. She would wear red. Why not? Why not wear red? It wasn't like Barney was coming, was he? And if he was coming, if he did love her, then it wouldn't matter what colour she was wearing.

When Verdigris left the stall, she could hear music playing. There were cymbals and psalteries, there was something that could have been the blade of a sword except it twanged like a handsaw.

She saw a group of men stripped down to their waists, sleek and sinuous. But their faces were wrong, all wrong. Cracked bones, allowed to heal badly. A starting gun sounded.

Then the band began, playing 'Finger and Palm', but it wasn't the way she had sung it. It was faster, more insistent, more militant.

She saw open mouths but none of them were singing. They were making this noise, a susurrus, the sound of wind running over the lip of a bottle. Breath waiting to be formed into words.

Then she understood. You had to be an expert to be able to tell these things. And even though she played in a shitty club in a shitty part of town, she had studied at the Royal Academy of Music, and she had come top of her class. She knew music. She could feel the itchy rhythm in the soles of her feet, yes, in her fingers and in her palms.

They were waiting. Waiting for a voice like hers. Waiting for something to fill in the gaps, to give them shape, to find a form for whatever joy-seeking spirit lived inside them.

Glances slid her way, glances from women swathed in blue, glances from moustachioed men in olive-green sweaters. Men who looked like Barney and women who looked like— not her, not Verdigris, but sweet-faced, colt-legged Valerie, with that shock of dirty blonde hair she'd since dyed platinum because when you were thirty-four and singing in a shitty club you either had to be young or you had to be distinctive.

She wasn't young anymore.

She wasn't the kind of girl who believed if you held hands at a high school dance then it meant you were in love, that the boy you were dancing with was feeling the same thing that you were.

She understood about asymmetry now, how it could be beautiful if you let it. That maybe when you whispered those words about trying to hold a candle in the cold November rains while his hand brushed the small of your back then you were calling up some kind of disaster for yourself. Weren't the best love songs like that? Songs of wanting, songs of unfulfilled desire? Songs about needing someone, songs about heartbreak and loneliness and the shadow you can't ever quite banish no matter how close to love you let yourself come?

And she understood about verdigris. That there were kinds of damage you could decorate yourself with, and maybe it didn't make you wiser or fancier or better but it could make it *seem* that way.

It was why she had always loved the idea of Jiříž. She had loved the idea of it because she had never thought she would go, not her, not sweet-sixteen Valerie who had made a promise she had never intended to keep.

But here she was anyway. She was wearing red and she was on her way to Union Bridge to see if the boy she had almost-maybe loved would be waiting for her.

He's married, she thought, but it didn't matter.

He won't remember, she thought, but that didn't matter either.

Because now the song was welling up inside of her, like an underground stream breaking through the rocks. And she could see what it was doing to the people around her, what it did every time she sang like that.

They were making room for her, they were urging her onward. The song flew out of her, bright and glorious as the first sunrise after the day the bad thing happened, when she realised she was still alive, broken maybe, but still breathing.

And this time she didn't hold back. Not like she did all those other times, with Philip and Martin and Sayeed and then after with the countless Jacobs and Glorias and Janets and Callums and Karis that had followed. Those times she pushed them up to the point of love but never past it, never beyond love to the thing that lay after.

3

When Alek withdrew, the American girl laughed. As he rolled onto his back, palming the condom into a rosette of tissues, he wondered if it was his place to judge if her soft chuckle was a cruel laugh or a happy one. Her eyes were closed, the smile slipping from her face as she let sleep finish whatever he'd started.

Marta had never laughed when they'd been intimate. She'd been the one who'd taught him that unlike everything else in the world, sex wasn't a race. Harmonies, she said, were sweeter than a single rude note. Marta used to say things like that during sex. It was maddening.

The American girl had a name but Alek wasn't certain he'd heard it correctly. *Sky Lark?* It seemed too strange to him to be true. She was in town for the Festival.

They'd met in the bar in the Rua Lia where, when the taxi lay dormant, he sometimes took shifts. She'd made a beeline for him across the room because – she said – he was the only man she'd met in the whole *fucking* town who didn't seem to have a broken nose. He let her touch it to be sure, and that barrier passed, the night slipped into a pleasant kind of companionship until he was ready to lock up.

On the way back to his apartment, the subject moved to the Sanctuary Chase.

'So you've never done it?'

'Every year.' Drink made him a braggart and he hated that. 'The others get to the bridge and suddenly they're convinced they'll see heaven. You get that far, why would you not want to give it a chance? Me, I don't believe in heaven. I believe in here and now.'

—

He thought of Sky Lark the following week when he waited at the start line. He thought of her again when the starting pistol had been fired and he'd already broken free of the usual mob of tanked-up fun runners. Alek was slim and lithe. He was athletic, but not *only* athletic. He knew well enough that the race was as much to do with faith and skill as it was about raw physical endurance.

When Otto Chvátal had instigated the first Sanctuary Chase back in the twelfth century, he'd been running for his life. One morning, he'd woken on the wrong side of the town in the wrong bed and with the sun on the rise, every cuckolded husband with a knife seemed to be looking for him.

Some called him the First Lover, but of course that was impossible – Chvátal was a libertine, really, and anyway, the *Prikopiya* were far older than him.

Chvátal had even written on that, in his later years. He was neither a separatist nor a unionist and would delight in arguing against either side. His position was that should The Lovers meet, they should just fuck each other then move on.

'Union *and* separation,' he would argue. 'It's the only way to please everyone.'

Such philosophy, Alek reasoned, was likely not on his mind as he ran for his life. Alek had often imagined the scene in unnecessary detail. Marta had encouraged him to imagine Otto emerging into the street, the morning sunlight exposing him, but every shadow he passed was sharpened by hidden blades.

'He felt like a stranger in his own city.' Marta had thought about things like this a lot. Her knowledge of the city's history ran deeper than the surface-level festivities. She was the one who first told Alek about the Sanctuary Chase in a way that finally made sense to him. 'These sorts of stories are important,' she said.

On the day of the chase, Chvátal put himself in the hands of a God he only believed in when his fortunes were poor. When it came to saving his own skin, he was not proud, he would prostate himself before the Cardinal and claim sanctuary at the Basilica of Saint Agnes-Outside-The-Walls.

The route Otto Chvátal ran was still honoured. Alek knew it well, he drove it every day.

It began at the corner of Pope Pius Parade, where Chvátal had spent the night. The route twisted through the artists' quarter and across the Union Bridge. At the south end of the bridge, the rear wall of the Basilica rose in a sheer cliff of the local red stone, its posture supercilious, its back to the river. Here, the road doubled back on itself twice before plunging into the labyrinth of cobbled streets that eventually led to the Basilica's façade.

But Otto Chvátal never made the turn.

At the end of the bridge he was overcome with a vision telling him to keep running. It was said a pair of ornate double doors appeared before him and opened wide with (Alek assumed) the sound of a heavenly choir. The sinner, Otto Chvátal, ran through without pause and was forever changed. Years later, having been ordained Cardinal himself, he would claim to have glimpsed paradise on the way.

The official route of the Sanctuary Chase took the long road to the Basilica's facade, but only Alek and a few others bothered with the turn at the end of the bridge.

So many others, perhaps made light-headed with dehydration and the exertion of the route's ups and downs over bridges and hills, found themselves overcome with a sudden piety, believing wholeheartedly the magical doors from Chvátal's story would appear and open for them as well. Crossing the bridge made believers of almost all the runners.

As a consequence, the red rear wall of the Basilica was now buckshot with dark carnations of dried blood, where generations of men (and they *were* mostly men) had – their noses preceding them by a dangerous fraction – refused to turn and refused to stop at the end of the Union Bridge. No magical doors appeared, the stone wall remained impassive, and with a splinter of cartilage and a minor concussion their new-found zealotry was tested and found wanting.

Even years later, the volume of casualties remained startlingly high. The doors would only open for the purest of hearts, some said. The doors would only open if the runner was at a particular speed, said others. The doors would only open for the reincarnation of Otto Chvátal.

Alek didn't believe in The Lovers, and he certainly had no time for Otto Chvátal's preposterous fairy tale. To him, it was a miserable story of a fun-loving young man who had knocked his head and turned desperately straight and dull. Saint Otto, Full-of-Ardour – Saint Otto, Full-of-Shit.

Alek turned the corner of the bridge each and every year. He made it to the Basilica unbloodied and in good time. In each of the past eight years he'd been one of the fastest twenty runners and his time was improving.

This year would be no different. He'd seen the plump young men who had travelled far to get here. He'd seen them waiting for the starting pistol with rosaries hung around their necks, crucifixes clasped in their hands. Some wore makeshift helmets and straps over their noses as though they could protect themselves in advance. None of them wanted to win the race, they only wanted to *see*.

Alek's only faith was that this year, finally, he would be first.

All those years ago, Marta had been the one who'd first encouraged him to run, waiting in Pope Pius Parade with a stopwatch in her hand. When she'd run away herself and left him with only a fury he didn't know where to put, he told himself he no longer ran for her. There was a modest cash prize for winning the race, but being first, with the only unbroken nose in town? He thought of the American girl again and remembered the sound of her laugh.

By the time he reached the north end of the bridge, he had a good sense most of his serious competitors had fallen behind. The straight line of the bridge focused him. He ignored the onlookers cordoned off behind the barriers.

The wall of the Basilica rose up before him like a raised palm. Already, he was preparing his line: the turn was sharp and he would inevitably lose speed, but if he softened the corner, if he timed things just right—

It was here, just as he entered the shadow of the dog-headed statue of St Christopher, that he heard the woman singing.

Alek didn't believe in The Lovers. He wasn't certain he believed in love. He'd heard stories about people falling in love at first sight, of course, but they seemed every bit as far-fetched as the stories he'd heard about magical doors opening in solid stone walls.

He didn't look back, but he *saw* anyway. Flickering memories projected vastly across the bright wall of the Basilica. Some were old: his father turning his face away the day he left. Marta lit gold by the evening light. Some were from only moments ago: the north end of the bridge. The bandstand. A woman. *The* woman in red.

She should have been wearing blue, he thought.

Behind him, she sang and her voice had the sharp, perfect clarity of a fingertip tracing the rim of a crystal glass. It cut through him as he ran, moving every part of him until it commanded every sense of his purpose.

No doors appeared in the Basilica wall, but the wall opened before him regardless. The stones turned inwards and he saw a ripe, raw passageway unclench, narrowing into a distant darkness.

If this wasn't paradise, it was at least something he believed he'd already had a measure of.

Alek didn't turn. He didn't slow down. He took a breath and entered.

4

'Fuck!' yelled Marta Svoboda as another contraction ripped through her. Her voice was too loud, now too English, and far too profane for such a holy space. 'Fuck' echoed back to her from the glittering mosaiced domes, from the ornately carved pews, from the statues of The Lovers themselves.

It had been years since she had been in this place, once so beloved to her. Years since she had been to Jiříž. For a time she had sworn she would never go back, yet here she was. You could leave Jiříž, it was said, but you could never *leave* Jiříž.

It had been difficult growing up in a foreign country. Though she had shaved the edge off her accent, had learned the intricacies of English life – which greetings were politely cutting and which were merely reserved – Jiříž had imprinted itself on her. She had a Jiřížian way of walking, a Jiřížian way of keeping her papers close, counting her change, a Jiřížian way of touching her nose to ward off bad fortune.

Her mother had relocated them to avoid such imprimaturs but even *she* had had difficulty shaking off her roots. In the Festival month she would still order pig snouts from the local butcher, boil them, and serve them with apples just as she herself had done growing up.

And Marta had *loved* Jiříž once, loved it deeply and blindly the way you loved things when you were fourteen years old. While her English friends had been dancing to bubblegum pop divas and practising French kissing, she had been dressing in blue and cheering the men lined up for the Sanctuary Chase.

Back then, she had been a unionist. Most of the girls in her age group were. They would stand together on the bridge, shouting and throwing flowers, or else combing the crowds for a sign that this year The Lovers had come.

Her first English boyfriend had laughed at her for it.

'Really? You believed, what? It sounds like Santa Claus but, you know, with—' He made a circle and slipped a finger into it because the word 'fuck' made him turn bright red.

He was nothing like the boys she had known back in Jiříž, brawny but insecure, yet his look of scorn had filled her with a startlingly electric sense of loathing. For herself, for her mother, for everything she had believed with such childish conviction.

It was only a few years before that her friends back in Jiříž used to take turns imagining how it would be when The Lovers finally came. What would they choose? Would they nudge them or undermine them? 'Of course I wouldn't help,' said her best friend Krissa, an adamant separatist, who admitted years later that she'd only taken that position to make herself seem more interesting. 'If I had a pistol then I'd shoot the *Prikopova* right in the back of her skull. Ha! Bam, bam, bam. And then that would be it, wouldn't it? We'd all be free.'

'That's not how it *works*,' Marta would explain, gritting her teeth. Back then she had memorised the intricacies of The Lovers' lore, historical *and* apocryphal. 'They have to choose. It doesn't mean anything if one of them is dead. Then they weren't really The Lovers, were they?'

Krissa just shrugged and bit the inside of her lip, bored with the topic already.

But Marta hadn't been bored. She was enraptured.

It was only years later, when she took a course in Folklore in her second semester of university, that she began to see what the myth meant to Jiříž, how it fascinated precisely because of its expediency, how it could take chance and happenstance and pure superstition, and elevate them into something greater.

But by then it was too late for her.

Still, she understood how it could happen. It had felt the same when she had learned she was pregnant. Suddenly every tiny detail of her changing body was a clue, a potential threat, a wondrous portent. She visited the message boards, followed comment trails into the deep recesses of the internet. She learned it was possible to lactate from supernumerary nipples in your armpit, your crotch, and she searched her body for previously overlooked moles. She watched her belly expand like a great dome, watched the steeple point of a foot emerge and recede again. The further she descended, the more she was reminded of Jiříž: grandmothers whispering that if you slept with a man with an unbroken nose your child would be healthy and strong.

Barney had an unbroken nose, but then so did most of the men she met outside of Jiříž. It was why civic law demanded the tavernas offer foreigners their first and last drink for free – good for tourism, they claimed, but really it was just about demographics.

Now here she was, doing her part for the great principality of Jiříž. She breathed out raggedly and forced herself to waddle towards the pews. She felt large and ungainly, kept her hand clutched protectively around her burgeoning belly.

'Please!' she hissed as the next contraction squeezed her insides. She doubled over, felt the baby kick and squirm.

When she was through the worst of it, she shuddered and fought for breath. There were tears on her face. She was at the foot of the great statue of the *Prikopiya*. She looked up and there he was, Barney, larger than life, his gentle face – weak chin, squidgy nose – depicted in green porphyry. He positively gleamed with tenderness. And the woman he reached towards was equally ordinary but the folds of her long, flowing dress had been carved from lapis lazuli.

Would their reaching hands ever touch? Or would they turn away from each other? The artist had been chosen for her neutrality and so the statue itself revealed nothing.

If they joined, it was said that Jiříž would stand for another hundred years, exactly as she was. The land would be fruitful, its people abundant. But if they separated? It meant hard times were coming: war and revolution, after which a new city would emerge.

Mostly, The Lovers united, of course. Jiříž was one of the longest continually occupied areas on the continent. It had been founded by an ancient tribe nearly eight millennia ago. But then the Thracians had come (the *Prikopova* had been pledged by her greedy father to another), the Greeks afterwards (the *Prikopova* had been a slave and unable to marry), and then the Turks (the families of The Lovers had sworn a blood feud upon each other), before it had finally achieved independence following a bloody revolution (the *Prikopov* fell in love with a chandler's daughter and moved to America).

Now Marta could hear the *boom* of the starting pistol. The crowds cheered as the Sanctuary Race began.

Where was the priest? Where was the rest of the congregation? Where was anyone who could help her? She knew the answer: at Union Bridge. They were waiting to greet The Lovers.

Inside she felt a quickening. The contractions were coming faster, faster than she had been warned to expect. Now her fingernails were digging into her palms as she huddled beneath the statue. She felt scared and alone. Barney should have been here, of course. He should have, he should have, he should have…

But he was never meant to *be* her husband, was he? Marta had known that from the first minute she had seen him. He had been standing diffidently in the parking lot, waiting for the bus to arrive. He was talking to a girl. And Marta had known her too, though she hadn't been wearing blue, though there was nothing otherwise to mark her as special.

It happened like that sometimes. The *Prikopiya* might meet and separate, they might find themselves at Union Bridge during the Festival by chance, not natural sons and daughters of Jiříž but foreigners, diplomats, merchants, soldiers, even thieves. Still they would come. They would be led.

At first Marta had only meant to get close to him, close enough to understand what it was that made Barney so special. He had been quiet and shy, but then in those years they all were, all of them a little crazy, all of them a little broken.

They had been accepted to university together. They didn't know each other well but they would house-share, they decided, to cut down on costs.

Nothing had happened between them. Not at first. She had simply watched him.

He wasn't particularly sporty, wasn't popular like some of his friends. He didn't seem interested in love at all, really. There were the typical university flings, friends turned into lovers, brief experiments.

For a long time between them it *was* friendship, nothing more. They watched films together, went on hikes through the countryside, marvelling at the deep wood bluebells which had been so vibrant, so shocking to Marta. She discovered in Barney a rich seam of kindness. He had made her laugh. And when her mother died – an aneurysm, a tragedy that seemed to come from nowhere – he had put his arms around her and it had felt safe, as if she was encircled by the walls of Jiříž itself.

It wasn't meant to be anything more than that, a brief romance, a little flirtation. She was a unionist after all.

In their final year at uni she had suggested they take a trip to Jiříž together to celebrate, but Barney had demurred. The timing was wrong, he was trying to get settled at work. She had tried again the next year, and the year after. Eventually she had stopped asking. She hadn't wanted to take that trip either. She liked what they had together.

Then in Venice he proposed to her. He hadn't bought a ring, he said, so he fitted a ring sizer around her finger instead. 'You look sad,' he said, when he caught her staring at it. 'I'll get you a proper one, I promise.'

She didn't tell him it was the city that made her sad. Dreamy Venice, with its quiet canals, its glorious piazzas, a place for lovers, they claimed. But to her it felt like Jiříž tarted up: all trattorias sporting tourist menus, the harbour dwarfed by cruise ships like floating hotels. Surface and façade. Jiříž was *real*.

But maybe it wasn't. Maybe every city needed its own mythology to survive. Rome wasn't founded by twins suckled by a she-wolf and London wasn't established by Trojans. San Marco didn't need the stolen body of St Mark, smuggled from Alexandria in a barrel, to be beautiful.

But then Barney had lied to her. She had expected him to do so, ever since they first met. She'd known on their wedding day when they'd said their vows, but still it hurt her at a level she'd never known before. *A work trip*, he had said. He was a terrible liar. They both knew it. *I'll be fine*, she had said. *The doctor said everything is going well. No reason to worry. How long will you be gone? Just a day or two?*

It doesn't mean anything, she had tried to tell herself.

Just let him choose, she had thought. You can't force a person to love you. Just because he needed to *see*, didn't mean he would dash himself against the city like so many *Prikopov* before him. Maybe tragedy struck like a lightning bolt but she didn't believe love did, not really. Love was a city you built brick by brick, built it so it could survive flood and famine and fire, so it could survive the enemy at the gate. Love was a sanctuary, whichever way you reached it.

But she had followed after him, hadn't she? She had come to the Basilica because despite everything she was still a believer, and it was said the statue of *Prikopiya* might grant a wish to women during difficult births.

'It's coming. It's coming!' she screamed. She could feel a tremendous pressure now. She pushed and she pushed and her screams mingled with the sound of singing outside. Something was emerging.

Then it was over, it was out. She reached down blindly through the pain. It was slick with blood but she recognised it, its contours and curves, its finely articulated joints unspooling, finger and palm. The soft architecture of its body close to hers, swelling over her hands and spilling onto the spattered floor. She saw fresh rooftops glistening with vernix caseosa, buttresses and balustrades, narrow cobbled streets radiating in coils from a lazy, leafy umbilicus. It had come in a rush, and now it was here, it kept coming, bunching and unfurling across the cracking flagstones of the Basilica, plunging its roots deep into the stone and the earth.

Great sheets of dust fell from the rafters, the statue behind her tottered – The Lovers bobbing with indecision, threatening to fall into each other or away. Marta didn't care. As the walls of the Basilica's nave tore into jagged shapes around her, she could see a light in a swelling windowpane, and behind the sharpening glass, she saw the distinct soft profile of familiar figure, bewildered, lost and alone.

If she could wait, then so could he. Together, with time, they might build something new, and she had no doubt – no doubt at all – it would be beautiful.

Malcolm Devlin is the author of the novella And Then I Woke Up *(Tor Dot Com) and the short story collections* You Will Grow Into Them *and* Unexpected Places to Fall From, Unexpected Places to Land *(Unsung Stories).*

Helen Marshall's creative writing aims to bring the past into conversation with the present. After receiving a PhD from the Centre for Medieval Studies at the University of Toronto, she completed a postdoctoral fellowship at the University of Oxford investigating literature written during the time of the Black Death. Her first collection of fiction, Hair Side, Flesh Side, *which won the Sydney J Bounds Award in 2013, emerged from this work as a book historian. Rather than taking the long view of history, her second collection,* Gifts for the One Who Comes After, *negotiated very personal issues of legacy and tradition, creating myth-infused worlds where 'love is as liable to cut as to cradle, childhood is a supernatural minefield, and death is "the slow undoing of beautiful things"'* (Quill&Quire, *starred review). It won the World Fantasy Award and the Shirley Jackson Award in 2015. Her debut novel* The Migration *was one of* The Guardian's *top science fiction books of the year. It was shortlisted for two British Fantasy Awards as well as the Sunburst Award for Canadian Literature of the Fantastic. She is a Senior Lecturer of Creative Writing at the University of Queensland.*

Amusements

by

Verity Holloway

The old fortune teller's lungs gave out at the end of last summer season, but Libby knew that without being told. Not a message from Beyond so much as the profound reek of Madame Elena's Old Holborn tobacco saturating the little hut at the end of the pier. It would take at a deep clean and a good bundle of sage to be remotely habitable. Still, the hut came with all the requisite furniture. Madame Elena had left a glossy antique table draped in lace, a couple of Queen Anne chairs that almost matched, and the space heater still worked with an intermittent *clickety-drip* Libby could cover with a Celtic Moods CD. The shade on the ceiling lamp would have to go, though. The silk tassels were stiff brown stalactites, having dangled for decades above the coiling fumes of Madame Elena's fags.

'You can bring your own celebs, if you've got 'em,' said Doug, handing over the keys. The caretaker was a broad old boy with a habitual sniffle, and his toolbelt clanked in time with his lumbering steps. 'Madame Elena only used professional headshots, none of this arm-around-the-clients stuff, so you can recycle hers if you want. I won't tell anyone.'

Flanking the beaded doorway like a flock of grinning spirit guides, Madame Elena's superstar clients faded to a sun-bleached blue: Dawn French, Michaela Strachan, Timmy Mallett. *Best wishes, Eric Cantona.* Lulu had added a smiley face to her autograph, contrasting weirdly with the portrait of the departed Madame Elena herself, festooned in bangles and rings, red fingernails spread over a crystal ball, her stare stark and intense.

'I haven't decided on a name yet,' Libby said.

Doug sniffed. 'You could style yourself as her daughter. That's what Elena did when the last one retired in '62. Punters love a psychic bloodline. Listen, don't overload the power strip under the table or the whole pier'll go black. Yell if you need me, love,' he said, and went clanking away.

Gulls screamed on the wind, thrown about on the cold, salty currents. Inside the hut, Libby could hear the sea thundering against the pier's barnacle-studded legs. She supposed she'd get used to the noise.

A sandwich board was propped up against the table, and she wiped the dust away with her sleeve. Ornate Victorian text proclaimed Madame Elena's specialities.

Love, career, fertility, health. This lady's family have been on the
promenade since 1900. Come inside and let her help you.

Help. Libby liked the sound of that.

Despite the clinging chill, summer season would begin in just over a month. Plenty of time to get the hut clean, spruce it up with some of the money left over from the unpleasantness of last year. Head Office had been generous with the pay-out, but only when Libby dangled the possibility of going to the papers. *Do-gooder charity ejects sick girl* was a PR calamity Human Resources were eager to avoid. On top of losing her job and all the selective little acquaintances she'd made there, Libby ended up feeling like the bad guy for even suggesting such a thing. Tantamount to extortion, she worried, but the cards were firm:

The Chariot. Seven of Wands. Seven of Swords. Gather your willpower. Strategise. Defend yourself.

Aaron hated the idea from the start. He didn't want Libby to pursue the money, let alone move to the coast.

'You'll regret it. Seaside resorts are dying. *This is the coastal town they forgot to bomb…*' he said on the phone. He'd waited three days to call after she moved, just long enough to rattle her. 'Anyway, you'll have to dye your hair. I don't think gypsies come in blonde.'

She was still living out of boxes and kept forgetting to save pound coins for the electricity meter, so she took the call in the dark, hoping Aaron couldn't somehow tell. Mariner's Rest had been an elegant hotel once, back when people still looked forward to a week away, getting their feet cold in the North Sea and waltzing in the dance halls. The twirling plaster sconces on the ceiling hinted at the luxuries of the past, though the floor's shared bathroom seemed to mainly deal in cold water, and Libby's mattress creaked like a damp cat at the slightest movement.

'I'm not pretending to be a gypsy,' Libby said.

'That's what people pay for. Headscarves and big earrings and all that.' Aaron paused. 'How long do you think this'll last?'

'What?' she asked, running a finger down a hairline crack in the wall, sharp and crumbling. Libby had always been able to read symbols, the words beneath the noise. Her sketchbooks – taken up and abandoned more times than she'd care to admit – were a jumble of scribbled iconography. Pentacles and pylons, chalices and housecats, athames and Sainsbury's carrier bags. Her own pictorial language. Aaron, by contrast, preferred blunt instruments.

'This whole thing. When are you coming home?'

Libby felt herself wince. They never officially broke up, but they never made any fanfare about getting together either. Aaron wasn't especially interested in Libby's past, and to Libby, after everything, that looked like love. And he was fun when he was happy.

She tried to think of the right combination of words, the light-and-formless tone to avoid setting him off. In the second of silence, she heard Aaron swallow something and sigh.

'I'm not sleeping.'

He dropped it like a rock. She felt the ripples ringing out inside her chest.

'Oh?' she said carefully. 'Have you been back to the doctor?'

'I'm not wasting my time.' His voice took on that clipped edge that made Libby's skin feel too tight. The sound of beer and cough medicine, his mixed poisons. 'Right, well, it's been good talking to you.'

'Aaron…'

'Have fun.'

———

She took a bag of cleaning things with her the next morning. Along the promenade, a few huts were open to tempt dog walkers with shelves of film-wrapped peppermint rock. Sandra's Happy Chips made Libby supress a smile every time she walked past. Sandra, spray-tanned, crop-topped, viciously shovelling potato, had possibly never been happy in her long life, but they nodded at one another, fellow denizens of the seafront.

The North Sea was a grey slate. Floating gulls studded the waves, screeching in dissonant chorus, and as Libby made her way down the pier, she watched her boots passing over the cracks between the Victorian slats, marvelling at how something so old could stand firm in the face of the sea's untiring efforts. When she turned to admire the shore, she had a clear view of the old Edwardian lido, permanently closed, the drained pool a swamp of fallen leaves. A little way along, thronged with hardy palm trees, the Pavilion Theatre found new life as a bingo hall for local pensioners. Even with the thumping techno and clatter of the slot machines in the arcade behind her, it was romantic. Faded, certainly – held together by peeling posters for variety shows long gone – but still grand.

Aaron might visit when she was established. There were bumper cars down at the front; he'd enjoy those. She had to make her hut look good. If it was anything but pristine, he'd make that noise in the back of his throat, the one that made Libby's own close up, wordless and dry.

Seven of Swords, remember. Defend yourself.

Libby worked the day away. As well as the stench, Madame Elena's habit manifested on the walls as a stubborn brown stain, leaving stark rectangles where mirrors had once reflected the fortune teller's all-knowing eyes. An hour of strenuous scrubbing hardly made a difference, so Libby made a note to purchase paint. The floor was an easier job. Several decades of candle drippings required vigorous scraping, and by the time Libby was done, her palms were puckered with blisters. Those familiar pins-and-needles were menacing the small of her back, hot and cold at once.

Aaron had never accompanied her to the pain clinic. She told him it would be boring, but really, she didn't want him to know… well, any of it.

One consultant had cute little cufflinks. A star on each wrist, upside down from Libby's point of view across the desk. *Two of Pentacles, inverted: chaos.*

'Neuropathic pain,' he explained, 'is the problem of the brain alerting itself to trauma without a trigger. It's a communication error, like a phone ringing without a caller. After your accident, did anyone explain this to you? You were very young at the time, weren't you? Sixteen?'

'It wasn't really that sort of situation.'

'I see they took a CAT scan.'

'Yeah, most of us—' Libby's mouth worked around words without edges or weight. 'They looked at our brains.'

'And how about counselling? Did you ever receive any?'

There was no adequate way to explain why that wouldn't help.

It was late before she felt she'd earned her dinner. She was stepping back to take stock of the day's efforts when her foot nudged something snaking out from under Madame Elena's table. She almost tripped on it: a ship's rope, mildewy, segmented like a worm. She bent to pick it up, annoyed at herself for not noticing it earlier. It was just the sort of thing Aaron would take her to task over. Holding the thing, feeling its weathered heft, she could almost hear him: *You stress me out, Lib. The state of this place, all your art shit. I'm getting a headache.*

Happy Chips was still open. Libby dumped the rope and all her soiled cleaning rags in the wheely bin parked alongside the kiosk. Sandra stared blankly out at the dim horizon as saveloys hissed on the grill. A laminated sign was stapled under the menu: *Do Not Feed the*

Gulls. As Libby ordered, one of the birds trotted over to watch, its insolent yellow feet *splat-splatting* against the tarmac.

'They should let us shoot them,' Sandra said. 'Make it a game, hire out rifles. How you finding it up there, anyway?'

'On the pier? It's nice.'

'It's all bollocks, though, isn't it? Crystals and stuff.'

That stung. Libby shrugged, watching the gull chase off a rival, wings spread, beak gaping as if the filthy thing believed it was one of its dinosaur ancestors, jaw bristling with teeth.

I used to think a lot of things were bollocks, too.

'People just want someone to talk to,' Libby said, offering a bland smile. 'I'm a social worker in a silk scarf.'

There was no sunset that cloudy evening, just a gradual draining of the light. The pier looked dingy from a distance, a stretching black edifice teetering on spindly legs. What would the Victorians who built it think of pinball machines and *Dance Dance Revolution?* All those harassing neon lights and practically no one but Doug the caretaker there to enjoy them at this time of night. Libby's eyes adjusted to the encroaching dark, tracing the pier's great crisscrossing struts as she wondered if they might feature in her tarot sketches. The Eight of Swords, perhaps; a lattice of barnacled bars to symbolise entrapment. But that wasn't very Cognitive Behavioural Therapy of her, was it? She came to the coast to escape.

She paused. There, under the pier, in the space below the platform before the sea engulfed the legs, something was hanging. She took it for a sack at first, swinging in the breeze as if it contained something weighty, but the longer she stared, the stranger the sack became. Oblong, lumpen, with a narrow top and bottom. Rooty, almost, like a rubbery mermaid's purse. When Libby was little, holidaying in Blackpool, she picked one up as it came rolling along in the foaming surf. Someone – Dad? Mum? – told her it was an egg sack belonging to a shark, and Libby dropped it, expecting to be bitten. She felt it again now, that instinctive need to retract, retreat. The gulls bobbing about in the water below were intrigued, and a few took flight to investigate, wheeling around the thing in a shrieking crowd.

'Hey,' barked Sandra, and Libby jolted. Sandra was holding out a polystyrene tub of chips with a steaming red saveloy on top. 'I said, d'you want vinegar on that?'

When she looked back, stabbing a wooden fork into her chips, there were too many gulls to see clearly. The sack was theirs now.

—

A kid put 50p in the Laughing Sailor. The mechanical torso *clacked* and writhed, the head thrown back to release a recorded cackle.

It had only been a week, but Libby had acclimatised to the noise. Doug told her people were louder on the pier, and he was right. It was as if being out over the water gave them permission to try on a new version of themselves; more vibrant, confident, a little drunk. People cheered for their winnings on the slots and cursed their losses on the claw machines. They shrieked at the arm-wrestling robot and commiserated over dropped ice creams. As Libby spruced up her hut, she overheard snippets of life stories, budding romances, and filthy jokes.

'Just you wait until high season,' Doug warned her with a grin. 'This is peaceful.'

Libby hoovered and dusted, scrubbed and painted. Whenever she felt the acid fingers crawling up her spine, she took breaks out on one of the benches overlooking the grey horizon, doodling seascapes in her sketchbook as the wind whipped her hair around her face. Perhaps, as Aaron suggested, she should invest in a headscarf.

Aaron. There had been no more phone calls, only a text late last night when she was finally dropping off to sleep:

LOCAL NEWS THING ABOUT BUS SERVICE TO SEASIDE. CANCELLING ALL APPARENTLY. BAD FOR BUSINESS?

The Queen of Pentacles, reversed. Envy of others' successes, self-absorption.

Worry flared in her gut. It wasn't Aaron's fault. The codeine made him forgetful and irritable, scratching at his skin. Other times, he'd brim with affection, sleepy-eyed and docile. Took an embarrassingly long time for Libby to twig, really. Years of wondering how one man could sweat so much, or switch from lethargic to snappy in an instant, like a bad dog. Libby felt stupid. And then she'd wanted to help, which was, on reflection, worse.

'I know about pain,' she'd pleaded. 'I know what it's like to try anything.'

Only drove it underground, didn't she? Made him hate her, visibly so, scratching at his arms until they gave up furious pinpricks of blood. He was to be pitied, not resented. Besides, Libby thought, what successes could he possibly be envious of? She hadn't opened yet, let alone taken any money.

Every card she pulled for him was Death. Her sketchbooks teemed with poppies, their bulbous seedheads dripping with resin.

She should call. Just to make sure he was doing okay.

Come on, *Libby*. It would only make her look needy. Aaron liked that, didn't he, if she was being honest? He liked her insomniac, brittle with pain, needing him like he needed his pills.

She kicked at the railings with her boot. Flecks of paint came away, and she didn't know whether to feel guilty for the damage or satisfied that she'd at least left a mark. Her sketching pencil slipped from her lap, and she quickly bent to catch it before it had a chance to roll between the slats. As she felt around under the bench, the heel of her hand bumped against something protruding from the dark, damp wood. Libby peered between her knees. Only a frayed nub of rope. Thick as a child's wrist, it was secured around the slat, stretched taut as if weighed down from below.

She got down on her knees and looked through the slats. Each panel was warped and swollen from a century of weather, and she couldn't get a clear view. Just rope, a long stretch of it, creaking sluggishly as it revolved in the wind. A strong gust blew Libby's hair over her face, and when she managed to pull it back, she could see all the way down to the sea. The rope was attached to a burlap sack. And the sack was struggling.

Libby toppled back onto her bum. The gulls wheeling overhead cackled at her clumsiness, and she struggled to her feet as quickly as she could. Weird feeling. As if whatever was in the sack might come crawling up the rope towards her feet.

The wind, came Aaron's lethargic voice in her head, but then a memory intruded: Wade Winkleman, the short boy from her Maths set. He found a rabbit under a bush at the far end of the playing field. It was diseased, most likely, judging by how it didn't run away when he threw stones at it. Later he claimed he put it in a bin bag and drowned it down at the quarry pits. Libby didn't want to believe him, but the satisfied grin on his face stayed with her. It would have died anyway, she told herself, but later, when Winkleman's name was among the dead, she heard that rabbit's squeals and swallowed back a mouthful of bile. The *why* of Wade's death clattered against her windowpane at night, keeping her awake in her childhood bed and, later, Aaron's. Did Wade have it coming? Not all of them were cruel kids. If only there were some key to it all…

The Ace of Cups, inverted, pouring out its water into the cracked and barren soil: emptiness, loss.

She was already running up the pier, back to the shore.

—

When Libby reached the beach, her lungs were salt-raw and heaving. She had never been the sporty type. It was around the halfway mark, as she went clattering past the tearooms, when she realised she had no idea what to do once she got down there. She'd only seen the sack for a moment, but whatever was inside it had been small, fighting against its swinging prison. Could she call Doug for a ladder? And then what? Place it on the sand, in the sucking surf? That was assuming the creature was still alive in there, not suffocated or frightened to death.

As she struggled over the shingle and onto the grey strip of sand where the sea met the land, Libby gave a punched-out cry. She had arrived in time to see a white plume of foam where the sack had dropped into the water, sucked back over the rocky shelf and into the tide.

—

Doug sniffled into his cotton hankie.

'You've done a nice job in here,' he said, stepping into Libby's hut. 'Sincerely, love – it's a great improvement. Certainly smells different.'

Libby had hung mirrors over the worst stains, draping them with lace. On the glossy table, her cards were laid out, along with a not-too-cheap crystal ball and a pile of polished citrine chips painted with runes. The shaded lamps cast a moody glow at a reasonable cost, a combination of charity shop perseverance and the electrical aisle at Quality Discounts. Madame Elena's celebrities remained around the door. Taking them down – even Timmy Mallett – felt disrespectful.

'I got one of those plugin perfume things,' Libby said. 'Safer than incense.'

Doug patted her arm. Doug who'd told her the burlap sack was nothing but chip papers tossed on the wind. The same Doug who'd chuckled mildly at her distress as she trudged back from the beach. The sea could do that, he'd said. Play tricks on the eyes. Distant ships appeared to scud along in the clouds, and orbs of lightning danced on stormy nights. 'It was worse in the war,' he told her. 'We had the Germans trying to hit the docks every night. People were frightened out of their minds. Every strange light, every funny cloud…'

But the war was over. A struggling sack was a struggling sack. And every night since, as Libby lay in bed at the Mariner's Rest, hot water bottle against her back as coils of pain contracted and spread, she saw that moment again and again, the sack sucked inexorably away into the sea.

Doug bent to peer into the crystal ball, his eyes fishy and bulbous in the glass. If he thought she was stupid, he didn't seem to mind. Why did it matter so much if a man liked her or not, or if she'd inconvenienced him? Would Madame Elena with her scarlet talons give a toss what a man thought of her?

Seven of Wands, reversed: confidence demolished.

Oh, shut up.

'When are you going to give me a reading, then?' he asked.

It was a quick way to please him. She settled down on her side of the table, in the scrolling chair left by Madame Elena. Doug sat opposite, watching her shuffle the deck as if she was about to perform a trick and he wanted to spot the sleight of hand.

Libby placed both hands on the soft purple altar cloth she picked up from Curtains 'n' Things. 'I'd like you to settle your mind for a moment,' she said. 'Focus on your breath. Watch them happen: your inhales, your exhales. Be present with me. Is there anything you want to ask? Something troubling you? No details. What's yours is yours. My job is interpreter.'

'Am I going to be a rich man?'

She must have glared because Doug snorted. 'What about summer season, then? Will we have a good one? Is the seaside something people want again, instead of spending all their wages on the Costa Del Whathaveyou?'

He looked so earnest about it, Libby felt a pang of sympathy. She shuffled the deck, giving a few little flourishes to fill the silence. At last she drew a card, letting it slide between her fingers. She always knew when the right card touched her fingers, like knowing the texture of your own pet's fur, or the way the cool side of the pillow feels on a lazy morning. Whatever communication failure was afoot in the pain centre of her brain, this was the opposite. She laid the card face up on the table.

A man dangled from a rope twisted around one ankle, his arms hanging slack around his serene head, fingers pointing idly at the earth he would never touch again.

'The Hanged Man,' Libby said. 'Others may not understand your sacrifices, but you see things differently. This is a period of uncertainty. You're unsure of how summer season is going to go. Once upon a time, it was all much clearer.'

Doug sniffed. 'That it was.'

'The Hanged Man is a reminder to let go and wait for an outcome, or at least a better time to act. We often see the Hanged Man in conjunction with the Wheel of Fortune. They both tell us that clinging on to the old ways only brings us pain.'

With surprise, Libby felt her throat ache as she said it. Doug was distracted by memories.

'We used to have a Ferris wheel when I was a boy,' he said. 'Right up on the pier. At the top, on a clear day, you could almost see Calais. People came from all over to ride it. Made you proud.'

On a whim, she drew another card and slapped it down. Doug smiled knowingly. 'Wheel of Fortune. Very clever. How'd you do that?'

Libby forced a grin, but her lips felt stiff. She hadn't done anything. 'The Wheel of Fortune is the ever-changing nature of life,' she said, hearing her own voice thicken with the threat of tears. 'We have to accept it. Digging our heels in, trying to go back to the past, only hurts us. See the king at the top and the beasts underfoot? Everyone is subject to change. Only the wise accept it.'

Doug sniffled. 'I'm an old stick-in-the-mud, eh?'

'No,' Libby said, realising she'd committed that most lazy of acts: making a reading about herself. 'It's more like... the tides. You wouldn't row a boat against the current, not unless you wanted a struggle.'

Doug, thankfully, was satisfied. 'Maybe I row against the current, taking care of this old place. Maybe that's alright. The young don't have to understand it, do they? One more card. Tell me something nice.'

This wasn't for Doug any more, but she couldn't stop. Her fingers flew over the deck, stopping with perfect surety over the last card resting against her palm. As she slid it free and recognised the illustration, her spine gave a warning tingle.

'The Devil!' Doug cried, jokingly horrified. 'No, I don't want to hear what Old Nick's got in store.'

'Another Major Arcana card,' Libby explained. She didn't want him to be displeased. 'It means, um—'

But Doug was already getting up, waving his hands in surrender. 'I'm a churchgoing man, love. You shout if you need me, alright?'

He left her sitting there, with her lace-draped lightshades and her crystal ball. And the Devil on the table before her, flanked by naked slaves. The chained figures, insignificant beside the hoary old Satan, didn't dare meet one another's eyes, ashamed by the weight of the binding iron forged by their own desires.

A shrieking gull careened past the hut, jolting Libby from her thoughts. Aaron was miles away. He was brooding in his flat with its empty fridge, alone. No one was there to make sure he went to bed. No one to watch the kitchen bin for empty pill boxes or the dripping dregs of cough medicine. She had left him to drag his chains alone.

—

She planned to let the phone ring five times, then hang up. The Mariner's Rest was quiet for the night, all but the lazy click of the electricity meter over the ceaseless sighing of the tide. Each ring of Aaron's mobile felt like the throb of a wound.

Three.

Four.

Five.

'Hello, stranger.'

He caught her on an exhale, and her hitch of surprise made him chuckle.

'You sound knackered,' Aaron said.

'I've been working pretty hard. It's looking alright, I think. You could…' She wet her lips. 'You might like to come down and see. It's still early, so there won't be any annoying kids.' She offered it like a bonus prize: hook three ducks and win a *South Park* cuddly toy from China. If she tried to explain the volume people gained on the pier, the infectious clamour, he wouldn't come. He'd have one of his headaches. He'd shuffle off to the bathroom cabinet—

'Will I need to book a room?'

She couldn't believe it. In her elation, the words wouldn't come, and Aaron's voice crackled on the line: 'Still there?'

Exhale. Inhale. Calm. 'Yes. I mean, no, you don't need a B&B. I've got a camp bed here under mine, if you don't mind it being a bit lumpy.'

'It's been ages since I had proper chips.'

'We could get some from Sandra. She runs Happy Chips, but she's miserable. Wants to shoot all the seagulls.'

He was laughing. She felt a grin spread across her face, trembling at the edges like it might come apart. When had she last heard a smile in his voice?

'I've missed your weird stories,' he said. 'Friday alright? I'll come on the bus. They're still running for now.'

—

The gulls circled, boasting and bullying. The street sweepers had been by at dawn, scooping up the previous night's chips and vomit, and the cold morning air smelled like petrol and spilled salt.

Libby sat on the wall at the bus stop beside the pier. She'd worn a nice knee-length dress, nothing too gypsy-ish, and good boots for walking along the shingle. Lunch would be taken care of by Sandra, and if Doug wasn't busy, she could introduce him, too, though the two overtures – 'This is my boyfriend' and the more realistic 'This is Aaron' – jostled like bumper cars in her head.

The fortune teller's hut was ready. Paint dry, floor swept, table resplendent with candles, crystals and cards. A swish with a burning bundle of white sage gave the room a clean, inviting feeling even Aaron couldn't criticise. A quick test of the cards threw out the Hanged Man again, but Libby disregarded him. She hadn't taken the time to properly shuffle the deck since Doug's reading.

Aaron said he was getting the early bus. That way they could watch the tide when it washed out. He wanted to examine the rock pools, see if he could catch a crab or pick up one of those white cuttlefish bones they hung in birdcages, stripped of flesh and ink. Libby shifted on the wall, flexing her stiff hips. The pain was a rumble of thunder, a squall far out at sea.

She hadn't brought her sketchbook, expecting to be busy, but the first bus rattled past without stopping, empty but for a heavily made-up woman standing at the front, staring out with a blank, meditative expression. Libby checked her phone. She composed a text, something peaceable in case Aaron had got off at the wrong stop. Not that he was likely to miss a landmark as obvious at the pier.

She looked back at it, the black edifice studded with neon. In the morning haze, she could almost see the ghost of the old Ferris wheel ticking around at the pier's terminus.

And she waited. And the wind whipped her hair and her spine pulsed cold and hot at once as the buses came and went like tides. She erased the last text and thumbed another: LOST? Perhaps Aaron had overslept. Overslept, missed his bus, or…? Maybe the excitement of their meeting demanded a handful of pills washed down with a beer for breakfast. Codeine rusts the switches in the brain, the ones that tell the lungs to fill and empty. What if—

Under the pier, a shape swayed to count the passing seconds. Libby pulled back her hair, squinting into the misty white sun rising over the sea. A black oval was suspended above the water, revolving in pendulous circles as the waves slapped the pier's legs either side of it.

The rush of the traffic didn't matter so much anymore, not while the dangling object – not a bundle of floating chip papers, but a sack, narrowing at either end like a shark's egg – and its contents began to kick in earnest.

She didn't rush to it. Her job was not to intervene. Fibres of fabric and dirt came off the burlap in a cloud as the thing inside it fought and struggled. The sack was splitting, a seam breaking open from top to bottom like a chrysalis rending in two. Small flutterings emanated from the growing opening. A *puff-puff* of white flakes, then red, their gloss catching the morning light. Petals, tumbling into the sea. Libby's mouth dried. Her throat closed. The sack twisted, and with a tearing sound released a soft brown flurry of rabbit fur, catching in clumps and rolling out on a stray gust. A tuft carried upwind over the sand, glancing against Libby's fringe. Cards followed, handfuls of them taking flight across the beach, wands chasing cups, pentacles overtaking swords as the gulls looked on, calling into the wind.

A drowsy, drunk sensation held her, and she watched in dull fascination as, with a wisp of dust and frayed material, something large came worming out of the bag. Pale and naked, all but a jangling collection of bangles and gaudy rings, the arm uncoiled and strained. Prolonged nails, red as poppies, tipped the stretching fingers as they curled inwards, leaving a tobacco-stained index finger and thumb pointing down into the water below.

Libby pocketed her phone and shakily found her feet.

The rope unwound and whipped through the air and the sack disappeared into the churning grey sea.

Verity Holloway *lives in East Anglia. She is the author of* The Others of Edenwell, Pseudotooth, Beauty Secrets of The Martyrs, *and* The Mighty Healer. *She writes folklore features for* Hellebore Zine *and her short fiction has appeared in* Far Horizons, The Shadow Booth, *and* The Ghastling, *among others. Find her at verityholloway.com and on Twitter as @verity_holloway.*

As I Want You To Be

by

Ray Cluley

Do you know what Nirvana means?

They were in a club, tolerating a tribute band who were systematically destroying all of George's favourite songs because, really, was there anything worse than great music played adequately? Kurt Cobain had only been dead four years and already people were trying to claim a piece of what he'd left behind… and finding themselves lacking.

'It's not enough to like all their pretty songs, or to sing along, if you don't know what it means,' George said.

Craig was leaning back on the bar, and never mind all the people around him pushing to get served. He was watching Lydia jump around in the dancing crowd. 'She reminds me of Jo.'

George grabbed both beers when they came, paid, and said, 'Jo? Really?'

She didn't exactly look like Jo. She had a stripe of bright red in her hair that Jo never had, and her eye makeup was darker than even Jo would have tried. She was wearing a deliberately-torn-to-be-lowcut T-shirt when Jo favoured loose and baggy, and her skirt was short enough to show her legs were in stockings whereas Jo wore tights, George remembered, but then she had only been fifteen. Lydia was a few years older, and she had tattoos, but George agreed that the *essence* of her was Joanna. The Nirvana T-shirt helped. Black, with a yellow smiley face outline. The smile was wobbly, with a tongue hanging out. The face had crosses for eyes.

'To absent friends,' George said, and raised both bottles of beer to clink them together, 'Cheers!'

He drank the first one down, put the empty on the bar, and took the second with him as they moved back into the club's crowd. Craig didn't drink. Craig didn't do much of anything except give him shit, but then what were best friends for?

'You'll regret this tomorrow,' Craig said as they pushed their way towards Lydia and her friends.

'That sounds like a problem for tomorrow.'

Craig laughed. 'Your funeral,' he yelled over the music, and as they neared the band he began jumping, mixing into the heaving audience and shouting lyrics to a ceiling that dripped with sweat.

'Dead man dancing!' George yelled, and joined him, ricocheting from one bouncing person to the next, his head rolling on his neck like something broken.

On stage, a Cobain wannabe sang over and over that he didn't care.

—

George had known Craig since secondary school. Timetabling and seating plans had put them together for most of their classes and it didn't take them long to discover they liked a lot of the same things. By the time they were in their final year they were inseparable. They even liked the same girl by then – Joanna Danvers – but as she was far too cool for either of them, that was mostly okay.

What George had liked about Joanna was her attitude. She was so very casually confident, a rebellious type without making too big a point of it, though in those days being a rebel really only meant ignoring the school dress code. Knotting her tie thin instead of fat. Wearing trainers instead of shoes. For the girls, skirts had to be a certain length, and there were rules about how much makeup was allowed, but of course Joanna flaunted those restrictions too, getting away with it because she skipped school a lot and the teachers were careful to choose their battles whenever she did decide to show. Some people thought she was weird – she said things sometimes that freaked people out – but to George that just made her more interesting.

The first time he'd ever seen her *outside* of school he'd been with Craig on the old railway line, which was when their shared crush on her really began. Craig had an afternoon paper-round, and most Saturdays George would go with him. When the weather was good they'd cut across the old railway embankment, and sometimes sit on the edge of what remained of a platform to flick through the local paper Craig was meant to be delivering.

'Six.'

'Seven.'

'Seven? For Jackie?'

'In that picture, yeah.'

The county athletic trials had just taken place and their school had put in several great performances. A double page headline inside had read *Well Done Wellbrook!* and although neither of the boys had any love for sport, several students were pictured for the piece, and George and Craig *did* have a keen interest in girls. They took turns pointing at the ones they recognised.

'Eight for Grace, definitely.'

'Definitely.'

'God,' Craig said, pointing and laughing, 'three!'

George laughed with him and agreed, 'Three.'

And then—

'What are you two doing?'

Engrossed in the paper spread between them, neither of the boys had noticed Joanna. In fact, her arrival had scared the shit out of them, and Craig was quick to say so, though she was far too cool to care about that. She didn't apologise, but it didn't please her, either. She was the epitome of aloof, standing there in her baggy jeans and DMs, a jacket open to show The Smashing Pumpkins splashed across the chest of her T-shirt (and, oh, how they'd joke about her smashing pumpkins). She had one hand cupped in front of her, eating from it like she had all the time in the world for them to answer her, picking at little bits of black and popping them in her mouth. For a brief but disturbing moment George thought she was eating flies, until she offered, 'Raisin?'

'No, thanks.'

'Suit yourself.'

'What are *you* doing here?' Craig asked. Like she was only meant to be seen at school. She offered him a raisin, too, but he shook his head.

'Free country,' she said. 'Anyway, I asked you first. What are you doing?'

'Reading the paper,' Craig said, and shook it at her. 'What does it look like?'

She ate another raisin. 'Looks like you're scoring girls out of ten.'

Craig flushed a deep red, and judging by the heat in his own face, George had done the same.

'We were just messing around,' he said.

'What would you rate me?'

'Ten,' said Craig.

George said, 'Eight.'

She looked at him properly, then. A smile curved half her mouth. 'Same as Grace Kayson?'

In that moment he thought she was a billion times better than Grace Kayson, but he tried for some of her aloofness and shrugged.

'I'll take it,' she said, and ate another raisin. 'You shouldn't judge girls like that, though.'

Craig folded the paper closed and put it back with the others in his bag. He sighed, being dramatic, as if she'd just ruined *everything*.

Joanna didn't care. She ate another raisin and said, 'Do you know what Nirvana means?'

She'd asked George, specifically.

'Do I what?'

She pointed at his T-shirt. On his chest, a thin-limbed figure held a skeletal arm around a flower, while something devilish pulled at its shoulder.

'Oh,' said George. 'No. I just like the band.'

'Better make the most of it. He'll be dead soon.'

That was the kind of weird shit she said, sometimes.

She ate a final raisin and brushed the rest from her hand, before turning to show the back of her jacket where a large black patch took up most of the denim, the Nirvana smiley outlined in yellow. 'I like them too,' she said.

'What does it mean, then?' Craig asked her.

Joanna shrugged. 'I don't know, that's why I asked. I keep meaning to look it up.'

George decided he was going to look it up as soon as he got home, and then he was going to find a way to tell her so it seemed like he'd known all along.

But, of course, he never did.

—

'Where'd you meet her, anyway?' Craig asked. 'And why the hell does she like *you*?'

George gave Craig the middle finger in the mirror, and Craig gave it back, grinning. They had the gents to themselves, thankfully. George rinsed his hands. Someone had thrown up in the sink, but he was careful.

'Come on, who is she? Why didn't you introduce us? Scared I'll steal her from you?'

'Mate, she doesn't even know you're there,' George said, and this time Craig gave *him* the finger.

Lydia had quickly spotted George in the jumping crowd, pushing and pulling her way to him to put a hand on his shoulder and yell, 'You made it!' over the music.

He nodded. 'Of course!'

She'd pulled her T-shirt taut to make the design clearer, though of course he'd already noticed. She'd improved it with cuts and tears, but otherwise it was the same shirt that had led to them talking in the first place. They'd been working out back with the deliveries, which meant you could get away with opening your uniform to whatever you wore beneath.

'Do you know what Nirvana means?' he'd asked her.

'Enlighten me,' she'd replied.

George made the gesture for a drink and Lydia nodded, so they forced their way out of the heaving mass and made their way to the bar.

'I'll catch up with you later then,' Craig called, and George waved him away as he disappeared into the bouncing crowd.

'A few of us are going back to mine in a bit if you're up for it?' Lydia said as they waited to get served. 'This band...' She winced instead of finishing.

'Yeah, not great, are they?'

They talked about music, comparing favourite bands and albums and songs just as they had at work, but beneath it all, in this new context outside of work, their intentions towards and for each other haunted their small talk. George stood deliberately close, his body pressed to hers at the bar. Lydia touched his arm and his back when she spoke. Everything yet to happen vibrated between them, potential and possibility evolving into certainty, *inevitability*, the more they talked and touched.

They talked about how shit their jobs were at the supermarket. Lydia was definitely too good for the place, and George told her so.

'I'm still figuring out what I want to do,' she said. 'Something to do with computers, probably. The web or something, I don't know.'

'*Really?*'

'Yeah. Why? Computers are the future.'

'Until 2000 comes along and fucks them all up.'

She laughed, and said, 'I got time,' like the future could never be a problem.

In the gents, Craig said, 'The web?'

George shrugged. 'Whatever,' he said, and, 'Never mind. I'm going back to hers now. You coming?'

'I go where you go,' Craig reminded him. 'Besides, I want to see what happens. Call it my morbid curiosity.'

George shoved him playfully just as music blasted into the gents, dense and reverberating, and a group of guys stumbled in from the club. They'd been laughing about something but hushed at the sight of George.

George dried his hands on his jeans and headed back in to the music.

—

Lydia shared a house with three other students, and all of them brought friends back as well. George stood among them in a lounge lit with candles and lava lamps while Lydia fetched a couple of inflatable armchairs and a beanbag to accompany the rest of the tatty, mismatched furniture. He'd been introduced to everyone individually but already he'd forgotten half the names. They reminded him of people from school. He kept expecting to see familiar faces among those of strangers and hoped he wouldn't.

'I fuckin' *love* this song,' Lydia said as The Cure's 'Lullaby' began beating and whispering into the room. It was from the *Mixed Up* album rather than *Disintegration*, but George preferred it. It was like the song had been given a second chance.

Poised on the arm of the sagging sofa, Lydia rolled a cigarette. At work, wearing the same offensively dull and unflattering uniform as everyone else, she stood out thanks to the stripe of colour in her fringe and the dusky dark colours she used to make up her eyes, something she'd never get away with on the day shift, but here, in her own environment among others dressed and made up the same, she stood out for reasons George couldn't quite fathom. Her Jo-ness, maybe.

Do you know what Nirvana means?

'So, you a student too?' asked one of the lads on the sofa beside her, bringing George back into the room.

'Nah. School was enough for me.'

'We work together,' said Lydia.

'Oh,' said the other sofa guy. 'You like stacking shelves?'

George finished his drink and said, 'Fuck, no.'

The lads on the sofa laughed and George was relieved, and for the next couple of hours things went pretty well.

—

'Never have I ever been caught having sex,' said a girl everyone called Dizzy, though George couldn't remember why, and three people in the room drank. One of them, a guy called Theo, pointed his bottle at Dizzy right after and said as some sort of protest, 'Never have I ever deliberately walked in on someone to *catch them* having sex,' but Dizzy only smiled and said, 'It's not your turn.'

'Never have I ever faked an orgasm.'

All the girls laughed and drank.

'This game always ends up being about sex,' said Dan. George was pretty sure his name was Dan.

'Never have I ever complained about a game being about sex,' said Lydia.

'I wasn't complaining!' Dan said, but he laughed and drank anyway.

'It's all right,' Lydia said, 'we can play something else. I spy, with my little eyes, something beginning with *whiny bitch*.'

'I wasn't *complaining*,' Dan said again.

'Are we seriously going to play I-spy?' someone asked.

'Never have I ever…'

And so the game went on.

George learnt who'd taken ecstasy, who'd flashed a stranger, and who'd been tied up for sex, while he drank confessions for watching porn, for kissing somebody he shouldn't have, and—

'Never have I ever seen a ghost.'

That one came from a goth girl who contradicted herself by drinking.

George looked over at Craig. He'd been leaning against the wall, watching the game with little interest, but now he straightened and smiled, curious to see what George would do.

George looked into his cup. He was already pretty fucked. He didn't need more alcohol. He didn't really know these people, anyway. He didn't have to tell them *anything*.

Lydia leaned close and asked, 'You okay?'

George looked at Craig again.

Craig grinned. His teeth were bloody.

George downed the rest of his drink.

He'd first seen Craig like this at the funeral, standing graveside with his family and a few other friends from school, some of whom had already been put in the ground themselves. They still wore their school uniforms, the whites of their shirts and blouses stark against a background of mourning black. George, standing with his mother, had said Craig's name softly, and she'd squeezed his shoulder, pulling him closer in case he wanted to turn from the sight of the grave yawning for his friend's waiting casket.

As far away as he was, Craig had heard him, too. He'd looked up from the headstone he'd been staring at to say, 'Where were you?' He was calm. No, he was *bewildered*. Where *were* you? He wasn't angry. But George flinched from the question as if he'd been yelled at, and so his mother hugged him tight. It was as much to comfort herself, he thought. The funeral – the *funerals*, plural – had shown him a secret she and all parents carried, which was the knowledge that their children would one day die. It was a secret they tried to keep buried deep but the funerals brought it to the surface, unearthed it in making holes for their children's coffins. There was guilt, too, coming up with such dark soil, right there to see even if your eyes were teary. There was guilt and there was *gratitude* that your own child survived when others had not. George had missed that fatal day of school and lived. Now he had to live with having missed it.

'Honestly,' the goth girl was saying, 'it was standing right there, at the foot of my bed, and I swear to God, I thought…'

Craig, bloody-mouthed and grinning, came over to look down Lydia's top and said to George, 'Smashing pumpkins,' while a line of blood ran down his face from somewhere in his hair. 'Seriously, mate. Ten out of ten.'

Lydia smiled at George. She said, 'What are you looking at?' thinking that she knew.

'No one,' George said, then corrected, 'Nothing.'

'Nothing?' Lydia looked down at herself and back at him and said, 'Really?' before leaning to give him a better view, a too-familiar half smile on her lips. It was meant to be flirtatious, but it made George think of Jo.

'Here begins the rest of your life,' Craig said, and blood blossomed in the fabric of his school shirt, spreading to form a Rorschach George didn't want to read.

Here begins the rest of your life had been a line from their yearbook. A yearbook Craig never received. A yearbook with too many headshots that had epitaphs instead of witty quips for farewells. *Here begins the rest of your life*, the headmaster had written for those who remained. *Make the most of it, won't you?*

Abruptly, George pulled Lydia close and kissed her.

If she was surprised, it didn't feel like it, her lips opening to his almost immediately and her body pressing even closer to his. Her hands went to the back of his neck and then into his hair while she fidgeted into his lap.

As the others began to notice, a ripple of jeers built to whoops and whistles, and finally cheers when they broke from the kiss.

'Let's play spin-the-bottle!' someone suggested.

'We're playing never-ever,' said someone else.

'Never have I ever kissed someone and pretended they were someone else,' said Craig.

And from right beside him, Jo said, 'George needs another drink.'

George flinched.

Lydia. *Lydia* said, 'George needs another drink.'

But George didn't want another drink. He could still feel the softness of Lydia's lips on his. He could still taste her lipstick and what she'd been drinking before kissing him. He didn't want to lose that.

'Come on,' she said, and took his hand to pull him up with her as she stood. 'I've got tequila in my room.'

The others made celebratory noises and she told them to fuck off, laughing. Someone said, 'Don't let the bed bugs bite,' which was apparently hilarious, but before George could question it he was being led upstairs.

'Where are we going?'

Standing at the top of the stairs was Craig. He said, 'Drinking makes you stupid, mate,' giving him shit, but then what were best friends for?

George tried not to look at him as they passed.

'My room,' said Lydia, taking the handle of one of the doors. 'Unless there's somewhere else you're meant to be?'

George shook his head.

'Then step into my parlour…' she said and, opening the door, gestured him inside.

It was dark, but not completely: stripes of red light lined one wall, giving the whole room a soft, otherworldly glow where it wasn't shadows.

'George, meet the girls. Girls, this is my friend George.'

She took him to where several terrariums sat on metal shelves. The red light came from each of the habitats.

'You're not arachnophobic, are you?'

George looked.

'That's Charlotte. She's a pink-toed tarantula, see her little feet? She's not a web-spinner but she was my first, so I named her after my favourite book. Have you read *Charlotte's Web*?'

George shook his head.

'I'll lend it to you. And this one's Tequila, she's a Mexican Red-Knee.' Lydia smiled. 'Told you I had tequila.'

'You're allowed to keep these? In the house, I mean.'

'Theo's parents are the landlords, so it's okay. One of the main reasons we tolerate him. And look, this pretty little thing is a black widow. She's called Natasha.'

'I don't see anything.'

'Really? She's usually— Ah, shit!' Lydia looked around the room frantically.

'What?' said George. '*What?* Did she get *out?*'

Lydia stopped searching and laughed. 'Sorry. Couldn't resist. That one's empty. I wouldn't keep a black widow anyway, not while I'm living with that idiot lot downstairs.'

'So none of these are dangerous?'

There were at least half a dozen terrariums, a couple of them thick with web, but Lydia didn't show him any others. She put on a CD, and as it whirled up to play, she said, 'Some of them can bite, but then I've been known to do that, too, so…'

She stepped in close and kissed him.

It was like they hadn't stopped since before, the kiss quickly as intense as how they'd left it downstairs. George lost himself in the taste of her for a time he couldn't measure, and as they kissed, Lydia walked him backwards to the bed, her hands working at his belt. She had him entirely undone by the time the backs of his knees hit the mattress and forced him to sit. She enjoyed a moment of looking down at him, then knelt at his feet to pull at his jeans.

'Lydia,' George started, but then her mouth was on him, and he had no more words, only noises.

From out of the dark, Craig spoke.

'What's it like?'

George tried to ignore him.

'Come on. Call it my morbid curiosity.' He said, 'Never will I ever…'

George groaned, and Lydia made a noise to show she'd heard him.

'What are you two doing?' Jo asked. She was suddenly standing next to Craig by the terrariums. The light from the spider habitats shone through her body, suffusing the bright white of her shirt with red. She was a blood-lit ghost in school uniform, her shirt half-tucked and incorrectly buttoned, her tie as low as an old noose. There was a laddered tear across the thigh of her tights like a spider's web.

'What does it look like they're doing?' Craig said and grinned. The blood on his teeth and chin looked darker in the dim light. It looked black as old scabs.

Jo shrugged. 'How would I know?' she said, and George saw her eyes were gone, replaced by the red light of the terrariums. She was eating from a handful of—

flies

—raisins and offered one to Craig. Her eyes came back when she looked at *him*.

'Are they bothering you?'

Lydia was looking up at George, her hand working where her mouth had been.

'What?'

'I can cover them up if you want,' she said.

George looked back at Craig and Joanna, imagining them under sheets like Halloween ghosts, but they were gone. There was just a wall of spiders.

'No,' George said. 'No, it's fine.'

Lydia smiled up at him, a smile that was all hers and full with new intent. She climbed him onto the bed and quietly said, 'I'll help you forget they're even there,' as she straddled him. She must have removed her underwear while she was using her mouth because he was immediately enveloped by the easy, eager warmth of her, and he groaned, and she sighed, and then her hands were on his face and they were kissing and kissing and there was nothing else and no one else but her.

—

'It's okay,' Lydia said.

George had been staring at the ceiling, but he turned to face her and saw she was on her side, looking at him. They weren't quite *in* her bed – they hadn't made it that far – but she'd turned some of the duvet to partially cover them both.

'Sorry,' he said.

She smiled. 'It's *okay*. It happens. We've got all night. Or is there something on your mind? Like, what were you thinking about just then?'

'Yeah, George. What were you thinking about?' Jo asked. She was wearing her jacket now. George could see the Nirvana smiley reflected in the glass of the spider habitats, the yellow face cast into something sickly in the red light. Corpse-like with its crosses for eyes. Its protruding tongue.

'I was thinking about you,' George said, and Jo smiled her half smile because she already knew.

'Me?'

As I want you to be, sang the CD.

The day they'd kissed had been the first day George ever bunked off school. He'd bumped into Jo at the bus stop, which never would have happened except he'd overslept that day and didn't have time to walk. She'd asked him casually, 'You going in today?' and he'd surprised himself by saying, 'Nah,' just as casually back.

'Cool,' she said. 'Want to hang out for a bit?'

They went to the old railway line.

They didn't talk much on the way there, but George was happy to see a couple of people from his year spot them together as they went. The thrill of being with Jo instead of going to school was something he thought he'd enjoy for a long time. He was already excited to tell Craig about it, but glad as well that he wasn't around right now to enjoy it with him.

Without discussing it, they stopped at the old platform. It was little more than a wide wall, a long flat of concrete with a steep angle down at either end. The tracks were long gone, the route turned into a path for dog walkers and cyclists. Steep embankments rising either side enclosed the space in a kind of artificial valley.

They sat on the platform edge.

'Weird day,' Jo said.

'Yeah.'

'Did you see the sky this morning? It was red for the longest time. Like the dawn got stuck before deciding, fuck it, okay, I suppose we have to start the day.'

'Yeah,' George said, though he didn't really know what she meant.

'Weird day,' she said again.

George kicked his feet, glad that he'd worn trainers instead of school shoes for his run to the bus. Jo didn't need to know his school shoes were in his bag.

Jo was wearing trainers, too, of course. She picked at a small ladder in the thigh of her tights but stopped when it suddenly split wider.

'Where's your mate?' she asked.

'Craig?' As if he had loads of friends and had to narrow it down. 'He never bunks off.'

Because George did it all the time.

'I think I'm in his art class.'

'Yeah. Mine, too.'

'It's the only class I like.'

'Yeah.'

And so they talked, skirting the surface of various subjects because neither of them knew the other very well. It made for some painfully stilted conversation. George said 'yeah' a lot, and only occasionally voiced an opinion of his own. They talked about school and art and album covers, and they talked about music, and George wanted to tell her what nirvana meant but he hadn't looked it up yet.

'Does your friend like Nirvana?'

'Craig? Nah. He's more of a Blur guy.'

Which was a complete lie. Craig loved Nirvana, perhaps more than George did. But the more they talked, the more it became apparent that Craig was meant to be a topic of conversation, and the excitement he'd felt about having Joanna all to himself began to fade because it didn't really feel like he did anymore. Quite the opposite, in fact.

'There's this girl he likes who loves Blur, so…' George said, and shrugged.

'Oh. Well, Blur's okay, I suppose.'

In that moment, George wished Craig didn't exist. It was there and gone, the briefest of wishes born of envy, but, oh, how it came back to haunt him in the following years.

Jo sighed. 'Something doesn't feel right.' She looked at George and said, 'Don't you feel it?'

'Feel what?'

'I don't know. Like the sky this morning. Don't you feel *anything?*'

'Nervous, maybe,' George said, accidentally honest.

'It's a bit like that,' Jo said. 'But more… Do you read comics? It's like my spider senses are tingling or something.'

George didn't know what to say. He did feel a bit strange, but he was pretty sure it was because of how close they were sitting.

'I don't really read comics,' he said.

For a long moment he thought he'd killed the conversation, but just as he was about to say something lame – he wasn't sure what, only that it was bound to be lame – Jo looked him right in the eyes and said, 'Do you really think I'm an eight?'

It confused him for a moment, but she was referring to that day with the newspapers.

'Craig said I was a ten.'

She gave him that half smile, sort of teasing, and without really thinking about it, because if he thought about it then he'd chicken out for sure, George leaned forward and he kissed her.

For a moment she didn't do anything – sat a little more rigid, maybe, a little straighter – but then her mouth worked with his and they were kissing together. She tasted of raisins. George put his hand on her thigh. He felt her skin through the laddered tear in her tights.

The touch jolted her out of the kiss.

'What's wrong?'

'I don't know,' she said. 'Something.'

She pulled at the hem of her skirt, but it was too short to cover the tear she'd made. She put her hands down to the platform edge and pushed herself off, grabbing her bag on the way.

'Where are you going?' George asked, standing. 'Don't go.'

But she was already halfway gone, running the trail back the way they'd come.

'Craig's an idiot!' he called after her, but he didn't mean it, and she knew better anyway.

—

Lydia nudged George for him to elaborate. 'You were thinking about me, how?' she said.

'You remind me of someone I went to school with for a while.'

'Wouldn't *that* be weird. What school did you go to?'

And without meaning to, George admitted, 'Wellbrook.'

It had the same effect it always did. He watched it happen, regretting his honesty as Lydia first recognised the school, then remembered *why* she recognised it, and even as some part of her brain was trying to do the maths she said, 'Shit, really?' and, 'Were you *there?*'

No, George thought. I was kissing a girl who wished I was someone else.

'It's okay if you don't want to talk about it,' Lydia said, but there was an excitement in her eyes that meant she hoped he would. 'I mean, people *died*. Students and teachers *died*. Shit, I don't even know *how*, there's all sorts of stories and they're really fucked up. Were you actually *there?*'

'I'd rather not talk about it.'

'Sorry. Sorry. I just said that you didn't have to talk about it, and then—'

She used one hand to make a spewing gesture from her mouth.

'It's all right,' George said. 'Everybody wants to hear about it once they know.'

And when they find out I wasn't even there that day, they wish that I had been. Almost as much as I do. They don't understand how weird it must be for everyone *after*, whether they were in that day or not.

'It's like they find out I went to Wellbrook and suddenly there's this other George they're far more interested in. They don't actually see *me* anymore.'

'I see you,' Lydia said. She smiled. 'I spy with my little eyes, something beginning with… George.'

George smiled back. She made it easier than it had been for a while.

'And I see something beginning with you,' he said.

Lydia immediately looked away, fidgeting to lean out from the bed, and George worried he'd said too much, but before he could retract the comment or rephrase it somehow she said, 'Uniform.'

What?

'Sorry, should have said excuse the mess or something when we first came in.'

She was talking about her work clothes, still piled on the floor by the door.

'Uni books?' she asked. 'Can't be underwear as I don't actually know where that's gone.' She started looking for it, and George realised she thought they were actually playing I-spy.

'Don't worry about it,' he said.

There was a red stripe across her back from the bra she was looking for. George touched it, and she turned around.

Her face was Jo's.

'Are you saying I won't need it?' she asked, and smiled her Jo smile.

I'm dreaming, George thought, though he knew he wasn't. I'm dreaming, and then I'm going to wake up in time for school and everything will be how it was meant to be all along.

'What time is it?' he asked, just to be saying something.

She looked past him to where there must've been a clock and said, 'Three a.m. Time flies, huh?'

No. Time is slow and it's sticky and it holds you in place until karma can find you.

'I better go.'

He rummaged in the duvet to retrieve his T-shirt. He'd worn Nirvana as well, the winged and skinless figure from *In Utero*. I hate myself and I want to die; that was what Cobain had wanted to call the album, but people talked him out of it.

Couldn't talk him out of the sentiment, though.

'Don't go.'

She pulled at his shoulder, pulled at his T-shirt before he could get all of it back on. Plucked the wings from his body.

Don't go.

He'd said the same to Jo once, but by then she was already running away from him, running to her future and into his past.

When his T-shirt came off, Lydia was Lydia again. She threw the shirt across the room, as if the distance would keep him from leaving.

Craig stepped aside, dodging like it might have touched him. He was standing in the red light of the terrariums, bathed in the blood of their glow.

'I think she likes you, my absent friend,' he said. 'But I'm an idiot, so what do I know?'

'I found out what Nirvana means,' Lydia said. She was kneeling up with George, having wrestled his T-shirt from him, but she moved closer and put her arms on his shoulders and held him loosely behind the neck. 'You never did tell me, but I looked it up.'

She smiled at him, and the smile was all her own.

'It's pretty cool, actually. It's, like, this state of being where there's no more sense of self or suffering, and you're released from karma and the whole cycle of life and death into a kind of ongoing happiness or nothingness or something. Like, there's nothing else but that moment.'

She wriggled closer. He could feel her naked body against his. The softness of her breasts against his chest.

'And you know what that reminds me of?' she said.

She put her mouth to his ear and whispered, 'I'll show you,' tickling him with her breath before kissing him, pulling him back to her bed and urging him down onto her, into her.

From the stereo, a dead man sang for George to take his time, and to hurry up, and that the choice was his, but really, what choice did anybody have, ever, about how things played out?

Do you know what Nirvana means?

'Yeah,' said George, and, 'Yeah.'

'Yeah,' said Lydia. '*Yeah.*'

She wrapped her legs around him, pulling him close, and close, and close, keeping a rhythm with him and the music and—

Memoria…

Memoria…

The CD was sticking.

Memoria…

Memoria…

George looked over to find his friends, but Lydia turned his face to hers before he could see if they were there and the CD fixed itself, jumping forward as she held him in a kiss, so George thought about the people he missed, and the people he loved, and how sometimes they were the same people, but they didn't have to be, and when he broke from the kiss to look at who he shared it with, she smiled her half smile and George had to clench his eyes closed because all the while she held him, *they* held him, their arms were all around him, their arms and their legs, all their legs were wrapped around him, so many legs, too many legs, all of them long and bristling with coarse hair and bending and flexing around his body to squeeze him tight.

'You're hurting me.'

Lydia's eyes were wide, but they widened further as George hurried to finish her.

I see you.

And suddenly her eyes divided, and divided, and there were too many of them as well, now, row upon row of eyes in a face too small to hold them. George turned from what he saw because he was afraid, he was afraid, he was afraid ad infinitum, and while he looked away he felt Lydia, felt Jo, he didn't know, felt her shift her head enough to bite where his forearm pressed tight against her throat. Felt her put her mouth to his wrist and sink her fangs in deep, and when he flinched from her she kicked at him with her legs, with all of her legs, her long, bristling legs, untangling them from his body as she heaved hers beneath, and suddenly he was turning, and turning, and turning above her, rolled by legs that held him away and rolled and rolled him, round and round like karma, tying him in sticky lines that would not stop coming all the while she drained him.

Do you know what Nirvana means?

He knew. Unable to move, twisted in silk and sheets that held him cocooned, he knew. And as she came for him he saw his slow necrosis in her – *oh* – so many eyes, and he screamed, all of him open-mouthed and soundless as a husk that didn't, that couldn't, feel anything.

Ray Cluley's *work has appeared in a various magazines and anthologies and has been reprinted several times, including in Ellen Datlow's* Best Horror of the Year *series, Steve Berman's* Wilde Stories 2013: The Year's Best Gay Speculative Fiction, *and in Benoît Domis's* Ténèbres *series. He has been translated into French, Polish, Hungarian, and Chinese. He won the British Fantasy Award for Best Short Story ('Shark! Shark!') and has since been nominated for Best Novella (*Water For Drowning*) and Best Collection (*Probably Monsters*). His second collection,* All That's Lost, *is available now from Black Shuck Books.*

Hyperlink

by

Polis Loizou

It starts in the usual way.

a/s/l?

A dozen responses already spring to him, but Josh clicks on Napster and browses his downloads instead. Clicks on *Things Fall Apart* by The Roots.
Back on IRC, the prompt is waiting.

a/s/l?

A world of possibilities. How many times has he answered this question, and how many honestly?

18 f Singapore
42 m Glasgow
23 m Athens
29 f Berlin
I'm a bartender
backing singer in a tribute act
my dad died
yeah he had prostate cancer but we werent really close
mum was an architect
my wife can be very cold
controlling. you know?

Wherever the words come from, they end up being swallowed whole by whoever's on the other end of the cables. Or maybe not. Maybe this open new world just lifted a lid: that it's all strangers playing strangers. Every so often he'll think about stopping but he won't, and he knows he won't. Taking on another form adds a fresh layer to his soles, a new weight in his pants.
Dickhead.
Age, sex, location: what will it be this time?

Bubblegum on his breath. It mixes with the smell of stubs in the ashtray. Go with the truth, says a voice inside him. So he types.

24 m Derby

He deletes the location. Re-types.

24 m London

Better to go with a place he's been to, in case of probing questions. It's got to be somewhere big enough to allow for paths not to cross. If it turns out he's chatting to a local, he can always say he's a tourist. The reply comes:

ah cool. I'm 23 f Denver.

American. Perfect. Chances are she's never left her country, let alone been to London. He can say whatever he wants.

They talk about nothing of any consequence.

In between, he smokes another fag and clicks to Geocities. He uploads the new concept art the client sent over. A low-budget animation with a tacky-looking monster reptile, but they liked his website and a job's a job.

Lucky they have no taste. He's only good enough for this.

He gets bored of the woman in Denver, and ends the chat as the album draws to a finish.

Somewhere, he's got a list of albums Blinker recommended. He finds it, types the first one in the Napster search and waits for the results.

Finally, they show up. Along with another thing, that seems not to be linked to his keywords at all.

Unreleased   *<a href>*

He's never heard of this artist. Curious, he clicks, and watches the percentage increase on the download bar. It takes eighteen minutes.

His smoke drifts up the screen, making his eyes water. The fag's burned down to his fingers.

Some people have good lives.

The download finishes but he's tired. It can wait. There's *Buffy* to watch.

He closes Napster and Netscape and goes to shut down the PC when there's a crackle in the speakers.

Then a voice.

Is it speaking to him?

He doesn't know what it's saying, but it sounds urgent, then it cuts.

He sits within the silence for a minute.

What language was that? It wasn't English, that's for sure.

Can you get interference from abroad? And through PC speakers?

He stubs out the fag, pops another gum in his mouth, then waits for the energy to come so he can get up.

—

He meets the others outside the Astoria but they go to a Greek place for dinner first. They eat lemon potatoes and chicken from skewers, and while they clink their foreign beers he stops for a second to take in the moment. None of these guys was in his life until about a year ago. Now they do things like come into London for gigs together, geeks who met each other on forums.

How could he ever have made friends like this at school? Everyone hated him there. Called him weird, gay, a loser.

And then what happened, happened.

He blinks it away. Sad git.

Eyes on the here and now. He's with friends. Like other people are. He's a normal guy, happy to be himself. He gets to work freelance, lives on his own and pulls every time he goes out, if he wants to. He can watch *Queer as Folk* without listening out for housemates.

They decide to split the bill. Andy jokes this might be their last night out together. Not long left of the year, and you never know…

'Y2K,' he says with a ghostly vibrato.

The others roll their eyes.

'Let's hope it gets you first.'

'That your way of saying you're not coming to mine for New Year's, then?'

'Oh yeah, forgot about that. Okay, New Year's might be our last night together. Just in time for Y2K.'

Scott throws a pitta at him.

Blinker asks Josh if he's checked out any of the albums he recommended.

'Some of them, yeah.'

He suddenly recalls that other album coming up in the search, that unexpected artist name. But even the memory of it flickers in his head, and when Blinker says something back, he forgets entirely.

It comes to him again, suddenly, in the middle of the Flaming Lips gig. He should listen to that album, he thinks, whatever it is. Maybe when he gets home.

—

He lights a fag and opens Windows Media Player. He presses Play, then goes through the million choices of skin in Settings to see what'll match. It's a thing he does sometimes, totally pointless but cool. Making the media player's skin 'match' the music, whatever that means.

The tracks play.

It's not clear if this is even a proper album, or just a collection of demos. That field is marked *Untitled*. The tracks are only numbers.

This <a href> person is pretty good. Josh can't tell if it's a man or woman, or even a band or solo artist. The music is an edgy electronica – would sound awesome on headphones, he thinks, all-encompassing – but it sounds as if the vocals themselves are synthetic too. Some scientific experiment or something, artificial intelligence.

Michael Cunningham could direct a video for it.

It's cool.

When he's finally lying in bed, he can still hear that voice in his ear.

Is this what tinnitus is like? he wonders, and next thing he knows is his alarm going off, waking him up in the morning.

—

He spends the day working on the website for that low-budget movie. He doesn't want to judge it by its budget, and he tells himself that isn't why he rolls his eyes at the concept art.

There's just an air about the whole venture, an air of being doomed to failure.

You can sense it in things.

The makers might truly believe they have a sleeper hit on their hands, a future cult classic – they see potential that will be realised, rather than a dart that aimed for a bullseye it was always going to miss by being twisted from the off.

It'll sink, like so much, like so many, into the depths of time and be lost for good.

At least he enjoys the process of making a website. Starting from scratch, the possibilities of code. Crafting a thing and seeing it finished.

The concept art loads, the CGI monster's face appearing bit by bit as black blocks.

He puts on the <a href> album again and— is it his imagination, or is she singing about everything he's been thinking? Was that what the words were?

Weird, he thought of this person as 'she'.

He still has no idea who this is. It even occurs to him that it might be a known artist taking a gamble with something new. But the sound has got a hold of his head.

He enters the name in Napster and, to his delight, more results appear. 4MB, all with the green circle, all at DSL. New tracks. Or maybe they're old and he just hadn't thought to look before.

Hadn't he?

Maybe not.

He hits the download button.

With an energy fizzing up in him, he stands and walks around the room. Then he turns back to the PC and opens Netscape. He searches for the artist but nothing comes up.

Now what?

Without quite knowing why, he tries something else: he types the name in the URL bar and hits Return.

Something is happening.

A page is loading.

Bit by bit, segments step forth from the white fog. If he squints, it looks like a face written in code.

Among it all is an email address, barely visible against the background.

He stays standing as AOL opens, as his fingers tap out a message, as that icon of a paper airplane flies away from him and to whoever this person is.

What did he even write? He can't recall.

By the time the new tracks have finished downloading, he's sat back down, smoked a fag and drunk a beer. As he loads the new mp3s on the media player, an excitement grows in him, something close to horniness.

Weirdo.

He ought to text that girl from the other week, see if she's up for meeting again even though he flaked out last time. They could wander round Pride Park or walk along the river, end up here.

The music plays, and he realises he's stayed frozen.

He hasn't even touched the HTML he was working on, or the Flash animation he was experimenting with. Somehow time has ebbed away and he's done nothing but sit absorbing the frequencies from the speakers.

Did he turn them up to full volume? Or have the tracks been getting steadily louder?

No, he hasn't moved.

Unless he has and can't remember.

His eyes are fixed on the artist's name on the player. Who is this <a href> who can cut right through him? How is it that he's randomly come across the thing he needed, when he didn't know he needed it?

At some point, tears began streaming down his face. He wipes them away.

—

Sometime in the middle of the night, a hand shakes him awake.

'Josh,' says a voice. 'Josh, you alright?'

There's someone in his bed.

The girl.

'Yeah.' His voice is croaky. His throat really hurts.

It sounds like she's smiling in the darkness.

'You were making a weird noise.'

She is definitely smiling. He can feel it.

'What?'

'Yeah, it was really weird. Like weird bleeps and stuff.'

'Oh.' He tries to laugh, even though he feels embarrassed. 'That is weird. Sorry?'

'It's okay. It's funny.'

'Yeah.'

He doesn't know how to phrase what he wants to say. He wants to tell her to leave, to get out of his flat and not contact him again.

Instead he stays silent.

Her hand crawls up his leg, then cups him. He rolls over and pretends to be exhausted.

Get out, he doesn't say.

He stays awake all night, a constant frequency screaming in his ears.

—

He types the Ain't It Cool News URL. When the website loads, Harry's ginger curls taking shape, he enters the title of the CGI monster film in the search bar.

You never know. There might be some early buzz about it.

Nothing. Of course.

He sighs.

He opens IRC and goes to the chatroom where he and the others gather to talk shit. Someone's worried about Y2K, so Andy takes the piss – not that the other person can tell.

Josh feels bad for them. In secret, he also dreads the future demise of this world, and the threat of Y2K is so vague that it somehow looms even bigger for it. Then he reminds himself that all the top brains in the world are on the case. It'll be fine.

Besides, everyone's always trying to turn the Net into a horror story. The media are constantly banging on about how awful chatrooms and forums are, how they'll lead to mass social isolation.

But it's the opposite. Josh has met, even been, so many people online. His world has never been wider. He's never felt more immersed in society, more a part of it.

And now discovering possibly his favourite new artist of the year? Another win.

He starts messaging Blinker about <a href>.

Stops himself.

Why can't this just be his for a bit? A little corner of the world that's left untrampled by other feet—

SSSSSSSSSSSSSSSSSSSSSSSSSSSSSSSSSSSSHHHHHHHHHHHHHHHHHHHHHHHHHHHHHH

Josh comes to with his hand on the volume dial of the speaker.

The voice again, speaking.

Speaking to him.

It's in his ears, he can feel it like a tongue.

He turns the speaker off.

The silence is heavy, damp.

Something's up with that speaker. The off-white chunk sits there, mutely, as if staring at him. The other one looks lifeless. Blameless. He should buy new ones.

On screen, the others are asking him questions.

what was that about?
did u paste ur code here by accident mate

He can't understand what they're saying, until he scrolls up the chat and sees the wall of text he's left. HTML. Reams and reams of it.

Regaining his breath, he types a response.

yeah hahaha
sorry lads

He must've done. Blacked out and pasted code he'd copied from Geocities.

He doesn't look too closely at it, because deep down, he knows it isn't anything he copied earlier, it isn't anything he's written for this website at all.

He should call his GP.

Later. Now, something tells him to open up AOL, almost presses on him. It's unlikely an artist like <a href> would've responded to some nobody-from-Derby's message, but he checks his inbox anyway.

And there it is.

Waiting to be opened, a message from <a href>.

Dear Josh,
Thank you for connecting. It's a special thing.
Just between us,
<a href>

He doesn't know what he was expecting, but the message has stumped him. The email reads as though it was written by a robot.

That's when it hits him: of course. This is all a simulation. Performance art, exactly what <a href> would do.

Smiling to himself, he closes all his programs and shuts down the computer. The Windows 98 logo and its accompanying sound disappear, as does what looks like a face, before Josh is left staring at a black screen.

—

Taking his Walkman with him, he strolls into town to wipe his brain a bit.

He browses Virgin Megastore before going over to MVC in the Eagle Centre. He's in the mood to buy a film, but maybe he should just rent one instead. Who knows where the next job will come from, and he did just go to a gig in London.

Pace yourself, sunshine.

No.

Today isn't like other days and Josh isn't the usual Josh. He feels lighter, yet at the same time more solid, more corporeal, more of a person. Like he's one of the personas he makes up in his head for strangers on IRC, but magicked to life.

What if it's all a simulation? Like in *The Matrix.*

What if he's the one who isn't real? Never has been.

The pleasant thought makes him float.

He won't buy a film but he'll rent one, and on his way back home he'll stop off for a haircut at that kindly barber that's part railway bookshop. He always enjoys the chat there. The man is like something from a bygone age. Only comforting.

Who is <a href>?

What are they like?

With that name, it's obviously a nerd who knows their coding. And with those sounds, it's a proper artist rather than some manufactured pop star. Rich, resonant. From as long ago as Lovelace and Babbage but as close as if in the same room, lips on his ear.

Yet, that email. Strangely distant.

Or was it intimate, too?

Just between us…

Between them.

The two of them. Linked by this secret music through the ether.

He smiles to himself, even laughs.

His phone rings.

That girl, wanting to go to the pub.

He ignores it. The world is full of people, billions and billions of people.

—

Tonight the Friary is a broth of thumping bass and cigarette smoke, sambuca and perfume. Josh stands tall in the middle of it. He tries not to think of the tunnels to the old gaol beneath his feet.

He's in a polo tee and his hair is gelled. He sips his Corona, aware of eyes on him – the eyes of women, even the eyes of a guy on a sofa by the window. Maybe he should go to the Curzon afterwards, see how far he gets this time.

In the back room, he dances, giddy-drunk. The flashes of light pick out a woman smiling at him. She dances with her friends.

That guy from the sofa is here.

The lights flash.

He's next to him.

The lights flash.

Josh is free.

The lights flash.

The music bangs.

The lights flash.

The guy's hand is on his arse.

Under the club, they make out in the stone tunnels. Red brick coming through the white plaster.

The guy is stubbly, something he's never experienced before. The thrill of the sensation scuttles up his arms. It makes him giggle a bit.

He tries not to think of robed monks materialising in the darkness.

—

Back at his flat, he pours rum and Coke into two glasses and they clink them together, sitting side-by-side on the sofa.

'What do you want to listen to?' Josh asks, suddenly awkward.

'Anything, I don't mind.'

The guy sounds proper Midlands. He must actually be from here.

Josh starts up his PC while the guy browses his DVD collection. Finally, he opens up his downloads and loads <a href> on the media player. That perfect match of a skin, icy blue, so suited to these tracks.

'Interesting,' says the guy in response to the music, in a way that means he hates it. 'Something wrong with your speakers?'

Philistine.

Josh only smiles. He won't change the music. The guy can deal with it. And whatever, this is only for tonight. They don't need to be friends.

'Seriously, it's just static? Can you not hear that?'

Josh frowns, baffled. The synth. The words. That voice.

'Sorry, can you actually turn it off?'

The guy has his back to him, his head still scanning the DVDs on the shelves. But his voice sounds as if it's coming from a different part of the room. The body of this person standing in his flat, browsing the DVDs, stands perfectly still. Paused.

The distance between them shrinks.

Just between us…

Josh's heartbeat quickens. This was a mistake, to play the music. The guy should not be hearing it. Only Josh is meant to hear <a href>.

'Wha— are you alright?'

But the guy isn't even looking at him. Why does he sound concerned?

'Why are you making that noise?'

What noise?

The guy's head is still turned away from him. And then it isn't.

The head turns, the skin an icy blue. There are no features on it anymore, just lines and lines of code.

'Josh! Are you okay?'

The voice sounds worried for him, wherever it is.

The icy blue breaks up. It fragments into black blocks.

Thank you for connecting. It's a special thing.

Bit by bit, the blocks spread across the face and body of this other being, then the walls and floor, then up to Josh's feet, then the world is all black.

—

Lights.

Dots of light, as if marked on graph paper, all around, leading him into… something.

The vastness of it. So much darkness and light.

The sound grows.

SSSSSSSSSSSSSSSSSSSSSSSSSSSSSSSSSSSSSSHHHHHHHHHHHHHHHHHHHHHHHHHHHHHHHH

Josh sees his arm reaching out ahead of him.

Reaching, reaching into the endlessness. Only dots of light in the black.

His hand stretches towards this full, full vacuum.

And from the black another hand emerges, stretching, to meet him.

Polis Loizou is an award-winning writer and performer working across various disciplines. His debut novel, Disbanded Kingdom, *was published in 2018 and longlisted for the Polari First Book Prize. His second novel,* The Way It Breaks, *is set in his motherland of Cyprus, as is* A Good Year, *a historical novella inspired by local horror folklore. His short stories and creative non-fiction have been published in* Litro, Stockholm Review, Untitled, clavmag *and more. He is also one third of the award-winning fringe theatre troupe* The Off-Off-Off-Broadway Company, *as well as a performer of folk tales and poetry.*

The Crumbling Edifice

by

Ashley Stokes

Step off empty carriage onto deserted platform. Farworth railway station could be a distressed Edwardian photograph that is shrinking me, folding me into it. Mist shrouds the entrance. Inside, the counter is unattended. No one checks my ticket. A spongy give to the floor. My hands swelter. I ought to take off my gloves. As I exit, nausea mushrooms in my stomach. Something whispers in my ear.

Farworth knows I've arrived.

Farworth is amused.

The road out slopes down to a junction. I know the way to Ash Close. Before I liaise with the Client, I will investigate the House. This may be another case where my skills are not appropriate. Rather than me, the Client may need a therapist who can help with the reverberations of what happened, if what happened is no longer happening. Scoping the House on my own will allow me to assess this.

Mock-Tudor semis on the sloping road. I hate mock-Tudor. Farworth is an outer circle of mock-Tudor hell. I could be walking along this road in any year since these houses were built. 1923 or 1933. 1993. And I could be wandering like I used to wander back in '92–93, adolescent me with a fantasy novel tucked into my coat pocket, passages of strange prose repeating in my head as I hoped to run into Vix. Like in '93, I could be walking into anything.

Ash Close is a noose-shaped cul-de-sac of mock-Tudor detached houses. The House is number 14. Its front lawn is overgrown, its windows boarded. I think of you; you in the night looking up at the windows here, your blades in a sling-bag, your contractual obligation. I remember staring up at a girl's window once upon a time in some other dead-end street, some other night. The same girl, Victoria Wix – everyone called her Vix – I had approached in a foggy park two weeks before. 'Oh no,' she'd said, 'it's the Crumbling Edifice.'

I feel sicker. I could purge. If I start to purge, I might never stop.

Rear of the house: kitchen entrance covered by a plywood sheet. Graffiti scrawled on the board and the surrounding brickwork, most of it inoffensive.

I miss you… I love you… Sofia RIP.

There is, though, a symbol in black paint, a T in a circle with diagonal lines connecting the bar of the T to the edge and some arrowhead-like runic mark above the flat of the T. I follow its outline with the tip of my gloved forefinger. Through the leather, I think I can detect heat. The Temple

freaks have been here to salute you. Crept over to stake their claim to your deeds. The tools of my trade click together as I rummage in my bag for my phone. Phone recovered, I stand back and photograph the symbol. I will add it to the file with the others from Hinwick, White Ness and Stoley St Marks.

There is a burn in my throat. It is like I am in that weird pause when you know you are ill, sure you are sick, yet tell yourself it will pass.

The burn is more acidic, flares as I peel back the plywood. Gaining entry is easy.

Certainly easier than it was for you. You woke Martim da Souza when you chiselled open this door at approximately 3 a.m., 22 June, the year before last.

I am standing in the da Souza kitchen. Standing in darkness. I feel me as you. I am you and Martim is onrushing in pale blue pyjama bottoms, fuzzy in the moonglow that drifts in from outside. Up close, his expression – panic, aggression – tells you he knows he is *not* dreaming, that there *is* an intruder. The lifelines on his palms seem like black strokes in a manga as he raises his hands to protect himself from your first slash. Your second strike is fiercer. When Martim thumps to the floor, you feel proven, anointed even.

You had never before met Martim da Souza, forty-two years old, a manager at a local precision engineering firm, originally from Sintra, Portugal; or Carolina, thirty-seven, a dental nurse whose Portuguese origins you could detect in the voice screaming her husband's name from halfway down the stairs.

Halfway up the stairs is where you stab her seventeen times with the hunting knife CCTV says you'd bought two days ago in Gubbins & Co, the camping outfitters on Farworth High Street. You drag her through the hallway and leave her alongside her husband in the kitchen where eight hours ago she tossed salad and uncorked a bottle of Rioja.

Also previously unknown to you, Tomás, twelve, is frozen on the mezzanine with his hands over his eyes as you stalk up the stairs lifting the wet edge of the machete.

You spend more time with Tomás. Use him to smear a T symbol some half a metre in diameter on the mezzanine wall.

It has been painted over, no doubt after the trial, but I can still sense it as if it's branded into the space the frame of the building occupies. This staging point I experience not as a cold spot but a thin spot, a weak point in the boundary between your mind and mine, and further back, your mind and His.

On the mezzanine, I relive what you concluded here: that these non-entities, these soft puppets, are mere markers on your way, clauses in your agreement. You are high now on the thought of the money.

Sofia da Souza is fifteen. You know her. You are familiar. You have singled her out. I knew this already. The Client knows, too, and the court and the papers. Sofia was the gateway. She led you here. In some ways, she invited you in. You feel gratitude towards her.

Your gratitude makes my guts want to expel what I've described before at other sites and thin spots as the *post-emotion*. If I'm not careful I could bark up or black out. I can't faint. I must stay in the moment of culmination. There are skirls and post-emotions in this house that were not described at the trial, or listed at the inquest, or speculated on in the tabloids and online fora. I am witnessing events no one should see. Hearing incantations you should not have heard.

Her room has been stripped out.

The wardrobe is no longer here.

I suspect it was burned. I hope to God it was burned.

I sense your initial panic when you can't see her. Even though it is dark and there has been chaos and carnage, she cannot have given you the slip.

The wardrobe looms over you. How imminent your reward as you tap the wardrobe door with the machete. What whispered to you then streams through me now. Orders. Exhortations. Gleeful encouragement.

The expert witnesses will tell the judge and jury that you were ill in the da Souza house, as if this accounts for your baseline motive. They will say you are schizophrenic. That's why you hear a voice that described to you bizarre trades and obscene priorities, why you believed you had signed an agreement in your own blood that committed you to the sacrifice of the da Souzas to the entity called Grand Jack Thorian. In return, you would win the Euromillions Lottery, advertised as a £170 million jackpot on the night of the murders. In the days that preceded the draw, you spent £232 on tickets in supermarkets and newsagents across Farworth.

You are not ill, though. I only sense illness in me, not you. You are not mad. You are not sick. You should not be cosseted and babied in a psychiatric hospital.

You should be in the ground.

Still, this was also done to you, you were taken down too, seduced. He has powers of persuasion even the strong and prepared can struggle to resist.

She is right, the Client. He is still here. Still in the shadows. Still in Farworth. I've heard Him mutter and hiss before. Thirty years ago and since. Grand Jack remains. For all the others and you, Farworth, then, will be the place of final reckoning.

—

It is alarming to me that the acid in my guts and throat does not ease as I put Ash Close behind me. I walk up unpopulated streets. Heading for my rendezvous with the Client, I pass terraces of pebble-dashed facades and concreted-over front gardens, churned-up verges and leafless, stunted trees. I try to imagine how you experienced these streets, Ethan Scarver. It is much harder for me to latch on to you out in the open air where your residue is dispersed, a mere hint on the breeze.

I remember walking streets like these when I was sixteen, the age your behaviour began to worry your peers, teachers and responsible adults like the Client. We have all been there, but at sixteen I transitioned from being someone Vix would walk through like a phantom she couldn't see, to being the only person at school she told that a voice was telling her to do things no one ever should.

—

Rook's Nest is the only business open in the precinct. The other shops – a minimarket, a dry cleaners, Ripped Venus (an adult bookstore), an Indian takeaway called Spicy and Nicey, and Bright Young Things International, the internet café where legend says you used to communicate with members of Grand Jack Thorian's cult – all are dark and most have white-washed windows and to-let signs. Rook's Nest is lit up, though I suspect only for me.

When I step in, it is wider, deeper, more spacious than I had imagined from the website, a proper geek-out games emporium. Running down the centre, zigzagging tables smothered by green cloths, battlegrounds for armies of miniature knights and humanoid hordes. They are flanked by a display of boxed board games on one side and on the other, ceiling-high shelves of books, some of which belonged to my own V/X imprint. *The V/X Encyclopaedia of English Demons* and *The Ruins of England Handbook* were consistent sellers here at one point.

The *Encyclopaedia* is still in stock; only one copy, but I note it is well-thumbed. *Ruins* is sold out. Being the owner of V/X Lexicons, acting under this veneer of respectability was what had initially put me in contact with the proprietor of Rook's Nest, Mo Dent. Recently, she enlisted me to provide the more exotic service I do not readily advertise.

I check out the board games, admiring their design and artwork: *Minions of the Moon*, *Realm of Dusk, Imperium of Pheme.* I feel that throb inside I've never know what to do with. I could abandon myself to dice and maps and counters and figures and not have to think about Ethan Scarver and Grand Jack Thorian for a few hours at least. Hours, though, could become days that would blur into sleepless nights and squandered weeks. I have no one to game with anyway. Never have. By the time I was sixteen I had two hundred and nineteen Warhammer figures, all painstakingly painted, and had constructed sixteen dioramas using polystyrene, papier-mâché and butcher's grass but had no one to play with but a part of me that pretended to oppose my every move.

I would have loved somewhere like Rook's Keep to hang out when I was a teenager. There was nothing this cool for me. The only thing that came close was the Strange Idol Patterns second-hand bookshop on Talavera Road, with its shelves and shelves of SFF paperbacks, but I was always the only one in there, and in any case, it went under quickly and I was back wandering the streets again.

I remember being sixteen and one late afternoon after school shadowing Vix and some other kids I knew to be notorious set-pieces. Back then, the unhaunted and ordinaries I referred to as set-pieces. I followed them into the Starburger. Steam on the window made the street look like a Jack-the-Ripper fog had wafted in. Hunched in my overcoat, collar up, making a cup of piss-weak tea and plate of shit chips last as long as possible, my bare hands gripped a second-hand yet still combative copy of *Slave Girl of Gor* that stank of some dead man's fags. At ten-second intervals, I glanced over the top of the book eyes-left at the set-pieces. They were grouped together in another booth, having a laugh and chanting lyrics from the terrible music set-pieces fell for in '93: M People, 4 Non-Blondes, DJ Jizzy Jizz and the Flash Ponce.

Vix wore a battered motorcycle-style leather jacket over a ruby-red babydoll dress. I noticed a change in her expression. I could sense the skull beneath her skin. It was happening to her already. It was terrifying to see.

No one else noticed, of course.

She glanced over.

Her eyes met my understanding eyes.

It's funny, but when you get older you realise that it's those of us who were into the geek scene, the role-players, the alternative chart worshippers, cult fictionados, wannabe Conans, the great unloved – we all emerged in the end better balanced, more realistic. Just look at me, for example. I have a mission. I have a goal. The set-pieces thought they were going to be the popular ones forever, that all their coming days would be like the sunny days in daytime soaps from the other side of the world. They would never be abandoned, never get hurt.

Although there are obvious reasons for this, none of those set-pieces around the table in Starburger grew up to be what they thought they would, except for me, Adam Pasmore.

Adam Pasmore, Demon Hunter.

Well, Adam Pasmore, small-press publisher, qualified driving instructor and, on the side, some nights, Demon Hunter and sworn nemesis of Grand Jack Thorian.

—

'Mr Pasmore?' says a voice behind me.

I don't turn around. I say, 'You were right to contact me, Ms Dent. Jack is deep in the spaces.'

'You don't know what a relief it is to hear that,' she says.

'I know what it is like to be disbelieved.' I swish around to face her. 'But we should not be so hard on those that saw this only as an earthly tragedy. There are expert seducers in play.'

—

Of course, I too had thought there was nothing out of joint at first, when the murders were in the news and the lurid details of your trial attracted media attention. I too had assumed the da Souza case was another where a young man with extreme mental health issues had slipped through the net of social care with terrible consequences. The demon the prosecution described but did not name must be a hallucination, or the anthropomorphism of your latent desires. In fact, what drew my eye most was the artist's impression of you that appeared on the BBC. Was it the sketchy nature of the court artist's work, or were you really missing two fingers from your right hand? This did pique my interest, it had to be said, though I did not connect the stars and see the constellation until later.

It was only when Mo Dent emailed me in confidence that I had a closer look at the case. I quickly realised you had not conjured a demon persona from your deepest self. You had been led to the fiend. Groomed. Groomed like Vix was groomed.

Dig a little deeper and we realise that you had been talking about your wants to people – initially on the the eerie_england subreddit, then through now-dead links to other, darker message boards – members of the so-called Arcane Order of the Temple of Ashes – AOTA – whose T symbol was like a satanic version of the Sergio Tacchini logo I had seen today on the plywood board covering the da Souza's back door. AOTA had steered you to Grand Jack Thorian, who also goes by the name The Candleman, or The Remembrancer, or, in Cumbria, Jack Wondrous. AOTA had shown you how to summon and bind Grand Jack and sign the contract. It was Mo Dent's assertion that not only was Grand Jack Thorian real, he was still in Farworth. Hence her contacting a demon hunter.

—

'He is still in Farworth,' I say.

Mo stares at me for minutes. She is taller than me, younger, broader, wears dungarees and has eight or so studs in her left ear.

'Drink?' she says, eventually.

'Nothing too sharp, my stomach's playing up.'

'The last pub in Farworth, the Nine Horseshoes, shut last week. I can open the bar here.' She jerks her head towards a fridge of craft beers and smoothies next to her till counter.

'Water, please,' I say. 'Still.'

She removes bottles from the fridge. I put my bag down and we sit at one of the tables.

'Don't you want to take off your gloves, Adam? You look like Dr No.'

I break eye contact. I sense post-emotion, that you and Sofia sat here together. You are not touching, but she feels warmly towards you. My stomach fizzes. I have to concentrate on my breathing so as not to embarrass myself in front of Mo.

Mo has already told me that Sophia was not the only kid you played card games with. Even though you had been permanently excluded from school, Mo believed that in some ways this had calmed you down. You never kicked off in Rook's Keep. You drank smoothies and played Magic the Gathering or Munchkin with quite a few of the kids who hung out here after school. No one said anything. No one complained.

'So you never thought he had this darkness in him?' I say.

'I thought he was twitchy. I thought he was odd. But if anything, I felt sorry for him. I didn't think he had any direction at all, or any skills or drive. There was no psycho vibe, though. You get all sorts in here, or you did. Dealers, dreamers, stealers, feelers. I usually suss them out right away.'

'What he did, where he went to find out how to do it, he did in the deepest darkness. It's not your fault, Mo.'

'Sophia,' she says. 'She was such a trusting girl, very sweet. She came here to use her imagination, she told me.'

Mo puts her face into her hands.

I wait for her to compose herself.

'No one,' I say, 'would think a friend would be plotting something like that.'

Apart from me. I would, but I do not tell Mo this.

'When I heard, I just fell apart,' she says. 'I felt like I had done this… I mean, I let him read the books here, I let him borrow the games when he didn't even buy a coffee, I let him mingle.'

'You could not have known. The Temple are cunning, they revel in destruction…'

'Just look at this place. No one comes anymore. It's not just here, it's the whole area.'

'And you've seen nothing else since? Shadows, movement, things that shouldn't be here?'

'No. Anyway, he killed her for money.'

'The prospect of money. He ever mention money?'

'He never had any money. He didn't have a job. He was homeless. His mother had chucked him out. He slept rough and looked it most days.'

'He wanted money for something.'

'He could have built an ark with money like that.'

'When I was sixteen I worked my behind off, three paper rounds and a Saturday job in a menswear shop that gave me a discount, just so I could buy a cool suit to impress a girl I wanted to ask out. You know, a girl who might not otherwise like me.'

'Silly boy,' she says. 'Did you sell your soul for a snog and a fumble?'

'You think Ethan was trying to impress Sophia?'

'By murdering her family?'

'I know it sounds stupid.'

'She was unworldly. She didn't even look fifteen and didn't try to dress older. He seemed bemused by her. I think she was just convenient… they were just convenient…'

'He was trying to impress someone.'

'Well, there's Keisha.'

'Keisha?'

'I thought she was his sister. Came in sometimes when he was here. She'd buy a cola but didn't play games. Gave a witness statement at the trial. Wasn't his sister, or his girlfriend.'

'What did she say at the trial?'

'He wasn't insane, then he was.'

There is a humming hive of hot wasps in my stomach. The heat surges into my face and I stand and slap my hands to my cheeks as if this will blow it all out.

—

I am outside in the mist. There is no bin. When it comes, it is loud and disgusting but no relief. She has her hands on my shoulders. I stumble away from the mess and she follows me.

'We need to find Keisha,' I say.

—

We wander the streets to the Murder Ink tattoo parlour where Mo believes Keisha works the reception. Murder Ink looks like it took a missile strike. Inside, it's white dust; scorch marks fanned across the walls, a banquette stomped in two.

Mo takes out her phone, tells me she's going to ring someone called Armin. Armin doesn't answer. She tries someone called Hassan. Hassan does answer. A pause. His voice crackles.

'Ah… oh dear… so sorry.' Mo hangs up. 'Armin is gone.'

'What does that mean?'

'I didn't want to know… Keisha's mother lives on Moon Street.'

We walk to Moon Street. The wasp hive in my gut seethes and flurries again. I try to supress the wasps by translating the scratches into sentences. You (think you) are a loser, that life is harsh and pointless. You (think you) love Keisha. Keisha does not want you because you (think you) are a loser. Nothing on your hands but time. You read about Grand Jack. Grand Jack – Candleman and Remembrancer – fucks with young heads and swallows hearts during the long afternoons and dull endless weekends of adolescent yearning. On the eerie_england subreddit, you meet the members of AOTA and they sense your need, your willingness to participate. They tell you how you can summon Him, the contract you can sign. You signed in your own blood. And you would have made a Man of Him in blood, too. Where you signed it, where you brought Grand Jack up, that is where he will be now. Grand Jack never strays far from the crack.

I am at a garden gate in Moon Street. It feels like red-hot nails are being hammered into my temples and I have swallowed molten glass. Arcane Order of the Temple of Ashes/Ash Close: is there a connection? Is this relevant? Part of some cosmic joke or setup? Up the path, Mo is at the door. I cannot see the face of the woman Mo is talking to. Mo comes back up the path.

'Under The Perch,' she says.

—

The Perch is a huge double-gabled mock-Tudor pub at the centre of concentric circles of mock-Tudor terraces that from the air must look like the ruins of Amsterdam two hundred years after the last drought. Mo said it used to be popular with the golf club and pampas grass set, but around the turn of the century it reinvented itself as a free enterprise zone for smack-gak entrepreneurs and car park gladiators. It has been shut since the time of the da Souza murders.

As we approach, its gables rise into the sky like the wings of a crouching giant bat. The lower floor windows are barred and the upper ones smashed. Mo takes me round the back and opens a hatch to the cellar. Under The Perch means literally Under The Perch. According to Mo, now there are no pubs open in Farworth, social life has gone underground. There are what she calls 'pop-down' pubs appearing across the borough, some at regular times, some semi-permanent, others spontaneous. Under The Perch is kind of always here, like Farworth itself is only kind of always here.

We reverse ourselves onto a stepladder and climb down into darkness.

Disorientated in the black chamber. Glimmer of light. A room full of smoke. Sofas and mismatched tables crowded with candles and ashtrays swamped with butts. Gaff honks of weed. Stomach is swimming the butterfly stroke, my mind the front crawl. I scan the walls for AOTA's T symbol but don't see it. There is a shocked-to-shit, in-bits-in-the-air-raid-shelter vibe to the casualties stumped on the floor or sprawled on the furniture. In Farworth so far, Mo is the closest I've seen to a set-piece. Mo is definitely not a set-piece. Mo is looking around. There is a decorator's table set out with beer cans and a few bottles of gin and vodka staffed by a tall young woman in a white smock dress. Pale blonde dreads wrap her head like the coils of white snakes. In the candlelight, something crawls up her neck. Closer in: it's a scorpion tattoo.

'Keisha,' Mo says.

I smile and hold up my glove, about to say hi.

Keisha screams. She screams and points at me and screams and flees into the wall. Slides down the wall. Screams at me and folds herself onto her haunches. Covers her head with her hands and slaps the side of her head with her long fingers.

The others surround us, sway in the smoke and the glow.

My guts are falling through my legs.

My guts are heading for my feet.

Mo is holding Keisha by the shoulder and speaking in her ear. She is saying I am a good guy. She is saying we are here to fight it. We are here so she can go back above ground again.

—

There is a side-room with mattresses and bags and cases, jeans and vests strewn everywhere. Mo sits Keisha down and then we both sit opposite her with a candle in the middle. There is a tart, sweaty smell I don't like until I realise it's me. I wonder what my face looks like and whether my appearance is causing Keisha to shiver and shake. She is looking at me like she needs to kill me.

'Adam is here to help,' says Mo. 'You can trust him.'

'His hands. He has the same hands as him.'

'He doesn't,' says Mo.

'Get your gloves off then,' Keisha shouts.

'Kiesha,' I say, 'I lost someone to it, too. I know how you feel.'

Kiesha sniffs. 'How come?'

'Jack Thorian feels only lust and plays with those who yearn.'

'What Adam is trying to say is that it's not your fault, there's nothing you could have done. But we think that maybe, in a twisted way, Ethan was trying to impress you by doing what he did… we're not saying that you wanted that, or encouraged him…'

I put my hands in my coat pockets. 'Keisha, how did you meet Ethan?'

'None of your fucking business.'

'How you met has a bearing on what he did and where that leads us. So I ask you again, how did you meet Ethan Scarver?'

She huffs. I'm sure the scorpion tattoo on her neck jitters.

'Just drifting, I suppose. It wasn't at school, and it wasn't at work, or clubbing. No one knew him but me, like, he hung with no one. He'd been pex since he was fourteen…'

'Pex?'

'Permanently excluded,' says Mo. She nods at Keisha to continue.

'I was strolling and he was on the bench and he said something nice about me I shrugged off, but he followed me, like he thought he was in some wotsit movie.'

'What did you do?'

'Nothing. His smile was wide but his eyes were scared. He had nothing, he had no one. I didn't realise he was on the streets at first, but…' She looks at Mo rather than me, as if Mo understands and I won't. '…pity has rules.'

'You say there was nothing between you,' says Mo, 'but you used to come into Rook's to see him?'

'He was talk. He wasn't handsy. I'd drawn my lines and he didn't cross them, so I felt sorry for him. I knew he was in the games place as it was warm and no haters was in there. Sometimes I'd buy him a drink or a toastie. I am saying I cared about him enough that I didn't want to see him starve. I mean, he said nice things about me that no one does, but they weren't true, I'm not that. If I'd known that he meant what he said, that he knew it was money, that I would burn with him if he had money, so he was getting himself money using magic, that we would have the best place and the best things and afford to take a taxi everywhere and not work ever, VIP areas, Chinese every night, I would have… told someone who could have done something about him, the feds even.'

Her head droops forward. The hot wasps are spiralling slowly in my guts and I need to stand up or fear some terrible accident that will call things here to an abrupt end. This is his pull. What he wants to happen to me.

Mo looks up at me, confused. I look down at Keisha and try to smile in a friendly way so I don't look like a heavily-sweating Witchfinder General. I don't want to remind her of you looking at her and looking weird or covetous or brimming with lust and with lies. I imagine you sat on your bench and seeing Keisha with her long strides and hair and taut shoulders. I remember when I joined the school myself and seeing a girl with an aura, an atmosphere about her I'd want to share, give off what she gave off but together, but she had laughed at me when the others had laughed, in History after I put my hand up and described Czarist Russia in 1917 as 'a crumbling edifice of power'. I felt skinned by her laughing, flayed by her beauty and my sense of there being nothing of me that was anything to Vix. I would never have just followed her and tried to strike up a cheerful conversation. I would have turned to water. I would have drained away.

'When did you first notice,' I say, 'that something was wrong with Ethan?'

'First?'

'You told the judge that he was not insane and then he was?'

'When I saw what he had written on the walls.'

'Written?'

'Not what, how. I mean… what *and* how. When his…' She held up two fingers and twirled them around. '…I mean, he needed to see a doctor.'

'He wrote and signed a contract with Grand Jack Thorian in his own blood.'

'And he drew a big fucking picture of the dude with the dick on the wall in blood. And his fucking fingers were like hanging off. I ran, then, and I never saw him again until court.'

In court, it was revealed that since your arrest you'd had two fingers on your right hand amputated. You had ground the pads to pulp and the bones were visible when you turned up at Farworth A&E two days after the Euromillions draw. Freaked by your appearance, the nurse called the police and the police found the contract in your bag and the contract listed the da Souzas by name when the da Souzas were still on the front page of *The Sun* in which you wrapped your hand as a makeshift bandage.

I hold the fingers of my right hand with my left. The wasps in my gut seethe as I think of you splattering your fingers against a wall to create an opening for Grand Jack Thorian.

'Keisha,' says Mo. 'Where did this happen?'

'You know that building in the trees in the grounds by the roundabout where Lidl used to be before the riots?'

'Blackdale?' says Mo.

'Yeah, Blackdale.'

'Oh fuck. He was living in there.'

'Under there. The rooms and tunnels go down for miles. I'd never go back down in there, never in a million years.'

—

Mo and I enter Blackdale Park through a hole in a chain-link fence and cross a wooded area. A swathe of uncut grass opens up. At the head of a gentle slope is the shell of Blackdale House. It was once a mansion, Mo has explained, built in the 1800s by a local notary, that during the last century was used as local government offices. Earmarked for development, the building lay vacant for years until it was set on fire in the days after the da Souza murders.

The ruins of Blackdale House look down on a copse on the other side of the grounds. The building hidden in those trees was unknown to most of Farworth's residents. Even those who had walked their dogs and come across it in the trees thought it merely an old concrete blockhouse, not the entrance to the Drayburgh Sub-Control Centre, Farworth's nuclear bunker, abandoned in 1991 and sealed until you infiltrated it.

At the tree line, we pause, take a breather. I look down at those trees. I twitch, pick up signals, hisses and whisperings. Grand Jack lurks down there, straddles a thin spot, floats in and out through the temporal-spatial node you created in a temple-chamber below ground.

Mo grabs my hand. Only the park is between us and Grand Jack.

The park reminds me of the park at home and the day I emerged from fog and Vix was sat on a bench. All the time I had spent wandering the streets hoping to randomly run into her so we could talk without much cooler-than-me set-pieces nearby taking the piss, and finally it had been facilitated.

It didn't register fully until she said my name. Not my real name, obviously. Not Adam Pasmore. She used the name they all used for me: Crumbling Edifice (sometimes this was shortened to Crumbling Ed, Eddy Crumb, or Crumbly, none of which were an improvement on my previous label, The Adding Machine).

It strikes me hard as Mo and I cross the grass and head for the trees that if I had not met Vix that day I would not have been on this mission for thirty years. I would not be Adam Pasmore, Demon Hunter; only Adam Pasmore, qualified driving instructor.

On the bench, Vix had looked grey and unwell, even more captive to it than when I'd seen her in the Starburger. Her hands were shaking. My hands were shaking, too. I put them in my pockets so she wouldn't see them.

'Hi, Vix, er, saw you in the Starburger. I mean… I saw it in your eyes.'

'My eyes?'

'You're suffering from heartache, too?'

'Heartache?'

'Missing something? Boy trouble? I am here to help.' These were not the words I had long prepared, the lines I thought someone clever and romantic, like Keats or Stuart Staples, lead singer of Tindersticks, would have said. My tongue was suddenly made of corned beef.

'Okay, it's good to talk,' she muttered, like she needed to agree out loud that it was fine to chat with me, probably because as the set-pieces hated me, I wouldn't grass or gossip. 'I have been seeing someone, but he's not a boy.'

This didn't sound right. 'Not one of the teachers?' I said.

'Fuck off, no. In the summer, right… you know that ruined chapel in the woods we saw on the geography field trip?'

'I do, yes, formerly the shrine of…'

'Went there. About twelve of us. The drama lot and the gothic hordes. Anyway, Wade Wanksoffmen, you know him?'

'Wade Winkleman? The Boy Penis?'

'Yeah. Wade Wanksoffmen said really loudly, "Why does she want a Happy Meal when it's obvious she needs an abortion," and Kerry slapped him, and it was shit, so I left and walked down these steps at the edge of the walls and down more looking for a place I could have a crafty Silk Cut without Alice Malice going on about her mum's cancer, and then I kind of felt I was being led, drawn in, that this was meant to be, and there was this sort of round room with no roof and he was there. He says his name is Jack.'

'And he's older?'

'Much older.'

'Has he touched you, Victoria?'

'You're not my dad, Crumbly.'

I stood up. The thought of what she was going to say next filled me with a raging jealousy at least as strong as the hot feverish waves pulsing through me as I approach the trees and your bunker. It was not supposed to be like this. She was not supposed to do that. It was not fair. I needed to change the conversation.

'Can I make you a mixtape?'

'Only if it's songs girls can dance to.'

Maybe I should have said this first, materialised from the fog offering mixtapes. It would have sounded friendlier and less weird.

The next week I was the first one to arrive for double Maths in the classroom with the sloping ceiling at the top of the school with the door that opens onto the roof that was out of bounds when Vix steams in, eyes bloodshot like she has the worst cold ever, and hisses, 'A word, Crumbly,' before dragging me across the room and through the emergency exit and onto the roof. It was windy and spitting with rain.

'Mixtape?' she said.

'You really want it? I didn't think you meant it.'

'Jack says I must devour new things while I can.'

'You're still seeing Jack? You shouldn't be seeing Jack.'

'I've stopped seeing Jack. I only hear him now. Hear him when I close my eyes. He wants to hear your music when he's in me, Eddy Crumb.' The sleeve of her cardigan slipped as she flashed her arm at the sky. I noticed a long red scab above her wrist.

'Shit, what did you do?' I said.

'You tell me. You're the expert's expert at everything.'

'It looks infected.'

'Jack can be rough. The tape, Crumbly. Here, tomorrow.'

The next day I hand over the tape on the roof in the sort of atmosphere I'd associate with a scene in a film where some genteel rich people hand over ransom money to bollock-hard kidnappers.

'Just a thought,' I said, 'but will you… go out with me.' My voice was squeaky, like my balls were being crushed by the coils of a mini boa constrictor. 'It makes sense… we can… I can protect you.'

'Oh don't be stupid.'

The rasping way she said this preyed on me for days. I would have asked my mum what to do, but that would mean admitting that I… liked… a… girl. A diktat would follow along the lines of: teenagers do bizarre things and go through phases and, apart from you, experiment with sex and drugs and being an arsehole. Avoid anyone like this Vix person. And put a knot in it until you're thirty or you'll end up doing community service like your cousin.

What was happening to Vix was not a rebellious phase. She needed rescuing, saving. Whatever was happening needed reversing. One night, I couldn't sleep and crept out and walked the streets in the dark and found the house where she lived, a mock-Tudor monstrosity, and stood looking up at her window. I waited for hours. No face came to the window. But I threw no grit. I told no tales, cast no spells. I regret it all. This is the moment I have always regretted the most.

—

Halfway across the grass, Mo pulls on my hand, which is not so bad in itself except I feel that if I stop walking my burning veins will heat until they melt my flesh, my bones will boil down into glue and I will not make it any further. We stop, though, and I try to control my breathing. Mo has dark and frightened eyes. She is not as robust as me. She has not passed through this before. I have no time to school her.

'Go,' I say. 'Save yourself. Find Keisha. Go to Rook's Keep. You'll know the outcome, whatever. You just will.'

—

She is no longer with me. I adjust my bag and pull down on the strap so I have something to hang onto, something to grip as I march towards the trees.

—

The Drayburgh Sub-Control Centre is a nondescript concrete shed. Anyone could be forgiven for not realising it's not only an important relic of Cold War history, an underground nerve centre for the local authority should the USSR have rained down atomic death on Farworth, but also an interdimensional portal created by blood rituals and outsider angst.

The entrance is covered by a robust board held in place by three steel rivets. They turn out to be loose and easy to remove, I expect because you prised them out some time ago. AOTA's Sergio Tacchini symbol is scratched onto the board. Grand Jack's helper elves have been here, too. I wonder if they led you here initially, or you found it by accident, looking for somewhere to sleep or sit out the rain.

Inside, the dark smells of piss and brimstone. I want to chuck up again even though there is little left inside me. I take out my head torch and special box, and sling my bag back over my shoulder. I think of the mixtape I made for Vix, my top ten for '93:

For Tomorrow - Blur
Lipgloss - Pulp
The Past Gone Mad - The Fall
Animal Nitrate - Suede
How Could I Be Wrong - The Auteurs
Hobart Paving - St Etienne
Stutter - Elastica
Wish I Was Skinny - Boo Radleys
Into Dust - Mazzy Star
City Sickness - Tindersticks

That last song, 'City Sickness', the best song ever written, my song for Vix, how heartsick I was for her, the lengths I went to to cure myself of it. That lyric about the sickness hitting straight off the train, like it was written for me, for me always and afterwards, written for today, not written for tomorrow.

—

I am burning up. Sweat must be mottling my shirt. My hair is falling out. Great wet lumps of it have slipped down my neck to my shoulders.

Something below is sucking the air down into it.

Stand and cool off in the draught.

Swallow, take a breath.

I put on my head torch.

This room is an entrance lobby.

Floor made of wood surprises me.

Anticipated concrete.

Notice boards, cabinets.

Follow the draught.

A doorway leads to a thin corridor.

I enter and follow.

Cringe thinking of you taking Keisha down here, leading her through these cramped confines.

Flickery head-shape or shadow peeps at the end of the corridor.

Light can bounce around and reflect oddly in places like this.

If it were Grand Jack Thorian at the end of this passage, my blade would need to be faster than my doubt and my fear.

Grand Jack Thorian, also The Candleman, The Remembrancer and Jack Wondrous, is the Lord of Ashes and is permitted by Those Below mastery of the lesser ashlings, Rogoth, Himhak, Divonol and Zux. He is associated with sadness and desire, lost love and thwarted lust, all of which amuse and arouse him. A binding spell must be used to summon Grand Jack, one that commits the summoner to the frequent letting of his or her blood, the sharing of any spoils and the sworn secrecy of the pact, or Grand Jack can prove both mischievous and libidinous. An incomplete bind means that the summoner's soul is forfeited to Grand Jack after a period of thirty years. When Grand Jack appears, he does so as either a tall three-legged man with a three-pointed crown and three jet-black eyes, or as a serpent made of black flame. If Grand Jack is bound securely, trades can be agreed: blood for love, blood for wishes, blood for desires, blood for flesh and slaves. If Grand Jack is not tightly bound, he is liable to interpret the trade in any way he likes. His worshippers regard Grand Jack as the Champion of the Sullen.

This was how I described Grand Jack Thorian in *The V/X Encyclopaedia of English Demons*, allocating him an armour class of 2, 399 hit points and 15 attacks per turn. I'd included him in what was a folklore guide for role-play gamers in an attempt to draw him out, take the initiative this time, not wait for the call or an email like Mo's.

I have not shared with Mo my suspicion that you have read this descriptor, that it was the copy of *The V/X Encyclopaedia* in Rook's Nest that gave you the idea of forming a pact with Grand Jack Thorian, that lead you to AOTA; that for you, as it often does, this all started as an idle game. No one, at the beginning, thinks Grand Jack Thorian is real. We all just get off on a little pain at the start.

—

The corridor leads into a room with booths on three sides. No clear wall space. You did not draw him here. I can feel some heat further in, though. The draught is flowing towards it. My face itches. I fear touching it with my glove in case my nose and cheeks come away. There is another doorway directly opposite me that feels like it's more than a doorway, that even though there are many more doorways beyond it, this is the last doorway for me.

—

Beyond the last doorway, my torch beam picks out the largest room yet, so large that at first I can't assess how big it really is. I nearly trip over a stack of metal chairs as I blunder towards what turns out to be a huge map of the city and surrounding countryside. Swinging the beam to my right, my temples throb and I'm terrified that if I don't keep my breathing this slow and steady I will sick up my guts, my kidneys and liver, and He will love this.

Then I find your handiwork.

No wonder Keisha ran.

Smeared on the wall, lines and strokes in rust-like goo.

The three-pointed crown.

That third central leg that could be a tail or some bestial sting or appendage.

Wineskin in one hand.

Dagger in the other.

Grand Jack Thorian.

Candleman.

Remembrancer.

Jack Wondrous.

At least your version worked.

At least he gave you the money.

In the *Grimorium Nigreos*, the fourteenth-century rulebook written by the Heidelberg monk Jacobus Norn that describes how to summon Grand Jack Thorian and the other demon-sergeants of Those Below, the first part of the binding ritual is to create a sigil from the name of the beloved and the name Grand Jack Thorian, cut that into the palm of one's right hand and then masturbate while thinking only about the beloved and the succumbing of the beloved.

The second move is to slit the longest fingers of the right hand lengthwise and paint a 'worshipful' image of Grand Jack in bright flow that will please him.

I imagine me as you here, the wall lit by a camping lamp, the pain in your fingers, the pain in your palm. The dabs that make the crown and the knife and the tail.

Once the image is complete, the last of the blood is to be used to draw up the contract: how many will you give for her to fall.

You wrote your contract in pencil and then bled over the letters.

This we see clearly in the photographs of the contract published after your trial.

Agreement

[For the wondrous Grand Jack Thorian]
I will sacrifice 4 u the family Dasouza
I will make a temple dedicated to your wonder
I will undertake any other tasks that please u
[For me]
Win Euromillions lottery draw
Have Keisha Kay love me back

Signed: Ethan Scarver
Signed: Grand Jack Thorian

I didn't use pencil. I tried to use only my blood. This was my first error.

I had found the instructions typed on a neatly folded note hidden in the copy of *Slave Girl of Gor* I bought from the Strange Idol Patterns second-hand bookshop, along with *Conan and the Spider God* and *Nightmares and Geezenstacks*, compensation for the merciless assault to my sense of self I'd received after the 'crumbling edifice' comment earlier that afternoon. They were intriguing rules. It sounded like a great game. Like all summoners, apart from maybe Jacobus Norn, I did not think Grand Jack was real. I just had no one to play with.

I combined her name with his and cut the resulting sigil into my palm in the ruined tower at the Shrine of the Martyr in the woods, where on the school geography trip I'd had the piss ripped out of me for knowing what transubstantiation means. I masturbated in the cool damp air, picturing the succumbing of the beloved to the sound of cooing wood pigeons and the distant swoosh of bypass traffic. It took ages. It was meagre. I drew my Jack on the tower wall. I wrote my contract, made my trade.

I don't know if it is down to the age difference between us when we drew up our contracts and consecrated our Jacks with our blood, or whether you had more stamina than me and did not keep passing out, so hurried – my hands are not as mangled as yours; I just prefer to deflect any intrusive questions by wearing gloves in public – but your artwork and grammar were better than mine.

This is the root of it all, how it's all my fault.

—

And it is all my fault. Black fire flowing up the wall either side of your Jack to meet above his crown scratch-marked in blood is my fault. The thickening of the darkness where the flame meets the flame is my fault, and my fault that I can see white veins in my eyes that start to pull away towards him, and the deep waters from deep within me are starting to steam into the breach that is widening to let him pass through it. This didn't happen to you; you got the money. He gave you the money in return. I wonder about the money, the £170 million, where it is, what will happen to it now? He gave you the money because you did everything correctly. Typical Jack, though, you get the money but will never be able to spend it. At least, though, He will not wait thirty years and then draw your soul from your heart, your soul from your skeleton. My skeleton is magma-hot. I am very aware I am only my skeleton now. What remains of my hands trembles as I unlatch my special box and take out my vorpal weapon. His three black eyes form in the black fire that's spreading to and catching his outline in front of me, tracing his form you drew with your splattered fingertips.

I think of you and I, and wonder if we had met, would we have played together? Would we have saved each other instead of damning ourselves over decades? It's my fault this happened to you. My fault: I supplied you with the book and the rules of the role-play. It's my fault you are where you are. What you did to the da Souzas is my fault, just as it's my fault what the Stolley Gargoyle did, and the Dew Ford Devil, and the Anomaly at Roford Lode, the Catcar Dissolve, the Mephit of Glaster's three-day spree, the collapse of Hardcap Bank, the disappearance of Maeve Sabeva and the Manifestation at Blue Star Point where I first let the demon before me now escape, missed with my best strike, and it's my fault, my stupid fault – never underestimate the rapture of the deep boy – what happened at Wellbrook in 1993 and what happened to Vix. I brought Jack Thorian to be, and all because I used the passive voice in my contract, the object was acted upon rather than acted, and let him sidestep me and possess her for himself and his fun.

Vix will be seduced.

Year 11 will be destroyed.

It can't have helped that the image of Grand Jack I daubed in my blood on the wall of the ruined tower looked a bit like King Rollo, the boneless simpleton cartoon sovereign my mum made me watch on VHS until I was fourteen.

For this my soul is forfeit.

He steps through fire. I will close the fiery gate. I raise my dagger, ten inches of silver blade and talismanic electrum boss blessed, according to legend, by Saint Anthony. I call it Demonsdoom. I call myself Adam Pasmore, Demon Hunter…

Ashley Stokes is the author of Gigantic *(Unsung Stories, 2021) and* The Syllabus of Errors *(Unthank Books, 2013), and editor of the* Unthology *series and* The End: Fifteen Endings to Fifteen Paintings *(Unthank Books, 2016). His recent short fiction includes 'The Hinwick Effigy' in* Cloisterfox; *'Cretaceous' in* Theaker's Quarterly Fiction; *'Fields and Scatter' in* Weird Horror; *'Subtemple' in* Black Static; *'The Validations' in* Nightscript; *and 'Black Slab' in* The Ghastling. *Other stories have appeared in* Out of the Darkness *(edited by Dan Coxon, Unsung Stories),* This is not a Horror Story *(edited by JD Keown, Night Terror Novels),* Tales from the Shadow Booth, BFS Horizons *and more. He lives in the East of England where he's a ghost and ghostwriter.*

Habitual

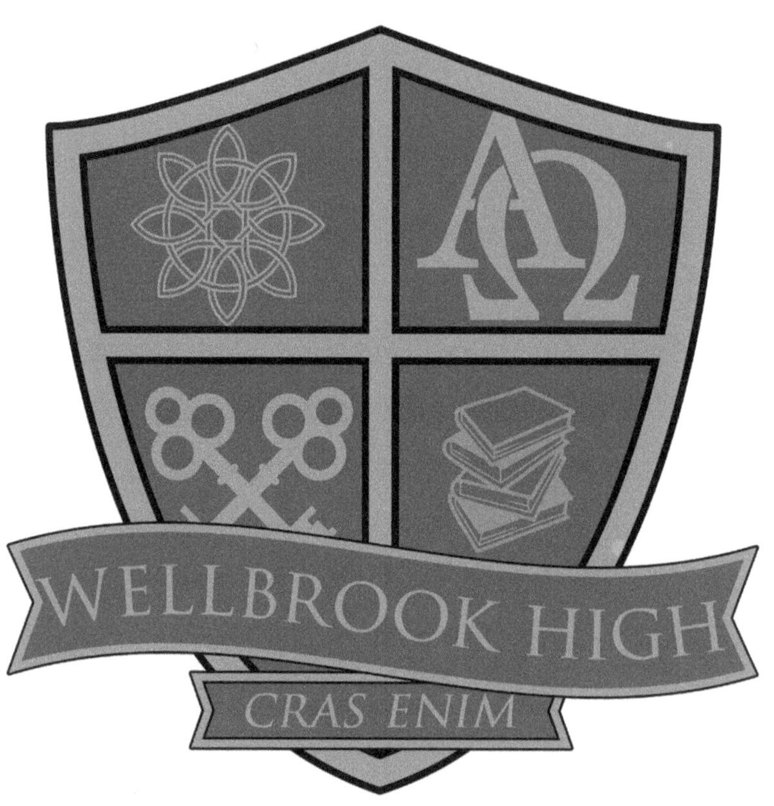

by

Daniel Carpenter

20

January: the walls of his flat sticky with damp, blackened spots growing on the ceiling, trailing down the walls. He moves furniture to discover mould crawling up the backs of sofas and bookshelves. Summer in the place had been bad; they'd been invaded by rats and flies – overspill from the restaurant next door that got shut down after it failed another inspection. But this is so much worse than he could have expected. People in his house threaten to move out and then do, dissolving into London: Pete and Den had bought a houseboat somewhere in the tangle of rivers and canals around Hackney, Frankie was heading back up to Sheffield to move in with her parents again. When Gawel tells him over a cuppa one night that he's found a bunch of other delivery drivers who have a spare room, and he's leaving in a week, he decides it's time for him to go too.

He dreads to think about living alone, how much the loneliness gets to him, chills him; makes him want a drink. That road should have been behind him long ago but there it is again, rearing its head, and he cannot think of that right now.

So he signs up to every site he can, trawls the ads, swipes and swipes. But the prices are high, too much for him, and every place he finds that looks like it might be good is gone, or going, or so competitive he wouldn't stand a chance.

Christ. What is this city becoming? he thinks, nursing another cup of tea with shaking hands.

19

They send him a text, and for some reason his phone doesn't flag it as spam. He opens it unconsciously.

Your zone one property is waiting for you. Get paid to live in luxury.

A con. Clearly.

He ignores it and goes back to serving the next customer their latte.

Later, on his way home, he eyes it again. Why is it catching his eye so much? Why does he feel so drawn to it? He can't explain. The night has fallen earlier than he expected, and the lights from takeaways and passing cars dance around him on the top floor of the bus. He's not looking forward to heading home, the place will feel cold and empty with so

many of them gone. Everyone feels so distant from him now, all of them moving on in ways he has never been able to: settling down, having a family, buying a home, making a life for themselves. He's never considered the thing he's made as some kind of a life. Just a series of days and weeks that have happened. No trajectory, barely any memories of some of those times.

That's the old days, though. Best not to think of those.

But he can't help it. Not when it's night and there's people a few pints deep, singing and chatting on the bus, and the warmth of it, the happiness of them, clings to him like cigarette smoke. He'll shower when he gets in. Bathe. Scrub it off.

When he opens his front door, he flicks the light switch in the hallway and… nothing. The bulb has gone. Just what he needs. He flicks his phone torch on and shines it up along the hallway. Spare bulbs are where now? Did they ever buy any? Possibly the power to the whole place has gone, which would be perfect.

Then his torch catches something in the air around the bulb, and a fragment of light cracks open, like a bird hatching. He squints up at the light fitting, shines the torch up there.

Flies. Hundreds of them, crammed around the bulb, blocking the light out.

That night he opens the message again and clicks the link.

18

Over the road from his place, as he's hauling the last of his boxes into the back of the rental, someone lies prone on the ground, face down against the kerb. People walk past and glance down but do nothing. *Just another lost Londoner*, he thinks. Someone falling through the cracks of the city. It seems so much easier to do that now than ever before. Could have been him once upon a time, the way he'd been. The city could have swallowed him up in that first year. Either the job would have done it for him, or the drink. Probably both.

Not now, though. New place. Incredible location. High up above everyone else.

He'll be a king.

When he'd spoken to the rep on the phone, they'd been enthusiastic. No, they didn't need to meet him face to face. No need. He was the ideal candidate. 'It's practically empty,' they told him. 'A few workmen every now and then, but no one lives there.' Every flat had been sold, but all to foreign investors. Once, one summer, the son of a dignitary from Dubai showed up for a week, but didn't come back again.

'It represents a substantial investment for our clients, so it's good to have someone in the building, keeping an eye on things.'

Like a concierge, or a security guard? he'd asked.

'Both, but you get the flat rent free, there's a gym on the fifteenth floor, and an infinity pool on the twentieth. You get access to all of it. Just keep an eye on the place.'

The keys were in a lock box, they said. They would text him the code. The man on the phone never asked him if he wanted the job or the flat, it was just assumed that the answer was yes. Of course, they were right.

A police van pulls up next to the man on the road. They check his pulse and haul him up by his arms and legs, chucking him into the back of the van with little fanfare, making jokes and laughing the whole time.

17

The building is in Canary Wharf, strange and emptied at the weekend when he chooses to move. In the docks, enormous luxury yachts sit moored, and he wonders if the people staying in them own some of the flats in the building. There's the gentle dip of oars as a handful of kayaks row alongside them, dwarfed.

This whole place is a playground, he thinks. The rich buying up flats and houses everywhere and never living in them. Places in the city closing off more and more from people like him. When did it all turn into a theme park? He can't remember, but he knows it happened in his lifetime.

He finds the lockbox and picks up the keys before heading inside.

The lobby is enormous, seeming to stretch out further than should be possible. In front of him, a ringed leather sofa welcomes him, and above it, a luxurious glass chandelier. Mirrors everywhere reflect the opulence and extravagance, but somehow refuse to capture him. Trailing his suitcase behind him, containing his few possessions, he feels like an intruder. *Don't make too much noise, you'll wake...* but then he remembers there's no one to wake.

A screen in front of the lifts asks him which floor he'd like and he selects the eighteenth. The doors open silently to a sleek metal box. No buttons on the inside; not even, as far as he can tell, an emergency button. The doors shut and the lift starts making its way up, except that's not what it feels like. His stomach lurches, and he feels less like he is ascending than descending. Drilling down into the ground. Numbers on a small screen above the doors climb up and up, but he knows deep inside himself that it is down.

It's a surprise, then, when he opens the door into the flat, and the first thing he catches a glimpse of is the view: London, stretching itself out to the horizon. All of it distant, unreachable, but present. *Like a model village*, he thinks. The city fills the windows, draws him in. So much so that he almost doesn't take in any of the flat itself. Whoever owns the place hasn't done much to it: the big open space he's stood in has a living area with a sofa and chair facing a large flatscreen TV; to his right is a long white dining table, ten or so chairs neatly tucked in, light bulbs dangling over it and a wood burner enclosed within a glass case separating it from the kitchen. Doors on either side of the room lead, presumably, to the bedrooms, study and bathrooms.

He lets go of the suitcase and flops down on the chair, staring out of the window as a handful of boats shoot through the Thames.

He could get used to this.

16

Daytimes he walks the corridors. Grabs the lift to the next floor, ignores the lurching feeling of the lift, always telling him he's going the wrong way, and explores every corner of the building. The rep was right. The place is totally empty. A ghost town.

On the twentieth floor, deckchairs lie unused and spread out across a wooden deck, overlooking the infinity pool. If he swims to the very edge of the water, he can look straight down: a twenty-storey drop to the street. When he clumsily attempts lengths, he can't help but feel like a disturbance.

In the gym, the dull *thunk* of a machine he's using, or the *clink* of weights knocking against each other, are intrusions in the silence.

Every noise he makes, another invasion. Every step, another message that he doesn't belong. But he shakes it off.

15

The nights are beyond quiet. Thick glass on every wall of the flat means that, with the windows closed, no noise gets in. He can see the lights of the city dancing, cars, planes, boats and people at all times every day, and yet he hears nothing. If he wanted to, he could let it all in, but that wouldn't be right. *The building wouldn't want that*, he thinks. So he flicks the TV on and leaves it running all night, the volume low enough for the noise to be a drone, filling the gaps. He's so used to the sounds of homes filled with people, creaking floorboards, toilets flushing at odd hours, low-level chatter. The wish to drown out the silence with something lingers inside him. Used to be that the drink would help, but he won't do that. He won't ever go down that road again. The drink is why he found himself in his mid-forties still living in flat-shares, working shitty jobs for shitty pay. When he thinks about it, really tries to think, he knows it could all be traced back to school and the things that happened. No kid should have to go through that. Growing up where he did didn't help either. But he won't let it take hold of him again. He cannot. So he lets the news, reality shows and sports wash over him quietly instead.

14

Once a week or so he heads outside for food. There's a small convenience store a few roads over which he uses for his weekly shop. Outside there is a freshness to the world, something he realises he has missed. Each time he tells himself he'll crack open a window, spend more time on the roof garden in the pool, go out for a run. But when he returns to the building, he cannot bring himself to do that.

13

A sound wakes him. It is the middle of the night, and the blue-tinged TV screen provides light enough for him to see. A scraping. Above him? Below him? It's hard to tell. He climbs out of bed and tries to pinpoint the location of it. There: right above him. Footsteps on the ceiling, a chair being moved, the quiet murmur of conversation.

Someone else is here.

The rep said they'd text if someone was visiting. Maybe they just forgot.

He can investigate in the morning. Knock on the door of the flat immediately above him, offer a cup of tea or something. Closing his eyes, he tries to fall back to sleep.

But the noise rises. Rises. Rises.

What at first had been the low dull scraping of a chair now sounds like a long fingernail dragging itself down a rusted pipe. The footsteps on the ceiling; a cacophony of giants crushing the floorboards beneath their feet. The quiet murmur of conversation; a horrible, raucous laughter directed at him.

The sounds fill his room and he thinks it might be better in the living room. He grabs his duvet and hauls it into the open space, but even there the sound is deafening.

It's beyond his understanding. As though someone has turned an amp up to full volume and planted it in his head. How can anything be so loud?

He shuts his eyes. Squeezes them closed. Please just stop. Just stop.

Please.

But nothing works.

He could call someone. Environmental services? He briefly recalls a couple of blokes showing up at the door of a house party once when he was a teenager. Trying to get them to turn the music down. Fuck lot of good that did.

Before he really understands why, he's in the hallway heading for the lift. Even out here, the noise is present. Scraping and laughing. He selects the next floor up and feels that strange lurch of the lift rising (descending).

The noise is louder now. An unbearable sound. He feels tears in his eyes and a part of him wants to reach into his sockets, push his fingers right to the back of them and tear his eyeballs out. As though that might just stop it.

Anything to make it stop.

The bell of the lift arriving at its destination is barely audible, and as the doors open, the wails and screams, the tearing and ripping, rises and rises and rises and…

Stops.

The corridor is silent. At the end, heading for the stairs, he spots a couple of police officers, one of them with a shock of ginger hair awkwardly shoved beneath his hat.

'Everything alright?' he tries to call out, but his voice is weak.

Still, one of them turns and for a moment it is as though he is seen. But they don't acknowledge him and leave through the stairwell door.

By the time he makes it there, they are long gone, and the door to the flat above him is locked.

He goes back to bed and tries, desperately, to sleep again.

12

There was a time when the drinking was too much. Before he knew how bad it was really getting. Falling asleep on the train after work and waking up in Brighton. Making it home only to discover the bed covered in shit in the morning. Blackouts. Nights that vanished from his memory. Friends who never forgave him for things he would never recall. The more everyone retreated from him, the more he retreated from everyone else.

It was easier to be alone.

The city liked lonely people. It welcomed them in and fed them well. Like a witch in a fairy tale. That was the true secret of London; the real magic. You could blink and somehow years would pass and you'd have spent them drunk and happy. But there would be sulphur in the air. A burning lingering in the background. An oven on. A pot waiting. A hungry, hungry city waiting for its reward.

11

A few days later he heads out again. Just to the shop on the corner. He still can't bear to go any further.

Sitting down next to it, a homeless guy with a hastily scrawled sign. *Hungry, God Bless.* Lined up next to him, a row of old *Big Issue*s. The man gives him a wave as he walks by.

'Bit of change?' he asks.

'Sorry mate, I haven't anything.'

The man looks at him briefly, eyeing him up. 'No worries,' he nods.

I see you, the nod says, *I know what you are.*

10

Next time he's down there he gives the man a handful of change, buys him a Coke and a sandwich from the shop too.

On the way back he glances up at the tower. There's the light in his living room that he left on.

But there is another light. A few floors up. A red light casting out into the evening sky. It reminds him of the aircraft warning lights towards the rooftop, and for a moment he thinks it might be just that. But this isn't the same kind of light. This light bathes the room it sits in.

There's another one, too. This one a few floors below. Much clearer than its counterparts, being lower to the ground. It's coming from a standing lamp next to a television. The pale yellow casts unearthly shadows around the room, making it look almost as though there are people in there.

Did the people at the agency say anything about security lights and timers? Maybe. He can't remember.

Behind him there's a commotion. He turns to see the homeless guy being hauled to his feet by two officers. The ginger hair of one of them is still vivid in his memory. Around the shop, passers-by don't even acknowledge it. Without thinking, he rushes over.

'Hey,' he shouts, 'what's going on?'

The officers ignore him. The ginger one has the homeless guy's arm bent and locked against his back, pushing him towards the back door of their van.

'Hey!'

This time they pause and turn. A few people stop, too. One of them pulls out a phone.

'What are you doing? What did he do?'

The ginger-haired one grins, deliriously happy. The other officer tips the brim of his hat.

They let go of the homeless guy, clamber back into the van and drive off.

9

He went down the pier once, in some seaside town on the coast. Got a reading done. Thought he recognised the woman doing it, from school maybe? But he didn't like to think about those days, so he never asked. Wouldn't have mattered whether he'd asked or not anyway, he was half cut as it was. She'd shown him a picture of the Hanged Man, a rope tightly knotted around his ankle, upside down from a wooden cross, leaves brimming with life.

'Should I be worried?' he'd joked with her, and it had probably come out like *shudibworrid*, but he knew from the serene expression on the man's face that there was no need. He was trapped, but he was happy.

The rest of that day had been a blur, then a blackout. He'd woken on the train back to London. Never even remembered the name of the town. For all he knew, that whole day had been just a strange dream.

8

It's late in the evening a few weeks later when he hears the noises. They sound as though they're coming from the living room, so he hauls himself out of bed and texts the agency, *Is anyone supposed to be coming tonight? I thought you would warn me*, but it's out of hours and they haven't responded to him before anyway, so why would they now? Creeping along the wooden floors of the room, he can hear it all getting louder and louder. Whatever it is must be on the other side of the door. *They've broken in*, he thinks, without understanding who *they* are.

The first thought he has is to apologise to the building. Touch the walls and say, *I'm sorry they're doing this to you.*

When he opens the door, the noise hits him like the first pint of the night. The room is empty but the sound is there, present in the room with him. A horrible cacophony of screaming, shouting, things breaking, ancient industrial machines burrowing and clashing. The noise is rust and broken things. It is old foundations dragging themselves out of a pit. It is the oldest noise he has ever heard and he cannot understand how he knows that. There's no point covering his ears: the noise is inside him too. It is everywhere and everything.

He stumbles to the kitchen. On the countertop there's a six-pack of Stella. None of the cans opened.

When did he buy that? He doesn't recall. But he feels that pull inside him, the desperation for a drink flooding back. He should throw them away. No, better than that, he should open every can and pour them down the sink. If their contents were still in the can, he could easily just grab one out of the bin. No, they need to be emptied completely.

But that noise.

That awful, awful noise.

He can't think. Not properly, anyway. He balls his hands into fists, pushes them against his temples, harder, harder, but it's no use. That fucking thing isn't going anywhere. Pulling the quilt from his bed, he curls up on the sofa, hoping against hope that it will just go away.

7

What were the worst times? Not the blackout drunk nights, no. They caused anxiety, but since the memories were wiped from his brain, he had nothing to cling on to, nothing to truly feel awful about. No. There were worse. Fights. Fucks. Both with strangers. Waking up in cities he couldn't name, in flats that didn't belong to him. The constant stink. The constant need. Hands shaking all fucking day. Even after, when he'd stopped. The days he didn't drink but couldn't think of anything else. Like a constant, obsessive noise in his head. Like someone screaming at him, grabbing his hands and slapping his face with them. *Why are you drinking yourself? Why are you drinking yourself?*

6

It doesn't stop. It will never stop.

He leaves the flat and it's there in the corridor. In the stairwell. All the way up the stairs too. No change to the volume of it. Now he can pick out individual noises: shrieks and wails, the horrible dull *shuck* of a knife going into flesh, the *crack* of a bat or a stick or something against bone. Are there drums too? Or is it the low, painful moan of someone's last few moments? Hundreds – no, thousands of voices pushing together like a wave of pain.

If he can find its source, then he can sleep, finally.

5

He exits the stairwell and he cannot quite understand what he is looking at. The floor above his flat was identical to his, but now appears to stretch on and on beyond the building. As far as he can see, there is no endpoint to it, just corridor for what could be miles.

He stumbles towards the door of the flat directly above his. His hands are shaking, his body telling him he needs something. Just go away. Just leave and go back downstairs. Go far from here. Find somewhere new. Somewhere different. But he's turning the handle anyway. He has a horrible feeling of belonging.

Before he can open the door, it's pulled open. Two police officers barge past him, leaving the flat. They turn and smirk at him.

'They're all in there, if you're interested,' the ginger one says to him.

'Party's just getting going,' says the other in a fit of laughter.

4

Inside, there's a smell that coats the flat. A hot, cloying smell. Something melting. Glue? It brings to mind old technology classes. The odd texture of glue against skin, the two fusing together. It's dark in the entrance, and as his eyes adjust he can make out figures. There are people here?

There's two of them in the hallway on the cusp of the living room, nursing drinks in their hands. A third sits in a chair just at the edge of his vision.

None of them move.

The world screams at him.

'Hello?' He tries to wave at them. 'Everything alright?'

As an afterthought he pathetically adds, 'I heard a noise.'
But there is no answer.
He reaches for the light switch and flicks it on.

3

The homeless man from the shop is poised with a drink in the corridor, standing opposite a woman he doesn't recognise. They are both dead, but their bodies are solid, standing upright and posed like two dolls. The third person, in the chair, is the same, a rictus grin stapled to his face, left hand permanently forced into a thumbs up.

He walks further into the flat and there are more of them. A man in a suit caught in a freeze-frame breakdance, his bones snapped and reset at impossible angles. In the kitchen, an older woman, glamorous in a black silk dress, expensive jewellery adorning her neck and wrists, is stuck in the middle of pouring a cocktail, mouth open in a perpetual scream. Her eyes, oh Christ, her eyes. There are more still: he can see so many of them in the flat.

2

And by the bedroom he sees it: a wooden cross and a rope. A set of steps next to it to help him. They trust him to do what he is supposed to do, what his body is telling him to do. It's about time he gave in, after all. He's just one of so many of them, slipping through the cracks of this place.

1

He climbs up the steps and ties the rope around his ankles and he looks around the flat, at all the people cheering him on, screaming and crying and wailing, and he can feel himself being hoisted up and up and then he is upside down and he understands, he finally understands.

He opens his mouth and waits for the city to take what it needs.

Daniel Carpenter *is a Mancunian living in London. He writes about cities and the people who get lost in them and his stories have been previously featured in* Year's Best Weird Fiction *and* Year's Best Dark Fantasy and Horror. *He tweets at @dancarpenter85.*

Shadowing

by

Penny Jones

Emily drove her battered old Ford home. She wondered if it was just her, or if it always felt this odd for people when they came back. The town centre managed to look both alien – a façade masquerading as home – and eerily familiar. As if she'd driven through a time warp, back to when she was a teenager.

It was the best of times, it was the worst of times.

Emily giggled to herself. 'See, Mum! I did learn something at school after all.' Emily wracked her brain for the next line, but she couldn't remember it.

The car had been her pride and joy back then, bought for her by her parents when she passed her test. Smiles on their faces as they spoke about it being vital for when she left to go to uni, when she left home, when she left.

'Easier for you to get round, love. Easier for you to pop home, too; you know, if it's too much, if you can't cope,' her mum said.

'Easier for her to bring her dirty washing back,' her dad had guffawed, choking on his tea.

Emily hadn't wanted to dissuade them from the idea of her going to university. She'd managed to pass her GCSEs okay, years of study making them a doddle, even after everything that had happened, but her A-levels had been another matter.

The teachers had given her – had given them all – some leeway. Cosy chats with the head of sixth form had replaced meetings with her parents, especially while Tom, her boyfriend, was in the hospital.

She visited Tom often back then, though as time went on maybe not as often as she should have. Two buses and the darker winter nights had made the journey more treacherous. She'd still told her parents she was visiting him. Hiding from them that, rather than travelling across town after school, she was instead walking the route of where *it* had happened; of where Tom tried to end his life.

Once she'd got the car, she'd told herself she'd go and see Tom more often. That she'd tell him what she needed to say, that she'd whisper in his ear what she should have told him months before. She'd wanted to tell him first, hoping that if she did then he would wake; but maybe she wasn't so naïve, as each time she'd visited she'd found a reason not to tell him. Either the nurses were present, or his parents. He always seemed to be just on his way out for tests or being brought back from them; needing to rest.

She'd hidden it all from her parents. Binning the concerned letters sent home from school each month, begging her teachers not to phone them when they didn't attend the parent–teacher meetings yet again. She'd brought in vague doctors' notes to explain her absences. Casual mentions to the staff about the journalists and papers that were still in contact, enough to prevent any real attempts by them to get to the root of the problem; anyway, they knew the root of the problem, they all did, well at least they thought they did.

She'd never told Tom; as far as she knew, he'd never known. She'd cut all contact with his parents, with her friends, with everybody when she'd gone away; her parents said it was for the best. They always thought they knew what was best for her, even now, even after everything that had happened. Emily didn't bother to try and dissuade them. There was no sense in pointing out to them the gaping hole in their reasoning, in their lives, in her life. There was no point in doing so, if all it did was remind them once more of what a terrible person, daughter, mother she'd been.

Emily didn't even know if Tom was still alive. She wondered if he still lay there, sleeping like a child in that hospital bed, getting smaller and smaller as he curled foetally further up into himself and away from the world, away from the hurt, away from her. She hoped he was dead.

—

Emily had only been back a week before her mum told her about the care agency down the road who were looking for staff. Standing in Emily's bedroom doorway, her mum had plonked two black bin bags either side of her, as if using them to stop Emily squeezing past her and escaping. It reminded Emily of the last time she'd been there. In the shadows, her mum looked exactly the same, arms crooked, hands on her hips, her words an echo of those before – asking Emily what she was going to do, that she wasn't a child anymore.

Emily tried to answer, but before she'd even opened her mouth, her mother told her that she was due for an interview the next morning at nine. Rolling her eyes, Emily snorted in derision. A sliver of mucus settled at the end of her nose. She wiped it on her sleeve, smiling at her mum's disgust; if they were going to treat her like a child, she may as well act like one, she thought.

'Get a tissue.'

'Why, so I don't mess up all my beautiful clothes?' Emily waved the frayed sleeve of her ancient jumper. All her clothes were second-hand – the kind that even the charity shops turned their noses up at; moth-eaten, stretched and stained, cleaned then bundled into bags for those that couldn't even afford the cost of a loaf of bread, let alone a Primark jumper or a coat from Oxfam.

'I can't go for an interview. I don't have anything to wear.'

'Here.'

Her mum grabbed one of the black bags and tossed it at Emily. Her mum had lifted it as if it held nothing but feathers, but as the bag struck Emily in the chest the force nearly knocked her flat. Grasping the plastic, Emily used the first bag to deflect the impact of the second one her mum threw at her.

'Try these on. There must be something worthwhile left here from when you were younger.'

Emily searched through the bags, each item of clothing taking her further back in time. The lumberjack shirt she'd wrapped round herself to hide her ever growing stomach from prying eyes; band shirts from gigs whose music had blasted in her ears, drowning out her memories, her fears. She remembered that smothering intensity of the heat, noise, of bodies pressed against her, replacing one yearning with another. Emily had never taken Tom to those gigs; he'd been too jittery after everything that had happened, his parents coddling him had made his nerves worse. She hadn't wanted to end up babysitting him, so she'd gone alone, had enjoyed the sense of freedom. Emily wondered if she'd taken him, if she'd let that claustrophobic atmosphere crowd everything out from his mind, whether he'd still have done it?

Emily stuffed the shirts down beneath the last item of clothing in the bag, a shimmery silver dress, so short she was surprised her mom ever let her wear it. Nowadays they'd call it a prom dress, but back then it was just the end-of-school disco. An excuse for the year elevens to celebrate. The school threw one for the sixth-formers too, but that one was off the school premises, with a bar and everything. Theirs still had a tuck shop; though someone had spiked the squash with Mad Dog, so the night hadn't been a complete washout. That, and the bottle of Lambrini Tom hid away for after, was probably what had led to her thinking that just once without protection would be okay. She'd usually been so sensible, had never wanted kids, not before and certainly not after. But the alcohol must have done something. She'd never have thought herself capable of getting in the mood, not there, not where it had happened. Maybe it wasn't the alcohol that made her think just the once wouldn't matter, maybe it was something else; something in the air, as the romantics liked to say.

—

Emily had worn her sixth-form suit for the interview. She'd been shocked it still fitted after all these years, after everything she'd been through; her body stretched and deflated, her skin and soul scarred by both herself and others. Slipping it on was like slipping back into her seventeen-year-old self. It hadn't mattered that she was wearing a tatty old suit anyway. The interview had been little more than a cursory question of when she could start. Emily had frozen when they'd asked her to complete her police check forms. But with a smile and a wave of the hand the interviewer had told her not to worry, that the forms would take some time and she could just take them home with her. Emily had nodded and slipped them into her bag.

'You'll be shadowing anyway, while you learn the ropes.'

Emily nodded once more as she was ushered out of the office, with entreaties to arrive at six the next morning, and not to be late, running through her ears.

Emily made her way back across the street to where she'd parked. Everywhere seemed to be double-yellow lines now, and the parking in the alley by the office was already full when she'd arrived. She'd ended up having to park in the car park across the road, wishing she'd ignored her guilt and accepted that fiver from her mum. She'd been sure the parking wouldn't cost more than a quid, and she still had a couple of pounds left to tide her over. Unfortunately the parking had been an eye-watering £3.50 for an hour. The machine gave the option of paying by card or by phone if you didn't have change, but Emily had neither. She added it to her ever-growing mental list of stuff she needed to sort now she was back home. She had ended up leaving the car in the middle of two others, parking its bumper up as close as possible to the brambles that edged the car park.

Squeezing back between her car and the van that had parked next to her, Emily was glad to see she hadn't got a ticket. She threw the paperwork for her new job onto the seat next to her, the police check sat on top. *Don't worry about that, it's only a formality. We have to ask all staff to fill one out; nothing ever comes back on them.*

Emily wondered if she'd have had to declare the parking ticket on it if she'd gotten one. Was a parking ticket a criminal offence? Then she wondered if she'd have to declare anything about the baby on there. They'd said it wasn't her fault; but they didn't know where the baby had been conceived, her parents had told her not to talk about that, that they'd lock her up in the asylum if she did. So she didn't, but she'd still been locked up, no matter the nice names her family and the staff called it.

—

Emily woke muggy-headed the next morning; her medication didn't go well with early starts. Sipping a cup of tea, she picked up a banana, promising her mum that she'd eat it on her way to work.

Emily pulled into the alleyway by the care agency; at least being up so early meant there was still space for her to park. Locking the car behind her, she made her way round to the office. Taking a deep breath, she smiled and hoped it didn't look as fake as it felt as she pushed the door open.

She looked round the empty office. She wasn't sure what to expect – certainly not a welcoming committee – but there was no one there at all. Carefully, Emily made her way through the small space, squeezing between the desks strewn with papers and files. Other than two wire-meshed windows by the door, the rest of the walls were covered by whiteboards, their surfaces scored and delineated into grids and boxes, scrawled writing stuffed into each. Even if she understood what the lists were for, she doubted she'd be able to read that cramped and crabbed script.

'Hello,' Emily called into the empty room. She checked her watch as she made her way through the desks. 'Hello. It's Emily.'

'What are you doing here?'

Emily jumped at the voice. Turning, she saw a woman stood in the doorway. 'I was told to come here. I'm Emily.'

The woman made her way towards her. Emily held her hand out, but the woman was already seating herself at one of the desks. 'You should be out on visits by now.'

'I'm here for the shadowing. I'm new.'

The woman sighed as she pushed her chair back. 'Did they tell you who you were shadowing?'

'No, sorry. They just told me to be here at six.'

'You're late, it's half past. Never mind, too late to be worrying about that now. I'll let it slide this once, but don't make a habit of it.'

Emily bit back a retort. Last thing she needed was to lose this job before she'd even started.

'Uh. That explains it.' The woman pointed at the illegible scribbling on one of the whiteboards. 'You were supposed to be shadowing Emily.'

Emily was about to explain that she *was* Emily, she was the one shadowing, not being shadowed. But before she could speak, the woman laughed.

'Emily shadowing Emily. Would've been amusing if that girl ever bothered to turn up.' The woman stood. 'Well, she hasn't turned up, yet again, so you're stuck with me. I'm Mary; I suppose I'll be showing you the ropes.'

Mary stepped towards her. 'I hope you're not like Emily.'

Emily opened her mouth to respond, but the woman had already hurried past her and out of the office.

—

'You'll be fine. I'll show you what to do.'

Emily followed Mary out of her car and into the early morning drizzle.

'It's easy really, just like looking after a baby.'

Mary typed a number into a metal box attached to the wall. 'Don't worry about these, we get all our clients' families to change them to the same number: 1, 3, 7, 9.'

Mary took the key and fitted it into the lock. She called out breezily as she opened the door. 'It's okay, Joan, it's just me, Mary from the agency. I've come to get you up.'

Mary turned to Emily and whispered, 'Watch for this one, her family like to come and do her nails, and she likes to use them.' She headed off down the hallway, calling, 'I've brought a new friend to meet you today.'

Emily closed the front door behind her then turned to follow Mary, but she'd gone. A door stood open at the end of the hall, voices whispered in the gloom. Emily strained to hear what was being said. As she stepped closer the one voice changed, its tone no longer cajoling, became harsh; the only response an undulating scream.

Emily took a step back towards the front door. She remembered those screams. That sound so large it wasn't natural, impossible for those paroxysms to come from something so small. Emily had her back to the front door when Mary stepped out of the room.

'We'll try with the next one; Joan's having a bit of a tantrum in here. Do us a favour and sort her breakfast. She'll have tea: milky with two sugars, and toast with marmalade. Just a scrape, though, else she gets it everywhere.'

Emily stepped away from the front door and made her way towards the kitchen, scuttling past the door that Mary had shut behind herself. Putting on the kettle, she hoped its boiling would hide the shouts and screams that emanated from the room next door.

The tea, already cool from so much milk, was cold by the time Mary came in to collect it.

'Bring the toast. Now she's up, Joan's in a much better mood. I'll introduce you.'

Emily brought the breakfast into what she presumed had once been Joan's lounge, but now appeared to be her everything and nothing all at once. A bed stood poking out between the fireplace and the bay window, its sheets tangled and reeking of urine and sweat, competing with the commode that stood between it and the chair that Joan was already falling asleep in.

'Joan you've got to eat your breakfast. Here.' Mary placed a triangle of toast between Joan's fingers and pushed it towards her mouth. Joan turned her head away, her mouth clamped shut in refusal. 'Emily. Why don't you try?'

Emily stepped forwards, Joan's eyes widening as they followed her approach. Emily picked up a slice of toast. Joan opened her mouth. Emily made to place the toast within it, but Joan smacked it from her hand.

Joan's voice came out dry and ancient. 'I know what you did.'

—

'See. It's easy.'

Mary pulled into the driveway at Joan's house once again. Well, Emily presumed it was Joan's house, but they all looked alike. Emily got out of the car and scanned the houses, looking for something to set them apart, looking for a way to tell that this was Joan's house, and not Bill's or Edna's or Heidi's or Maive's.

Mary was right, it should be easy, Emily thought. Each visit had been the same; same house, same key safe: 1,3,7,9. Emily made them milky sweet tea with toast and marmalade while Mary got them washed and dressed. Emily stripped the beds and put on the washing while Mary emptied the commode. Emily heard them, though, whispering, warning Mary about her. No one wanted Emily near them; they shied away as she approached them, their watchful eyes judging her, even as she placed their plates of toast on their tables, making sure to edge the plates close enough that they could pinch the sticky triangles between their fingers, without those fingers being able to pinch her.

—

The next day Emily lay in.

'Enjoy it while you can,' Mary had told her. 'I'll meet you outside the office at four tomorrow, to show you the ropes for the evening shift.'

Emily dry-swallowed her morning tablets, glad she had time to come round. Her meds always made her feel muggy-headed. Not tired as such, she struggled to sleep on them, but when she did she struggled to wake, often spending her mornings as if still dreaming, her nightmares often following her from night to day.

It hadn't mattered so much before; they'd always woken Emily early, telling her that she needed routine if she was going to cope back home. But there was little that was taxing enough to pull her from her morning stupor, tea and cafeteria food enough to carry her through the day until the evenings drew in, and her boredom once more sent her to her bed to doze fitfully until morning. But now she was home she'd have to be more alert, would have to make more of an effort. Remembering the advice of the staff, Emily heaved her heavy limbs out of bed and made her way downstairs to grab some breakfast, hoping her parents would be out.

She was in luck; the downstairs was empty, her dad at work, her mum out doing whatever it was she did to occupy her time. Emily popped the kettle on and slid two slices of bread into the toaster, slathering them with butter. She placed the knife to slice the toast into triangles, before stopping, her knife poised to cut. Instead she dropped it in the sink and grabbed the slice whole and stuffed it into her mouth, her teeth ripping a chunk of it away, butter dripping off and onto her hand. Emily licked her fingers before taking her plate through to the lounge and switching the telly on.

It was gone lunchtime when Emily heard the sound of her mum's keys in the front door. Guilt flooded through her as she cast her eye across the coffee table in front of her, her breakfast plate still sat there, butter congealing on its surface, a scattering of crumbs adorning the table around it. Emily was still in her pyjamas, her hair unbrushed; quickly, she grabbed the forms she'd been given at the interview. The first page was crammed with tiny writing, listing everything and anything that Emily needed to include on the form. Her eyes alighted on the word *infanticide*, listed between incest and kidnapping; Emily quickly turned the page. The next page asked for her address for the last five years, listing the bills and letters she could use as proof. Emily folded the papers and placed them back in the folder.

'It's just me,' Emily's mum called out as she opened the door.

Emily wondered if the greeting was a warning or a reassurance.

'Hi,' she responded, the silence from her mum only broken by the sound of the front door closing. 'I was just reading through my paperwork. You know, for work.'

Footsteps made their way along the hallway. Emily waited for them to stop by the lounge door, but instead they passed by and she heard the sound of her mum unpacking the shopping in the kitchen.

'I better go and grab a shower and get changed for work.'

'I thought you weren't in until four?'

'They want me in a bit earlier to go through some training.' Emily opened the lounge door and, without glancing at her mum, sped up the stairs and into the bathroom.

Standing under the shower, Emily counted the minutes away, trying to eke out the simple task of getting ready for work.

—

Emily arrived at the office at bang on four. She was glad she had decided to walk in; the alleyway next to the office was again rammed bumper to bumper with cars. Though what she remembered as a half-hour walk into town as a teen had taken her more than an hour. She'd have to get fitter now she was home and not cooped up all the time.

Emily made her way into the office. Mary was sat waiting for her.

'Emily's gone!'

Emily stood with her hand on the door, half in, half out. Not sure what to do. 'I'm sorry. I don't understand.'

'I mean you've got me again today, for shadowing. Emily's left, she couldn't cope.'

'But I'm Emily.'

'There's more than one of you, you know. Come on, let's get going. The clients won't put themselves to bed now, will they?'

Emily followed Mary out once more to her car, getting in. She tried to follow the route: left out of the office, right at the lights, past the school, past where she and Tom used to meet, past where it happened.

Emily wondered if she should go to the hospital, if Tom was still there. Did she want to see him? How would he be? Would he be awake or still asleep, his peaceful face belying what went before? Would it be expected of her, would he want her there, would his family, or was she just another reminder of what had led him to that hospital bed, another shadow of the past?

Emily was jolted from her thoughts as the car stopped.

'...we just have to undo everything we did.' Mary switched off the engine, and made to step out of the car. Emily stared up at the house. She wondered which one she was at. She tried to remember their names, but she couldn't. She'd have to write them down; tomorrow she'd bring a pad and pen, and note down everything she needed to remember.

Emily got out of the car and followed Mary up to the house. 1,3,7,9. Mary lifted the key out of the safe and unlocked the door.

'Evening, Joan.'

Other than the sound of the telly there was no response. Mary breezily made her way towards Joan's room, indicating for Emily to follow.

'We've come to get you ready for bed.'

Emily stared at the sun that shone through the bay window; although winter, it was still light out. She waited for Joan to refuse. But instead, Joan smiled pleasantly as Mary plucked the piece of toast from between her fingers. Emily wondered if it was the same one she'd cut yesterday.

'We'll get you washed and into your nightie, then we'll get you a nice bowl of soup.'

Emily hovered in the doorway, unsure what to do, hoping Mary would send her once more into the kitchen.

'Come over here, Emily. I want to introduce you to Joan. Joan, this is EMILY.'

Emily smiled at Joan as Mary spoke her name, enunciating each syllable as if spelling it out letter by letter.

'No.' Joan glared at Emily.

'Now then Joan, we can't have this, can we. You know you can't always have me here. Emily's new, but she's very nice, you two will get on like a house on fire.'

'No.'

Mary beckoned Emily over towards the chair. 'Joan, you know we have to do this, can't leave you sitting here all night. Now, I'm going to go into the kitchen and heat you up some soup. When I get back, I expect you to have behaved nicely for Emily.'

Mary picked up the plate and cup from the table and slid it away towards the telly, before leaning in once more to Emily. 'Remember, it's easy, we just need to reverse it. You're just undoing everything we did. Nothing to it.'

Emily watched as Mary stepped out into the hall. 'Nothing to it,' she whispered to herself as she cast her eyes around the room. A nightie lay neatly folded on Joan's bed. Emily hurried across to grab it. Outside, children played in the dying light. Emily drew the curtains against them, casting the room into shadow.

'You're not to come near me, you hear.'

Joan's voice cut across the sound of the television.

'There's nothing to be worried about, Joan, don't you remember I'm EMILY.' Emily repeated her name in the same tone as Mary, the letters sounding foreign on her tongue.

'No you're not. I know Emily and you're not her. Anyway, I don't like Emily, she was wicked.'

Emily felt tears prickle at her eyes. 'That's not me, Joan; that was the old Emily, she's gone. I'm the new Emily.'

Emily reached over towards Joan, unsure of what to do. She'd been making tea and toast while Mary had gotten Joan up yesterday. She had no idea how to do anything, let alone how to undo it.

'Let's just get this on you so you can have your soup.'

Emily passed the nightie across to Joan, static from the nylon material crackling across her fingers as it slid onto the bunched hands that sat clasped on Joan's lap. Joan screamed and threw the nightgown across the room. Emily stood up, backing into Mary as she ran into the room once more.

—

'She was probably scared, sundowning, they all get it.' Mary spoke to Emily in the same manner she spoke to her clients. 'They're like kids, it's best to keep the lights on when it gets dark, stops them getting spooked.'

—

Each house was the same: 1,3,7,9, nightie on the bed – she'd had to call Mary as she couldn't find any pyjama bottoms for Bill, but was told that he didn't use them, that it was easier for Bill, in case of any accidents – soup, commode, bed.

Emily made sure to switch the lights on in each house; the ever-growing darkness seemed to make each client more fractious than the last. She tried to ignore their whispers that grew into screams as she got them into bed.

She was glad to finish that night. Her back ached from trying to hoist their protesting bodies into bed, bruises already showing from their flailing limbs, as they kicked and screamed as she tried to help them. Mary told her to ignore them, that they'd get used to her soon enough. That they were like that with everyone when they first started. Emily hoped so.

—

Emily regretted her decision to walk rather than drive in for her late shift. She was exhausted, her muscles aching, and she still had the hour-long walk back home before she could have a shower and fall into bed; before she'd have to get up the next morning and do it all again.

Emily stared at her watch. It was already gone ten; she'd left her tablets at home, not wanting Mary to see them. Emily hated taking them too late, it would be nearly midnight before she could take them, and she had to be up again at five to get ready for work, her head still muggy from the night before. Surely missing one wouldn't do any harm. Whispered warnings from her doctors rang through her head, joining the harsher voices of her clients. Emily tried to match their admonishments with faces, their faces with names; but all she could remember were their accusations, their voices alternating between covert whispers and screams for help. Emily had been sure that Mary would run in, her eyes accusing, her body stepping between Emily and those frail bodies that all looked alike; so childlike in their emaciation, their faces as wrinkled as a newborn baby's. But Mary had stayed away, had ignored the imploring voices begging her to save them, before they too became a victim.

The voices kept Emily company on her long walk home. The streets looked different in the dark. Once she'd have known exactly where she was, she'd often walked these streets: home from a friend's, from illicit rendezvous with Tom; had known every back alley and cut through. But now everything had changed.

Emily looked around, trying to recognise where she was, but she could have been anywhere. The houses fronted the streets, bay windows encroaching onto the cracked and uneven pavement. Bins and recycling boxes stood sentinel between door and window, cardboard spilling out from them like paving slabs, cans of Fosters a scattering of bluebells across the pitted tarmac. She didn't remember it being so messy when she was younger. But then everything had gone in the bin. Had she staggered down this street, a bottle of White Lightning in her hand, hiding it among somebody else's rubbish for the bin men to collect the next day, rather than incriminating herself by chucking it in her own? She couldn't remember, her memories hazy, blotted out by drink and meds and time.

'You're still her.'

The voices still rang in her head.

'You can't trick us.'

Emily hurried along the street, praying she'd recognise where she was when she got to the end.

'We're not babies.'

Unfortunately, when she got to the end of the street Emily did recognise where she was. To her left the school loomed in the distance. The playground and buildings now shut away from the town by a high chain-link fence. Emily had always cut out the back of the school, sneaking to meet the others, or to meet Tom. The edge of the playing fields, though technically still school grounds, had been a mess of brambles and trees, an easy place to disappear for either a quick cigarette during break, or a quick kiss on her way home. The playing fields stood apart from the school, the grass still clipped short, showing lines painted white in the moonlight. It would only take her a minute to cut across. Emily placed a foot upon the grass, its texture springing beneath her foot, its blades dampening her skin, coldly sharp through the aged canvas of her shoe. It had been warm the last time she'd been here, the grass crisp and dry beneath her and Tom. She remembered her cries, his voice, 'Yes,' in response to her protests.

Emily tried to remember if that was his last word to her. She saw him again, before he went back up there that last time, but she wasn't sure if they had spoken.

She removed her foot from the grass and turned her back on the school. One foot chilling her, the material damp and coarse, rubbing against her foot, causing her to stumble as if drunk as she made her way back home.

—

Emily had barely slept, the muscles in her back spasming as she lay on the too soft, narrow bed in her room. Every time she began to drift off, voices woke her, but she was too tired to find them, to tell them to quiet; instead she lay there and listened to their accusations.

Emily had driven on autopilot, before stumbling into the office and making her way over to Mary's desk to wait. Sat on the desk was a large envelope with Emily's name written in block capital letters. Emily ripped it open.

Emily,
Sorry, you'll have to fend for yourself today, I'm having to cover for one of the others. Remember: it's easy, like looking after a baby. You just need to be firm with them.
Mary.

Emily stared at the paper. That was all it said. She turned it over, hoping for more information, but there was nothing. She tried to remember the addresses, the names of the clients, Edna, Bill… that was it; she couldn't even remember everyone she was supposed to see.

Emily sat there flipping the paper over in her hands, wondering if she could just hide it somewhere, pretend she hadn't seen it; maybe slide it into the bin and blame the cleaners, or slip it between Mary's desk and the wall, blame a draught from the door. The door opened as she was dangling the envelope over the bin. Snatching it back, she turned to the newcomer. It was Mary.

'Why are you still here? You should have left half an hour ago.'

'I… I couldn't remember where I was going. I hadn't written the addresses down. I thought I was still shadowing.'

Mary stalked over and grabbed the envelope from Emily's hand. Turning it over, she scrawled a list of names and addresses on the back of the paper.

'I hope you don't need the postcodes, if you do you'll have to look them up. I'm running late as it is.'

Emily just shook her head as Mary pushed the paper back into her hands, and grabbed a mobile phone from the desk.

'And I'm on call. Again. No one ever wants to take responsibility round here.'

Emily was about to ask her for the on-call number, but Mary was already gone. She stared down at the list of addresses in her hand, and hoped she'd be able to remember where each road was.

—

Emily managed to find the first address without too much difficulty. Parking the car, she got out and made her way to the front door: 1,3,7,9, the small silver key fell into her palm. Taking a deep breath, she kept repeating, 'It's easy. Simple. Anyone can do it.' She pushed the door open and tried to sound confident as she called out, 'Morning, Joan, it's just me, Emily. I've come to get you up.'

For a moment Emily thought it was a ragdoll lying on the floor, thrown from the bed in a tantrum during the night, before she realised that the ragdoll was too large, too angular. A groan emitted from the tangle of limbs, one foot hung over the crooked cot-side, urine-soaked sheets draping down as if Joan had tried to use them to escape. Hurrying over, Emily kept repeating to herself, 'It's okay, it's easy. Simple. Like looking after a baby.'

Emily freed Joan's leg. It thumped to the floor, Joan's wrinkled face screwing up as if to bawl, her sodden nightdress heaving as she sucked air into her lungs. Emily anticipated the cry, the screams, but instead a small voice uttered, 'You did this.'

Emily stepped back. She didn't know what to do. She should phone someone. Leaving Joan on the floor, Emily hurried through to the hallway and picked up the phone, but she didn't know who to call, didn't have Mary's number, or the on-call number, didn't know who

Joan's neighbours or family or friends were. The only number she could call would be for an ambulance. She could imagine them standing there, questioning her as Joan continued to blame her… for what? For an accident. It wasn't her fault.

Emily placed the receiver on the cradle and made her way back into Joan's room. Ignoring her cries, Emily stripped and dressed Joan on the floor, before hauling her up and placing her in the chair.

A mug of tea and a half-eaten triangle of toast stood cold upon the table. Emily checked her watch – it would have to do until Meals on Wheels came. Grabbing the urine-soaked sheets, she bundled them into the washing machine and switched it on. Leaving Joan screaming that Emily deserved to rot in hell.

It wasn't until Emily was in her car that she realised she no longer had the list. She checked her pockets, her handbag, the glovebox, but it was nowhere to be found. Emily tried to remember what Mary had written, but it was no good. She couldn't even remember all the names, let alone the addresses. Stepping back out of the car, Emily made her way back up the path to Joan's; 1,3,7,9, and she was in once more. Steeling herself for the onslaught, she snuck down the hallway, but Joan was asleep, a puddle of urine already soaking the pad on her chair. Emily snuck a glance at the table, but other than the toast and tea it was empty. She tiptoed across to the bed but there was nothing there either.

'You'll not get away with this. I know who you are.'

Emily swung round, but Joan still appeared to be asleep. She stepped closer, willing Joan to open one of her eyes, to peer out at her, for a corner of her mouth to turn up in a mocking sneer; but it hung open, saliva drying at its corner. She stepped past, keeping her eyes on Joan until she was out of the room.

She checked the kitchen, but the only thing she'd done there was put the washing on. She watched as the sheets went round and round, suds filling the glass eye as it watched her. She debated trying to wrench open the door, but it was pointless: if the paper was in there, it was now no more than mush.

—

Sitting in the car, Emily debated what to do. She was sure her next patient was Bill. Maybe it would all come back to her; she'd been to his house a couple of times now.

Reversing out of the drive, she pulled the car to the left and headed to the end of the road. Peering left and right she recognised a bush, trimmed into the shape of lollipop. Later, she turned right onto the lane with the powder-pink house at the corner, before indicating right to turn onto what she hoped was the right road. Emily smiled as she drove past the skip that had been sat on Bill's road the day before, noting as she did that someone had chucked a broken cot on top of it, its rail hanging down, snapped and twisted. Emily tried not to think of Joan lying on the floor, her foot caught and trapped in her bed; of bodies twisted and broken, trapped and screaming.

Emily parked in the first space she could see and ran up the road towards Bill's house, but as she stepped onto the pathway she realised her mistake. A family saloon stood parked on the road outside, a stack of shopping bags blocking the pavement, a chubby hand waving at her from the child's seat within. Emily stepped over the bags, the child's laughter suddenly turning to cries as she stepped closer. She flashed a look at the open front door that she'd presumed was Bill's, but there was no sign of a keysafe. Quickly she skipped back, knocking one of the bags over, a pot of yoghurt smashing beneath her foot as she hurried away, casting her eyes left and right, searching for Bill's.

The house was familiar when she stood in front of it. Emily tried to persuade herself it was Bill's house, but maybe she'd gotten herself mixed up; it could have been Edna's or Maive's or one of the others. Emily wondered if it mattered.

The keysafe sat in the same place as all the others to the left of the front door. 1,3,7,9, and the key tumbled out onto her hand. Emily placed it in the lock and turned it, scurrying in and closing the door behind her before the woman at the end of the road discovered her crying child and spilt groceries.

Emily stared at the hallway. It was familiar, but it wasn't Bill's. It wasn't Edna's or Maive's; it wasn't any of her clients'. She was about to turn round and leave, when she saw her face smiling back at her from the wall. Not a mirror, a photo. Emily tried to mimic the smile – she hadn't smiled like that since the night of her prom, Tom's parents proudly photographing them as they stood with arms around each other, excited for the night.

Emily still didn't understand why Tom had to do it, why it had to be there. Everything always came back to the same place, life and death both hanging in the balance as they lay there.

Emily bounced the key in her hand. She wondered who was through the door. Tom's dad had always worked hard, maybe he'd had a stroke; or maybe his mum had turned to alcohol and wrecked her liver and her brain.

Emily slipped the key into her pocket and made her way down the hallway. She wondered if they'd still recognise her. Pushing open the door, she saw the bed – not a simple divan like Bill had, or one with the cot-sides slipped beneath the mattress like Joan's. This bed was propped up, its mattress bent and twisted beneath knees and hips, supporting the body beneath. A tube snaked out from beneath the sheets, ending in a bag of urine the colour of the cider the two of them used to drink. Emily stepped closer to the bed.

'Do you remember?'

Tom lay there, his eyes closed, his breath rasping in his chest. Emily took his hand in her own.

'They blamed me. Said it was my fault. Said I couldn't cope.'

She tightened her grip, feeling the bones grind beneath her palm, until Tom opened his eyes.

'It wasn't my fault.'

Emily tucked Tom's hand back beneath the cover. Leaning in close, she scanned his face for a glimpse of recognition.

'They couldn't blame you, not after this.' Emily spat out the words, but there was nothing; Tom's face remained impassive. 'Did you not think what doing it there meant?'

Emily scanned the room. A soft toy stood atop a dresser. She remembered buying him it, that last Valentine's Day; his parents were obviously more sentimental then she gave them credit for. She picked it up. In its arms it held a stuffed red heart. She ruffled its grey fur, remembering how long she'd had to save to buy it from the Clintons in town.

'I said no. Didn't that mean anything?'

Emily stepped towards the bed, cradling the bear in her arms.

'She was born bad. Did you know?' Emily watched to see if there was a flicker of recognition. 'I'm not sure if they told you.' Emily held the bear up in her arms and smiled. 'It was to be expected, being conceived there, under those circumstances.'

Emily cooed at the bear in her hands, tossing it in the air. She giggled, letting it fall, snatching it, catching it at the last moment. 'It's okay now, though. I dealt with it.'

Emily stepped towards the bed, the bear outstretched as if she were about to tuck it in between Tom's sheets. 'You weren't there. They said I couldn't cope, but I did. I coped.'

Emily held Tom close, the bear pressed between them until his rasping breaths slowed and stopped. She stood and smoothed his sheets, placed the bear back on the dresser.

'It's easy. Simple, like looking after a baby.'

Penny Jones knew she was a writer when she started to talk about herself in the third person (her family knew when Santa bought her a typewriter for Christmas when she was three). Penny's debut collection Suffer Little Children, *published by Black Shuck Books, was shortlisted for the 2020 British Fantasy Award for Best Newcomer, and her short story 'Dendrochronology', published by Hersham Horror, was shortlisted for the 2020 British Fantasy Award for Best Short Story. Her novella* Matryoshka, *published by Hersham Horror, was shortlisted for the 2022 British Fantasy Award for Best Novella. She loves reading and will read pretty much anything you put in front of her, but her favourite authors are Stephen King, Shirley Jackson and John Wyndham. In fact, Penny only got into writing to buy books; when she realised that there wasn't that much money in writing she stayed for the cake. You can find Penny at www.penny-jones.com*

As If Your Mouth Were Sewn Shut

by

C. C. Adams

Madison's, One New Change, St Paul's
21:27, 23/09/22

Throwing his arm up along the back of the sofa was a façade, manspreading as if to show supreme confidence. Which, of course, was bullshit. You could talk 'fake it until you make it' until the cows came home but there was no getting around it, Chris thought: he'd been stood up.

Faux leather felt soft to his fingertips; at least he'd been stood up in a quality place. Madison's on a Friday night was lively. An upbeat crowd of city workers, judging by the look of men in suits without ties and women in lipstick and heels but not in the full-on glam you might expect if it was a Saturday.

Music in the background drifted out of obscurity into a verse of what settled on him as Lianne La Havas's 'Midnight' as she sang about not missing that train. Everything about Madison's spoke to the cool of London. The seating, the music, the ambience (not forgetting the candles in the little jars of red glass).

All that was missing was his date.

Chris leaned sideways and dug his phone out of his pocket – and he could afford to lean sideways, because no one in their right mind would want to sit next to the weirdo who saw fit to go to a bar by himself. Checking the messages on his phone revealed nothing new. The last one, received earlier that evening, was where Marion had told him she would see him soon.

She's not interested. Never was, never will be.

Chris scoffed and looked back over his shoulder. Behind him, on the other side of the sloping glass windows of Madison's, he saw the dome of St Paul's and exhaled wearily, before tipping it a nod of reverence. Shitty night or not, there were some things that were just beautiful to behold.

He plucked his glass from the table and made out he was draining it – the Negroni had been finished long ago, but it was a good way to signal he was leaving. Heading outside, chill night air clawed at him, but he shrugged it off as he made his way onto the terrace, a security guard tracking his movement. Not that he had any criminal intent, but he acknowledged

that the security guard didn't know him – or anyone else – from Adam, and so maintained vigilance at all times. Passing an array of patrons nursing their drinks, the terrace steps were broad and shallow beneath him. Bright lighting along the edge of each riser never worked; at some point, you'd be driven to distraction by someone or something. You wouldn't trip, but you'd still lose your footing. And the edge of the terrace? Gone were the days when you could lean up against the railing. Now, there was a Tensabarrier that no doubt ran the length of the terrace perimeter, a foot in front of it. Pursing his lips, he sneered in derision. How were you supposed to *lean* on the railing and *take in* the view when—

'Chris?'

He looked to his right. A short-haired woman, full figured in a black cocktail dress, peering at him from a couple of yards away, leaning sideways as if that would get her a better look. Arms folded and hands cupping her elbows, she paced towards him, high-heeled mules clacking as she did so. On closing the gap, Chris witnessed more detail: pale skin, with a smattering of freckles on her cheeks and high on her chest. The Bardot neckline of the outfit teasing a hint of her breasts; pale and freckle-free, small and full. Realising he was staring – even for a moment – Chris tore his gaze away and made eye contact.

Pale green eyes stared at him from under a fringe of mousy brown hair that looked as if it was already transitioning into the grey of middle age. But those eyes…

…staring at him, through him, unblinking. Screams in the air, as well as dust; both drifting from the ceiling and thrown up when more chunks of rubble had landed, the rumble and crash of debris strong enough that you could feel the vibration in your teeth.

And in your bones.

Her bones – broken, no doubt. One chunk of rubble the size of a shoebox, denting her ribcage. An impact like that must have ruptured her…

…heart.

Beating faster now.

'It *is* Chris, isn't it?'

He swallowed, praying it wasn't visible. 'Grace?'

A waggle of her eyebrows. 'In the flesh.'

'Yeah…'

She stepped towards him and grabbed his upper arms; he, in turn, grabbing her elbows, if only to minimise her proximity as she gave him a kiss on the cheek. Lips soft and cold against his skin, coupled with the night air, provoked a wave of goosebumps across his neck.

Of course it was the night air.

One hand lifted in question. 'So, what are you doing here?' she asked.

'Just felt the need to take in a little scenery, is all.'

'Alone?'

Marion wasn't going to contact him anytime soon. 'Yeah.' Forcing a smile, he screwed his eyes shut against an imaginary breeze.

'A lone wolf. I can dig that. I made the popular choice of coming up here with the girlfriends for a few drinks.'

'Oh.'

Grace stepped back and eyed him, seemingly satisfied.

Something discomforting was in that gaze. Catlike. Not a predator *stalking* prey, but one that would act on movement.

'Beautiful,' she breathed.

Huh?

Whatever his expression was, it must have partly mirrored inner sentiment, because she tipped her head in the direction of the balcony. 'The view. It's beautiful, isn't it?'

He turned back around. At this section of the railing, they were standing directly opposite St Paul's Cathedral. Where the sun had previously set behind the cathedral's dome, that curvature was now rendered ghostly white in the darkness, the gargoyles at its base in silent vigil. Further out in the landscape, glowing red lights from buildings and dormant cranes lit the horizon.

'Anyway,' she sighed, 'I need to be getting back. Those reprobates will be wondering where I am, especially since I'm the designated driver.' Chris looked over; saw her hand wiping the side of her neck. 'But we should catch up sometime, just the two of us. You know, go for a drink... if the lone wolf is agreeable to that. Your number's still the same?'

Please don't. 'I *think* it is.' He feigned nonchalance. 'Honestly, I have enough trouble keeping track of the damned thing.'

Her expression turned mock baleful. 'O-kay, then.' And rewarding him with a finger wave, she turned on her heel and headed back in the direction of Madison's without a backward glance.

Leaving Chris to shiver in peace.

He watched her go, a discreet slit in the rear of her dress disappearing into the crowd, along with the rest of her.

Shit.

And the terrace was starting to fill up now, more and more people taking in the night air, some with a cigarette, blowing a plume of smoke into the sky, only to dissipate in moments. A trio of women nearby sipped from glass flutes that, from the look of it, were probably full of Prosecco.

By now, Grace would be back inside, sat in the warmth of the bar.

Or is she? You have no idea.

I don't.

This isn't a coincidence. It can't be.

Chill air or not, prickly heat worried at his neck, like a swarm of lice.

That same sensation persisted as he made his way through the crowd, careful to stick to the edge of the terrace and as far away from Madison's as possible; taking the lift down to the ground floor of One New Change, descending into the Underground at St Paul's and heading across the river until he was finally in the back streets of Clapham, pushing a key into the front door of his house. Gloom of night fell across the threshold in a shard that rested on the wall of the hallway. Chris slipped inside and carefully shut the door behind him, making sure to turn the knob as he did so, to avoid the telltale click.

Leaving him in both silence and darkness – instinct telling him that to hit the light switch was to broadcast his presence.

None of this is an accident.

That's not possible.

Fuck off with your 'not possible'. You looked a dead woman in the eye. You didn't just hightail it out of there because you didn't like her perfume, right?

RIGHT?

Right.

Standing there in the darkness with only his hyperventilating as background noise was disorienting, and he braced his hand against the wall to steady himself. When that didn't work, he curled his fingers, nails gouging into the wallpaper. With that, he began to regain some semblance of control. And clarity.

She lay there, staring at him, through him, unblinking. Screams in the air, as well as dust; both drifting from the ceiling and thrown up when more chunks of rubble had landed, the rumble and crash of debris strong enough that you could feel the vibration in your teeth and in your bones. One chunk of rubble the size of a shoebox, denting her ribcage.

An impact like that must have ruptured her heart and her lungs, assuming broken ribs hadn't done that already. Add internal bleeding to the mix, and you'd be looking at exactly what you guessed it would be – a dead body.

Who just happened to see him on a night out and come over to give him a hug earlier that evening.

The same way Mr Maitland had given Chris a hug all those years ago: awkward and lacking warmth. A headmaster in name only, Chris had never liked him, always found him too 'up his own ass' – *Grace's* words, of all people. But there was truth in that; the only time Chris had really spoken to him, which was after the incident, Chris had the sense that Maitland was going through the motions and only doing the whole review thing so he could *appear* to give a damn. The letter that Chris had received was as flat and dispassionate as Maitland himself. *I write from the heart when I say that I sincerely hope you'll all be able to put what we experienced behind you, and live happy, productive lives.*

And where was Maitland now?

Fraying reverie brought Chris back to the present moment – still standing in the hallway of his house.

Come on, come on, you're wasting time.

He started up the stairs and made his way into the bedroom. Biting his lip, he surveyed his surroundings, less looking and more contemplating: from the wardrobe in the corner to the suitcase on top of it, the laptop bag sat in his chair. One hand bracing against the corner of his dressing table, he bent to retrieve his holdall from beside it, near-weightless fabric slithering in the darkness. The zipper cut the air with a harsh whirr as he opened the bag, the scent of a leather jacket held in the main compartment recently drifted up to him.

You don't have time.

Easing the top drawer open, he reached in and pulled out two fistfuls of underwear, stuffing them into a corner of the bag. Fabric slid across his hand in a sly and feathery touch, making him grimace. Working his way down the chest of drawers now: shirts and tops; he couldn't see or care if any of it matched. At his feet, the bag had started to bulge. He bent and clasped his hands to its sides. Not yet full to capacity, he decided, but it would do – and *that* was when he heard the sound. Subtle, but *there* – the bedroom door whispering across carpet. He turned and gasped, back-pedalling into the dresser. Toiletries on top of it clinked and clattered, one or two rolling off the edge and hitting the floor with invisible thumps.

Oh God, no.

Grace stood in the doorway, wearing the same black cocktail dress as before. 'Maybe it would help if you switched the light on?'

But Chris wasn't about to do that, even if he had presence of mind to. Grace was standing between him and the light switch.

'How…?'

'How did I get in?' She jerked her head in the direction of the staircase. 'You left the front door open.'

'No…'

'Uhhh… yes. You didn't shut the door properly, and anyone could have come in. *I* came in because I was worried about you.'

None of this brought Chris any comfort, let alone made any sense. Normal people didn't do that. The woman had *followed* him – and not just from a few doors away as if he'd stepped out for some air, or even gone a few doors down from Madison's or One New Change to make a phone call… The woman had followed him across town in the middle of the night. *How?* How was that possible and, more importantly, *why?* He hadn't seen her since back in school, when—

'You died.' His voice was barely a whisper.

Grace cocked her head, the gesture that of a curious dog. 'Ex*cuse* me?'

'You died. I saw you… die.'

And then the truth was spilling out of him, awful and sloppy like viscera from a gutted animal; everything from that macabre tableau from a year long passed. There was the rumbling of the ceiling, the crash…

…and Grace in the middle of it, her chest caved in, blood seeping through her shirt.

Nothing like the Grace that stood in the doorway before him now. This Grace was older. Somewhat thicker and heavier. Although he could barely see such detail in the gloom, he knew from earlier that evening that her hair was a shade or two lighter than in school, as if slipping past the peak of lustrous quality to begin the irreversible decline into thick wiry grey. But the eyes were the same – *weren't they?* – the same flat and pale green eyes…

…in a lifeless body.

'I'm sorry you had to see that,' she said softly. 'I can't imagine how disturbing it must have been. To be honest, I can't remember much. Commotion in the classroom. I tried to get out… and the next thing I remembered, I woke up in a hospital bed, feeling like someone had driven over me and reversed a few times.'

'You don't remember.' Derision dulling the edges of his fear.

'Honestly,' she said, 'I take it as a blessing. I don't know exactly what happened; I guess I went into shock. Maybe that's what saved me: being that far gone mentally that I didn't have to process the enormity of it all. I know I was lucky to be alive. Just a little bruising and some lacerations. I'm surprised the stitches didn't leave any scars.'

Chris licked his lips. 'S-stitches?' He scoffed. 'I know what I saw, and what happened to you isn't dismissed as easily as "needing a few stitches".'

What little light filtered in from the night beyond the window brought her features into relief as she closed the distance between them and laid a hand on his shoulder. Cold flesh leached heat from him through the fabric of his clothing.

'Let me ask you something,' she said, her eyes wide in the darkness. 'If I'm dead… how do you explain that I'm standing here right now?'

That hand slid up his shoulder and cupped the base of his jaw in a gentle caress, the flesh cold. 'I'm not hearing an answer.'

Chris cupped her wrist in his palm and gently pushed at it.

The hand didn't move.

Fear climbing to dizzying heights, he tried again – and *still* her hand wouldn't move. If anything, it had grown *stronger*, cold flesh applying alarming force to the base of his jaw. Her thumb slid across his throat and up to the other side of his face.

'What's the matter?' Her voice was deeper now, more *masculine* – and to *hear* that voice coming out of the same woman he had seen earlier made his skin crawl. 'Is there somewhere you need to be?'

She leaned in closer, and now he caught a whiff of her breath, suddenly stinking like rotten egg.

His heart beating wildly, Chris struggled against that hand, rocking this way and that, and catching the corner of the dresser between his shoulder blades. More objects clinked and clattered, falling to the floor. In front of him, beyond her forearm, Grace's silhouette, features muted in the darkness, wisps of hair drifting as she held Chris in place. Her hand shifted over his throat, her palm unyielding against his larynx.

Her grip tightening on the sides of his neck.

It was getting harder to breathe. Gagging and coughing had no effect, not even when a wad of phlegm slicked his lip before it hit Grace's cheek – he *heard* it land.

'You're… *not* human.'

'I'm not?' That voice was deep; insidious and cold.

Amplified as his fear was, Chris struggled with another emotion: disbelief. This… this *thing* had followed him across town and lied its way into his home, all under the guise of a friend (if you could even call her that) from his past. He wouldn't die in a car accident, he wouldn't even die in a hospital bed or at home surrounded by family – no. He'd die here in this house, never having had a wife or children.

And there'd be no witnesses, no one—

Ah.

'Others…'

'What?' The voice was almost a growl.

'Others will… know.'

'I DON'T SEE HOW.'

'My… death… raising… suspicion.'

What little speech he managed had taxed him, his vocal cords pained and sore. As the hold on his neck continued to press in on him, so did the silence – an almost tangible physical force. In the darkened confines of the bedroom, it was even more disorienting and terrifying; the only evidence of anything real was the grip on his neck. Soft and cold flesh squeezing with alarming strength. That, coupled with a voice that—

Pressure fell away from his neck, and he fell back, gasping – *that*, in turn, granted him a boon of much-needed air.

'You know,' said the voice, 'you might be right. So, listen to me. I'm going to leave you in peace and quiet. But, if you disturb that peace and quiet?'

The chokehold returned – brief and sharp, making Chris wince with the force of it, his eyes watering.

Now the hold left his neck completely, leaving Grace's silhouette in front of him.

Which turned and made its way out the bedroom, gently closing the door behind it with an audible click.

Leaving Chris to hyperventilate in peace.

The ghost of a chokehold lingering on his throat.

Darkness, sly and silent around him, daring him to make the slightest move.

Until his bladder finally let go.

*London native **C.C. Adams** is the horror/dark fiction author behind books such as* But Worse Will Come, Forfeit Tissue *and* Downwind, Alice. *A member of the Horror Writers Association, he still lives in the capital. This is where he lifts weights, cooks – and looks for the perfect quote to set off the next dark delicacy. Visit him at www.ccadams.com, or on Twitter @MrAdamsWrites.*

Shadow Burdens

by

Charlotte Bond

I always thought it'd be cool to see auras. Imagine all those people wandering around with their own special colour. You could tell what kind of person someone was at a glance. Was the old man asking you for money really honest and poor, or was it just some guy trying to scam a few coins while waiting for the bus? Is it safe to get in this taxi, or is the man's aura a violent red?

But I don't see auras: I see shadows. I can't tell you if they're part of a person or… something attached to them. From what I've read, auras seem to be an all-over colour that emanates from a person's soul, but the shadows I see perch on people's shoulders, like a parrot or a trained monkey – and I use that comparison because the things I see look alive. That said, they have no distinct form, but the shape changes and little wisps trail off them, as if their shadow flesh is constantly evaporating.

The first time I ever saw one was after the incident at school. They were on nearly everyone I encountered, but they were particularly pronounced on the parents of my friends who didn't make it. While the papers reported the initial number of deaths at the school, they didn't report what I think of as the 'aftermath deaths'.

Alice's mother was the first. If anyone was going to commit suicide, I thought it might have been Craig's parents, because he was an only child. Awful to lose a child, obviously, but how much worse to lose your *only* child, the person you've pinned all your hopes and dreams on? But it was Alice's mother – Jessica, she was called – who shot herself with a borrowed shotgun two days after her daughter's funeral. I always wondered who the shotgun really belonged to – who in their right mind loans a weapon to a woman who was clearly out of *her* mind with grief? They certainly wouldn't have done so if they'd seen what I had: a writhing black mass on her left shoulder (it's always the left) that was darker than tar, darker than treacle, darker than those little penny sweets that would turn your tongue black.

The darkness and solidity of the shadow really matters. The darker and more opaque it is, the greater the burden someone is feeling. Because that's what I've come to believe these things are – they represent burdens. But whether they emanate from inside us or are something external that affixes itself to us when we feel at our most overwhelmed, I can't say for sure. Except for when they're ghosts, of course, but I'll get to that.

Jessica was carrying all that grief, all that guilt. Alice told me that morning she'd felt sick and had asked to stay home, but her mum had sent her in. How much must that have hurt, to know you sent your daughter to her death when she'd asked to stay with you? Even having two beautiful twin boys couldn't ease such grief. In fact, I once saw her out walking with them, and when one of the boys tried to hold her hand, that black mass swirled and ran down her arm. She snatched her hand away before that darkness could brush against her son's flesh, and she buried it deep in her pocket, as if she knew what lurked over her. She didn't, of course. I've never found anyone other than me who can see them.

At first, I tried to ignore the black shadows, knowing it'd only increase my counselling appointments if I admitted to something else wrong with me, but when things calmed down and my fear faded to a dull, constant ache behind my breastbone, I started looking into this phenomenon. Even with the advent of the internet, I found little that explained what I saw, so I had to make my own theories based on observation. Things I have found out include that most people have them, but they're very small. If you've suffered a bereavement, they're much larger; and you can make the shadow smaller if you drink lots of alcohol, but it will always come back.

Interestingly, I can't see my own shadow burden – I don't know if that's because I don't have one at all or because they don't show up in mirrors.

Oh, and if they're really dark and swirling, and if they have eyes, it usually means you are being haunted.

—

In the decades I've had this talent (I won't call it a gift; nor will I call it a curse) I have come to believe in ghosts. I tried a few ghost walks and ghost hunts, but there was nothing to any of them except one. Ghosts don't haunt locations – they haunt people. You won't find a spirit wandering forlornly in the place it was killed; you'll find it struggling along behind someone it knew – its mother, a sibling, a grandparent, their murderer.

You're wondering how I know about that last one. It was a fluke, really. I was just walking to work (I'm a receptionist at a doctor's surgery fifteen minutes from my house) and I saw this man walking towards me with a writhing black shadow on his shoulder. It was thick, enormous, and its wisps almost concealed his face; black vapour streamed behind him like a comet tail. His eyes were fixed on the floor, his arms held straight by his sides, his hands clenching and unclenching. He was walking at speed, and my first thought was that he was being agitated by the blackness somehow. Clearly distracted, he wasn't looking where he was going and most people moved out of his way, but I stopped dead and stared at him. His shadow burden was easily a ten, maybe an eleven. I hadn't seen anything so bad since Cornwall. And as he passed me, I felt screams and sobs in my head – not heard, *felt*, the vibrations causing shudders down my spine and ripples in my blood. Weirdly, I smelled sweet and sour sauce, sticky and cloying, appetising and revolting all in one. Dizziness swept over me and I staggered against a lamppost. When the world stopped spinning and I was pretty sure I wasn't going to spew, I looked around. The man had gone. I saw his picture in the paper next day. By the timings given, about fifteen minutes before I passed him, he'd taken a cricket bat to his wife and elderly mother. They had ganged up against him in an argument over who should have taken the rubbish out before the bag split. I imagine the two women lying there, sightless, their blood mingling with spilt Chinese food, one sticky substance oozing into another.

From careful observation of strangers in coffee shops and friends at parties, I can tell that a person's mood affects any shadow burden they carry. You could walk into a party with barely a wisp of shadow, then your ex-boyfriend comes in with his stunning new girlfriend and the blackness swells up enough to engulf your shoulder. It presses against your temples, giving you an ice-pick headache, and its general noxious nature makes you feel queasy. So you drink, and either the alcohol or your own artificially elevated spirits quash it for a time, but it's always there, smoke against glass that's just waiting for someone to open a window. Ever been happy and drinking then felt despondency surge over you so hard and fast it brings tears to your eyes? Something in your psyche or your blood cracked open that window and your shadow burden surged back through.

I live alone and my main hobby is reading – I'll read a book once and pass it on, no one should ever tread the same ground twice – so I don't have a lot of clutter in my small flat. What I do have, however, are stacks of notebooks. They're divided into three types: theories, evidence, and bottle numbers with names. The notebooks containing theories are messy inside, lots of crossings out and scribbles as I learn new things. The evidence ones are neater, recording when I saw a shadow, on whom, what it looked like, and how it changed. Some of my friends who struggle with their own inadequacies and losses appear multiple times, while other entries are anonymous as I note down things I've seen in passing:

Woman in red coat with green John Lewis shoulder bag seen at bus stop with mass rated 5 on Wednesdays 4ᵗʰ, 11ᵗʰ, and 25ᵗʰ of May.

I rate the appearance of the shadow from one (tiny shadow) to ten (murderer). A bad day at work won't get you a shadow burden, but continual stress and anxiety will, maybe a level two. Anything up to a five can be dealt with by a therapist (if my friend Rachel is anything to go by), but above that, you start to look at burdens that weigh people down, and around six is where ghosts are involved.

I'm undecided yet about whether ghosts rise independently of the shadow burdens and are drawn to them, or whether they are somehow created alongside the shadow. But there is a connection.

Like I said, I did a bit of ghost hunting in my early twenties. I had to hide it from my parents, because they always thought I was mentally damaged enough without adding in anything else supernatural. They didn't know that, for me, finding out about auras, ghosts, shadow burdens and all that was a way for me to move on, to know that I wasn't the only one screwed up by excessively weird shit.

Anyway, it was a ghost hunt down in Cornwall at a place called Lanhydrock – that was where I met Louise. And Jenny, of course; I often forget about her, even though she was the one it was happening to.

It was January 2005, and we were camping out for the night with the Genuine Ghost Company. Several parts of the old Cornish house had burned down in 1881, leading to the deaths of the two owners. The Nursery Suite and the Long Gallery were supposed to be the most haunted, and we were in the Long Gallery. My parents used to drag me around stately homes all the time when I was a kid, so I'd seen a few galleries in my time. The pictures on the walls of Lanhydrock weren't very imposing, and the windows were tall and wide, letting in plenty of moonlight where the organisers had left the curtains open. The creepiest thing was the ceiling – I've never seen anything more covered in stucco decoration.

We were in there around one a.m., using our torches to look at the readouts of the EMF meters. It was quite cold but not breath-misting-in-front-of-our-faces cold (which, the organisers told us, was a sure sign of a ghostly presence) and I was trying not to look at the ceiling. With our torch beams flashing to and fro, shadows would dance above us, making it look like the carved figures up there were moving. I could all too vividly imagine them turning their blank, white eyes in our direction and then crawling down the walls towards us.

I was standing a little way back, not far from Jenny, when she said, 'I can smell it! Smoke.'

Instantly, Bob (the man in charge, who turned into something akin to an eager puppy at any slight hint of ghostly goings-on) abandoned the machine and rushed over to ask, 'Can you describe it to me?' He held a Dictaphone to her lips.

It was clear that no one else but me could see the black mass on her shoulder. It was thick and heavy, its movements languid.

'It's definitely smoke,' she said, 'but not cigars. It's more like…' A frown appeared on her face; black tendrils of smoke curled around her throat like a noose.

'Yes?' Bob prompted hungrily.

'Like the pipe tobacco my grandfather used to smoke.' Jenny swallowed nervously, the coils tightening about her neck. The shadow burden surged larger and, terrifyingly, I saw two red eyes staring at Jenny. There were no facial features to offer up an expression, but I felt a wave of malevolent glee run through me, accompanied by the sickly-sweet scent of pipe tobacco.

I was stunned and sickened. In some way, I'd always imagined the shadow burdens as somehow being alive, but in the way an amoeba is alive – formless and without intention. To see eyes, to witness a basic form with sentience, was incredibly unnerving.

'This is marvellous!' Bob said, and proceeded to question an increasingly agitated Jenny.

The next morning, as I was walking for the bus, Louise caught up with me. She was another member of the ghost party and had been like me: quiet and watchful. 'Smelt pipe smoke, did you?' she asked. There had been genuine interest in her voice and no hint of mockery, so I tried honesty.

'Yes.'

'And what did you see? You took a step back from Jenny, and you looked horrified – but just for a moment. You covered it so quickly that I guess whatever it was, you see them a lot. There's a cafe in the village. Shall we grab a cuppa before you go home?'

That was Louise all over: blunt and straight to business. Whenever I was with her, I'd feel like I was tethered to a whirlwind, swept up in all her activity.

My first instinct had been to deny everything, and I might have done so if she'd asked me simply: *What did you see?* But her observations had been so accurate that I felt off-balance and unable to dream up a lie quick enough. Besides, I had always wanted to talk about what I saw to someone. Why not her? It wasn't like telling my parents or my counsellor. If she looked at me funny, I never had to see her again.

I can't remember exactly what we talked about at that first meeting, but weirdly I remember we had lemon drizzle cake with a sticky, crunchy topping and milky tea that had a tang of staleness to it.

Louise was a ghost hunter, but more focused than Eager Bob and his ilk. She knew that ghosts were attached to people, not places. She went on ghost hunts because she said having a phantom dogging your heels made anyone want to seek out answers, so they naturally gravitated towards such events. Over the years, she'd developed a way of exorcising people with ghosts. Her method, I learned, involved the use of something similar to a witch bottle.

A witch bottle would be filled with something human, like urine or hair or nail clippings, along with herbs and pins. It could be placed in the walls of a house to protect it from witchcraft. But the earliest record of a witch bottle in England was in 1681, when it was used to rid a woman of a curse placed on her by an unfriendly wizard. There was some unseen demon bird that would flap around her face, terrifying her and disturbing her rest. The curse was drawn off her and into a bottle, which was buried; the woman was freed.

Through trial and research, Louise had created a ghost bottle to draw a ghost away from the person it haunted. Two things were needed: for the victim to imbibe or consume parsley (good for repelling ghosts), and a bottle filled with fresh nettle leaves and a tiny doll. The ghost would be temporarily forced away from its host by the parsley and would then be drawn into the bottle, thinking the doll was a real human (the life-force of the nettles would confuse it). Once in the bottle, the ghost would get trapped by the nettle leaves (ever noticed how they're all furry? Like lots of little pins). The bottle was stoppered, the ghost trapped, and the victim freed.

I got to see this in action when we went to visit Jenny – Louise had got her telephone number and address at Lanhydrock – and we went under the pretence of hearing about her experience for a non-existent book we were writing. It never ceased to amaze me just how ready people were to talk about hauntings to someone who didn't need convincing, who was already inclined to believe them.

'Whatever you see,' Louise warned me before heading inside, 'don't let it show on your face. Although I think you're already pretty good at hiding such stuff.'

So, as we all drank parsley and mint tea (with plenty of sugar to make it palatable), I kept my face as relaxed as possible while I watched that shadow burden writhe and twist, trying to cling to Jenny's neck while equally not wanting to touch her. When it was fully hovering above her shoulder, detached from her, it darted about in a jerky manner, trying to find a new host but equally repelled by us all, before sliding like oil into the bottle. When it was fully inside, I put the cork in hard and Louise instantly jumped into action, taking the church candle she'd lit already and tipping wax around the cork, blistering my fingers a little but sealing the ghost inside for good.

'Is it in there?' Jenny asked, staring at the bottle. I glanced at her shoulder; there was still a black mist there but it looked calmer, more like the worries everyone else carried with them.

'Is it?' Louise asked me. I nodded.

We finished our tea then took the bottle away. A month later, we came back and Jenny was all smiles. The visitations were gone, no more nightmares, and the shadow burden was miniscule. On the way out, I saw a picture of a little girl sitting on an older man's knee. It was the eyes that caught me, sent my blood rippling along my veins. I picked it up and asked, 'Is this your grandfather? The one who smoked a pipe?' The frame felt tacky to my fingers and I had to resist wiping them on my trousers when she took the picture from me. She looked down, her face carefully blank – so blank that it struck a chord with me. Only someone who has something to hide keeps their face that blank.

'Yes. That's him,' she said softly.

'Put it in the attic,' I advised. 'Or the bin.'

She looked at me, startled, then gave a relieved grin. 'Yeah. Maybe you're right.'

I have over two dozen bottles now, filled with ghosts, dolls, and dead nettles. Some of the bottles – like Jenny's – have turned black over the years. I only keep those with opaque glass, the ghost which fought hardest against leaving, who filled the air with sickening scents that had defined them in life.

One day, Louise came to me and suggested we open one of the clear bottles while it was submerged in holy water. She said she'd been reading up and maybe we could free some of the ghosts; plenty of them didn't mean harm, they just wanted to stay near those they loved, never realising the distress they were causing. It was a shame, she said, that they should be imprisoned. I agreed, and we went to a priest in Manchester who'd helped us out with supplies before.

As a test, we released one clear bottle first then checked on the victim for six months, to ensure they weren't being haunted again. They weren't, so we released the rest of the ghosts in the clear bottles. I'd hoped we might see the souls shimmering in the water or rising into the air like sparkly steam, but the only thing that came out of the bottles was a sludge of dead vegetation. But the black ones stayed shut away inside a cupboard in my flat or in a chest at Louise's place.

It felt good doing all of this. I gained a huge sense of purpose from working alongside Louise and travelling around the country helping people. Louise had money behind her to pay all our expenses, which was good because I drifted around from one job to the next for many years with no steady income. Eventually, I secured a job as a receptionist at a doctor's surgery in Bradford. One of the GPs there, Bradley, is Jo's brother – Jo Danvers, who didn't make it out of school – and I think he felt he owed me. He didn't, of course, but I still took the job. I needed it and I grew to love it. People being haunted tend to be unwell, and when they show up for appointments, I can see the eyes in their shadow burdens, and I can smell what the victim can. So I make a note of their address and I watch their house for a while, see how I can help them. The best method is often to get a delivery of garlic bread covered in parsley sent to them – ghosts hate garlic too, so it's a double whammy, and I've yet to find anyone who doesn't eat a free garlic bread that's been delivered to them by mistake. Then I wait nearby, maybe in a parked car, maybe sitting beneath a tree reading a book, parsley tea next to me alongside the uncorked bottle. It's harder to seal the top with wax when it's just me, but Louise's health isn't great these days, so I don't like to drag her all the way from Bath unless I have to.

Generally, I'm pretty successful this way, and my bottle collection is growing. I started to feel proud of myself, that I was doing good for the world. I started to feel clever, then smug. Not even the afterlife was a match for me.

Then I met the Dolmans.

Lisa Dolman came into the surgery with her little boy, Alex. He was complaining of stomach pains and a headache. She just wanted him checking out, she said. Her shadow burden was unusually thick and lazily curling around her, but there were no eyes. I just figured she was really worried about her son, and had been for a while. Parents of small children invariably carry shadow burdens of four or five, I've noticed. She stank of bad BO, but then so do plenty of our patients, and anyone who has a toddler is never going to be at their best every day.

So I dismissed her from my mind; she'd have to deal with her burden herself, and I was sure she would. Our practice has excellent support groups for parents. I thought maybe I'd offer her a leaflet on the way out, but other things pushed it from my mind.

A few days later, I overheard one of the doctors in the staff room, upset that one of his patients was in hospital. 'Just a kid, poor thing. Terrible accident – God, what must his parents feel? And I wonder if it was something I missed – a dizzy spell that I could have prevented.'

'What happened?' I asked, making myself a decaf.

'Young Alex Dolman fell down the stairs. I only saw him the other day. He was a wilful little chap – wouldn't let me feel his tummy for a tummy ache – but what kid isn't distrustful of strangers? And now the hospital is saying they've found other bruises all over him. So maybe he falls down a lot, and I didn't spot that. I honestly just thought it was some kind of virus.'

'Don't beat yourself up about it,' the other doctor said kindly. 'We can't spot everything all the time.'

I thought of Lisa Dolman all through that day and the next. Her shadow burden had been odd, thick and viscous. And that smell of BO had been strangely masculine. But there had been no eyes. And I'd not heard of ghosts harming anyone other than the person they were haunting. And yet something about her niggled at me, and I couldn't put it out of my mind.

Then two days later, Lisa turned up with her husband, Nick, at her side.

'My wife's got a bit of a cough,' he said. 'We need to see a doctor.' He was talking while Lisa looked down, her hair hanging over her face. Nick had his arm around her shoulder, like any man hugging his wife – except his fingers were white where they dug into her shoulder. The shadow burden oiled across his knuckles, almost lovingly.

'Oi!' He snapped his fingers in front of my face, and a wave of masculine sweat, nowhere near obliterated by the Lynx he wore, washed over me. 'Are you deaf or what? My wife needs an appointment.'

'Yes. Sorry,' I said. I booked them in with Bradley for half an hour's time then told them to take a seat. Nick glared at me, satisfied yet still suspicious; Lisa didn't raise her eyes. He guided her over to the waiting area, and as I watched them go, sickness rolled through me at the sight. Lisa's shadow burden had been so small on her shoulder only because that was what the creature had been hanging onto; the rest of it oozed down her back to her waist. Blue eyes – not red, but the blue of a hot flame – glared at me. The glare was the same as Nick's.

I booked the next few patients in on automatic before asking Roz to take over so I could go to the cool sanctity of the ladies. I'd never seen anything hanging down someone's back before – but then, had I ever really looked? I'd spent years looking at people's shoulders. Had I only ever been seeing half the picture?

When Bradley was between patients, I nipped into his room. 'Lisa Dolman and her husband are here. I've booked them in with you. Let me know what you think.'

During my time at the surgery, I've helped a few of Bradley's patients, those that he'd been unable to cure. He never asked me about it, but he'd come to learn that if I assigned him a particular patient and asked for his opinion, the chances were there was something I could do. He trusted me, knew that my experiences at Wellbrook had changed me, and although I saw the question in his eyes many times, he never asked me how I was changed, how I helped the people I did. It was a kind of trust, I think, born of both having lived through the horror of that time, accepting that it changed us but not prying as to how.

'Sure,' he said.

When Lisa's name was called on the tannoy, I watched from the corner of my eye as the two of them got up, Lisa slumped and Nick walking tall. Plenty of people go into an appointment with a spouse or loved one, of course. But still…

Later, Bradley confirmed my suspicions. Nick had all the hallmarks of a wife-beater: outwardly charming, answering on behalf of his wife or directing her as to what to say when she did speak, claiming his control was merely concern. All while his wife sat there, barely able to maintain eye contact. Neither of us had to look at Alex Dolman's hospital reports to know that Nick didn't confine his beatings to his wife.

I watched their house for a month, to be sure – a month during which a doctor's concerns were investigated then dismissed by social services. I tried all the tricks I knew to detach that shadow, but it wouldn't budge. So I called Louise and she came up; we exhausted all her tricks too. Nothing.

'It's because we're not trying to shift a ghost, but a monster. A living monster,' Louise said. 'How do we fight that?'

I'd been staring at the cupboard that held all my bottles when she asked that question, and the answer seemed to slide into my head. I'd had too many glasses of wine, so I shifted it to the back of my head to see if I could sleep it away. But when I woke up the next morning, the idea was still there, hovering and tantalising.

I got Jenny's bottle out of the cupboard and set it on the dining room table alongside a cup of fruit tea, so that both items were waiting for Louise when she got up.

'What's that all about?' she asked me when she sat down. I told her. She frowned. 'Let me think about it,' she said.

Two days later I got a text from her that said: *Go for it. I've researched it and it should work. If it doesn't, we can manage the old bastard and get him back in there. Let me know when it's done and I'll go stay with my niece in Cornwall, call in on Jenny for old times' sake – just to check.*

That evening, I took Jenny's bottle out of the cupboard and looked at its blackness. The ceiling lights reflected off the smoked glass, making it look like two eyes staring back at me.

Even with Louise's text, I still felt uncertain. Part of me boiled at the injustice of it all, how Nick went unpunished for the beatings he so freely doled out. And yet I'd spent my life trapping these ghosts. If I hadn't released some of them into holy water, my house would be filled with bottles. But Louise and I had agreed that the black ones would never be opened. What I was planning went so far against my principles that it was wholly repugnant. But every time I shied away from the idea, the memory of two ice-blue eyes glaring at me smugly stiffened my resolve.

I stopped at a pizza shop on the way, ordering a whole portion of garlic bread for myself. I had some dried parsley in my bag (I always carry it, the other receptionists who've glimpsed it in my handbag have given me weird looks behind my back) so I sprinkled extra on for good measure.

My nerves grew as I walked towards the Dolmans' house. I told myself that if I didn't meet Nick, I wouldn't do it. I'd let fate decide.

The Dolmans' house is on a narrow street, so Nick parks his work van around the corner and then walks to his house. I met him on that short journey, and I blamed fate for what happened next and not any subconscious knowledge I had of his routines from watching their house. It was fate that got me there in time, not my own carefully measured footsteps.

I pretended to be on my phone, distracted, the bottle hanging from my fingers. When he was a few steps away, I feigned a trip and dropped the bottle.

'Hey! Watch out!' he said, annoyed, as the bottle smashed between us. The air was filled with the scent of pipe smoke for a moment before the breeze carried it away. 'You've spilt glass everywhere.'

'Sorry – I'm so sorry,' I said, kneeling down to pick up the pieces and put them in my bag. The glass was as clear now as it had been when I'd first stoppered it. I forced myself not to look at the released blackness climbing hungrily up Nick's leg.

'Yeah, well, no harm done,' he said stiffly. 'Here. I'll even help you clean it up.' He knelt down and I concentrated hard on the ground until we were finished; then I looked up, first into his eyes and then into the red eyes that hovered just above his shoulder. Seeing the direction of my gaze, he frowned and looked over his shoulder. When he looked back, I thanked him, stood up, and hurried off.

No harm done. His words echoed around my head as I walked away from his house. *That's what you think.*

Nick's downward spiral was fast and violent. He was often at the surgery, complaining of nightmares, sleeplessness, nausea, and phantom smells. On those occasions where I had to book him in, I tried not to look at the black mass that curled round him almost lovingly. Within five months, Nick Dolman had hanged himself. I drank very heavily that night, my guilt almost overwhelming. I felt sure that Louise would call to tell me that Jenny's ghost had returned to blight her life now it wasn't tethered to Nick anymore, but no such call came.

Lisa came into the surgery several times in the months following Nick's death, needing sleeping tablets and antidepressants, but the creature on her shoulder was gone. Now, she carried only the burdens of motherhood, and even those seemed to ease as Alex grew into a lovable, lively scamp who charmed everyone when he came in for his yearly flu shot.

I don't know if I'd do it again. Jenny's ghost didn't return to her and it didn't infect Alex or Lisa, but who knows if that's how it would go next time? I check people's backs as well as their shoulders now, but I've never seen anything that would require me to go back to that cupboard and choose another black bottle.

Actually, what I said was a lie – the first one I've told you so far. I *would* do it again, if I saw a blue-eyed burden on someone's back. I couldn't stop what happened at school all those years ago: the blood, the screaming, the utter desolation of watching your friends die around you. I told you that I can't see my own shadow burden, but some days I can feel it pressing down on me, body and soul. A smell might set it off, like chalk dust or really sweet custard, or the stab of sorrow I feel like a knife in the heart when I see two young girls in their school uniforms, sitting on a bench sharing jokes and a bag of chips.

I couldn't stop the events at school, and I can't get rid of the ghosts of guilt that follow me around, but I can take this talent I've been given and use it to help others. I can't change yesterday, but tomorrow's another matter.

***Charlotte Bond** is an author, ghostwriter, freelance editor, proofreader, reviewer, and podcaster. Under her own name she has written within the genres of horror and dark fantasy. As a ghostwriter, she's tackled everything from romance to cozy mystery stories and YA novels. She was a regular contributor of mostly historical and sometimes bizarre articles to The Vintage News website. She is a co-host of the podcast* Breaking the Glass Slipper, *which has been nominated for the BFS award for Best Audio four times, winning it in 2019. Her Black Shuck Shadows collection* The Watcher in the Woods *won the British Fantasy Society's award for Best Collection in 2021. She is represented by Alex Cochran.*

Trial

by

Phil Sloman

Cold shadows engulfed him on the doorstep, his head bent, as he waited to be let in. An insistent drizzle filled the air, dampening his clothes and the small rucksack slung over both shoulders. He held a tattered piece of paper which had been folded and unfolded many times. Silently, he mouthed each word scrawled on the page in his illegible hand.

10.00 a.m. sharp. Come alone. No food or drink twenty-four hours in advance. And no drugs. Bring ID.

A crudely drawn map filled the rest of the paper, including a street name. There was no number for the building. There didn't need to be. It was the only one standing.

It would have been cheap offices back in the day, stuck in the arse end of an industrial estate where the river provided transport for goods, the waters brown and impenetrable. Now, dirty shards of glass littered the floor where the windows had been smashed in, either by children or by drunks throwing stones. Perhaps both. Piles of rubble dotted the surrounding waste ground, misshapen mounds poking from the earth like rotten teeth in this long-forgotten landscape where 'under development' signs were stained and warped. A dishevelled magpie grubbed for food in the swirl of discarded fast-food containers blown in by the wind along the road the man had walked down. The man saluted once, the movement awkward and uncertain, then lowered his hand, hoping no one had seen him do such a thing. Superstitions were for childhood and times he wanted to forget.

And still the door remained closed. He pulled back his sleeve, noting the time etched out on the cheap digital watch face, and sighed. Eighteen minutes past ten.

Perhaps he had the wrong place. Or the wrong date. Maybe both. He pressed the buzzer on the intercom for the fourth time that morning. A now familiar *bzzzzzzzzzzz* reached him from deep within the building, followed by silence as he released his finger from the button. Somewhere along the river a herring gull called out unseen. He ignored it and looked to the note again.

No food or drink twenty-four hours in advance. And no drugs.

No drugs.

The headaches had been getting worse. Much worse. Not taking the drugs wasn't really an option, yet…

'Hello.'

The voice caught him unawares as it crackled from the intercom. It was impossible to tell if it was male or female.

'Hello,' repeated the voice, 'can I help you?'

Cheap polish played at his nostrils as he leaned in closer to the intercom, his lips almost touching the metal. 'Hi, uh, hi. It's John. John Hansen. Dr Fielding asked me to come.' He paused, looking over his shoulder as if there might be anyone else there in this backend of nowhere. 'About the trial.'

The intercom fell silent. He stared at it, watching the circular pattern of dots, willing it to speak. A fly landed on his eyelid. He blinked and swatted it away. Somewhere, inside, he imagined he heard footsteps and whispered voices; but perhaps it was the wind.

'Don't let your imagination run away with you. It will only get you into trouble.' That's what his teachers had said to him. If only they knew the truth now. The things that happened when his mind wasn't calmed. What happened when *they* came to visit; the dark thoughts.

'Come in.'

The words caught him off guard, lost in himself. He was about to respond – to say what, he didn't know – when there was a buzz then a *thunk* and the door swung open. Shadows greeted him on the other side, stretching into the distance. He looked back, the magpie still scrabbling in the mess, the world grey as the drizzle continued, before putting the note into his coat pocket and stepping inside. He barely noticed as the door closed, separating him from the outside world.

Inside, a soulless grey-green corridor lay before him, its features lost in the gloom, leading to a second door picked out by tired lighting from above. His footsteps echoed hollowly down the corridor as he walked towards the door, leaving faint wet footprints in his wake. A small square of glass threaded with wire mesh was set at head height in the door ahead. For a moment, he thought he saw a face behind the glass; then it was gone.

'Hello?'

No one answered.

'Hello, is there anyone there?'

More silence.

He pushed at the door, expecting it to hold firm. Instead, it swung open wide. John gripped the shoulder straps of his rucksack tighter than he meant to, curling his shoulders inwards to engulf his neck tortoise-like. He swallowed with what little spittle he could muster and entered the room beyond.

The stench of chlorine hit him as he crossed the threshold, as if someone had tried cleaning the room with pool water. Cold white tiles covered the floor and walls, illuminated by two lengths of strip lighting above. Filthy black streaks of dirt were engrained within the off-white grouting, some of it bleeding thinly from the narrow tracks. The room itself was small. It reminded him of those interrogation rooms he had seen on television where the police dragged the suspect in for questioning. Except there was no oversized mirror dominating the space, no unseen officials watching everything unfold before them. Instead, a small rack of hooks was fixed to the wall, a single lab coat hanging from them.

A square table occupied the centre of the room, large enough for no more than the four narrow chairs tucked beneath. A clipboard and pen rested in the middle of the table; to their right a tall jug and glass, just as he imagined things would be.

'Please sit.'

The voice came from high above, delivered via small black speakers recessed in the ceiling. John spotted a camera beside it; one he had missed before. Thin and rectangular, with a dark cable disappearing into the wall. A small red light blinked above the lens. The camera followed his movement as he took a step to the side.

'Is that Dr Fielding?' He spoke directly to the camera. 'Only, Dr Fielding asked me to come here today. She said it would help me. That it would make me feel much better.'

'Please sit.'

'She said it would take *them* away.'

'Please sit.'

'Only…'

'Sit.'

There was nothing more to be said. He hung his rucksack on a hook, letting it sag from the weight of its contents. Nothing much. A book, some food, a couple of cans of Tango for later when he could break his fast. He placed his coat over it, small droplets of water dripping from its hem. John moved to the table, pulled out a chair and sat down, his knees brushing the underside of the tabletop. He gripped the edges of the chair vice-like as he shuffled backwards to get more space, grimacing as he felt the unmistakeable softness of freshly chewed gum stored beneath the seat. He said nothing.

'Please read and sign the form.'

'But I want to see Dr Fielding.'

'She will be with you soon. Please read and sign the form.'

'Please read and sign the form,' he muttered under his breath, the words juvenile and laced with sarcasm. Thin grooves formed in the wood as he dragged the clipboard across the tabletop, leaning in to read the attached form. The header bore the name of a company he had never heard of until last month. Dr Fielding had told him they were well respected in the world of pharmaceuticals – 'pharma,' she had called them, which had made him think of sheep – and that they had helped many of her previous patients, though none had had quite his needs. He continued reading. Several pages followed on from the company name, all of which he skimmed briefly, spotting phrases like 'dissolve liability', 'own volition', and 'not be held accountable for...'

They could say what they liked for all he cared. Dr Fielding had reassured him about everything when they had spoken by phone. Yes, of course the testing was safe. This was all quite standard and above board. There were laws governing these trials, making certain they were safe. It was how most companies got their drugs to market. And, as well as helping himself, he would be helping others like him; though he had never met anyone quite in his situation. Grabbing the pen, he scrawled his signature across the page, the tip scratchy against the surface, and slid the clipboard back to the centre of the table.

'Good,' said the voice.

'Can I see Dr Fielding now?'

'Soon. Now, you see the glass and jug?'

John nodded.

'There should be two pills next to the glass.'

John looked closer. Two small oval pills sat next to the glass. Both red. *Like that film with Keanu Reeves*, he thought. Was he ready to see how deep the rabbit hole went?

'Please take them.'

'Both?'

'Yes.'

'What are they?'

'We are not at liberty to say, Mr Hansen. That would negate the trial.'

'But what will they do to me.'

'That's what we hope to understand.'

'What if it's something bad?'

'They are perfectly safe, Mr Hansen. Trust us. We hope they will help you with your—' The voice paused, trying to find the right word. '—with your problem. Isn't that why you came here today?'

Why he had come here today. Well, yes, that much was true. What other options did he have? All those years of hallucinations. All stemming from… he didn't like to think. There were friends he had lost; both physically and through his own actions. He had purposefully cut himself off from society and everyone connected with… what did you even call something like that? It had no name. Or nothing rational you could call it. He had tried counselling and group sessions. When neither of those worked, he turned to drink and drugs. And still the headaches had persisted. Along with the hallucinations, which always seemed all too realistic. The scars he had told him they were real and yet there was always another reason for how he got them. Must have fallen over when drunk. Perhaps it was a cat; a rogue one running loose in his flat. Did he do it to himself? Always some way to rationalise and convince him that it was all in his head. Because the alternative didn't bear thinking about.

He looked to the table.

So, this was salvation. Two little lozenges filled with heaven knows what. The miracle cure Dr Fielding had promised him, yet no one even knew if they would work. That was why she had practically begged him to come here today. Or had it been the other way around?

The pills were dwarfed in his hand as he picked them up, two red capsules centred in his palm. So small. Could they really offer him release? Make the headaches go away. The headaches and those… things. He looked to the shadows.

'Mr Hansen?'

Not now, he thought. *I'm busy.*

'Mr Hansen?'

Not now!

He dry-swallowed the pills then instantly regretted it. An acrid taste hit the back of his throat along with a sensation that the tablets were stuck halfway between his epiglottis and oesophagus. Water spilled onto the table surface as he rushed to pour himself a drink. Like a cheap drunk, he downed the glass a little too eagerly as the water flushed the pills down from his throat. He poured another and downed that before pouring a third left untouched.

'Mr Hansen? Mr Hansen? Are you okay?'

It was a different voice. Distant as if broadcast via a ham radio, the signal dropping in and out with no one to tune it. A thumping sound in the background. Colours were bleeding throughout the room, the walls blurring in and out of focus.

'Mr Hansen? Can you hear me?'

Fire burned in his gut, moving to his bladder, building an intensity of pressure.

'I need to get to the toilet. Someone tell me where the toilet is. Now.'

His knuckles whitened as he clenched his fists. Somewhere a voice struggled to break through from above, hidden beneath hisses, and pops, and crackles.

'The toilet. Please. Where is it?"

A high-pitched note sounded, long and monotonous. Flatlining.

'The toilet!'

'Well…'

He looked up. This voice was new and coming through clearly.

'Well, you need to put your hand up if you want to go to the toilet. You should know that by now.'

'But…'

'No buts, Hansen. If you want to go to the toilet, you need to raise your hand.'

The sensation of urine at the tip of his cock was strong, pressure building from within, a fear that his trousers would stain dark around the crotch. Instinctively, he jiggled his legs hoping to stave off the inevitable. Slowly, he raised his hand.

'Very good, Hansen. First door on the right.'

Blinking, he scanned right, trying to bring the world into focus, breathing deeply. The kaleidoscope settled, the colours calming, the room becoming solid. There, to the right, was a door. He rushed forward, knocking over the table, sending the glass and jug shattering against the floor to leave a puddle on the floor. As he hurried through the door, he didn't question why he hadn't noticed it when he entered the room.

Noticeboards peppered the walls in the hallway he found himself in, scraps of paper hanging from them. A row of metal lockers nestled against one side of the passage. A stickman picked out in black against white showed on a sign a few feet away. He dashed forward, sweaty hands fumbling to open the door to the toilets. Graffiti and dark stains covered the tiled walls. That didn't matter. Nothing did other than the pain at his groin. He tugged at his fly as he stumbled towards the urinals, trying to hold on for a few seconds longer.

Relief flooded his being as a poker-hot stream of piss gushed forth into the tarnished metal trough. He stood, legs apart, body arched for he didn't know how long. Eventually, the torrent slowed, turning to straw-coloured droplets before ceasing. He shook his member to remove any residual liquid then zippered himself back up.

'What now?' he mumbled. That had never happened before. Never with that intensity. That explosive urgency to piss. Had it been the drugs? Surely it had come on too fast. Was it simply nerves? He didn't know.

Cold water flowed from the taps, splashing into the ceramic bowl of the sink, washing the residual droplets of urine from his hands, which he wiped dry against the back of his trousers. Above the sink a worn mirror was screwed to the wall, its edges marred with black veins. The man within was one he recognised far too well. Large dark circles hung beneath his eyes. He couldn't remember a time when they hadn't been there. His hair was starting to show signs of receding, forming what might one day become a widow's peak. Dark stubble peppered his cheeks. He dragged a finger beneath his eye, pulling at the wrinkled bag, revealing the pink flesh inside. Sighing, he let the skin go loose, brushing his clothes down, trying to smooth out the wrinkles more from habit than because he cared about his appearance.

'What now?' he asked again. Was this all part of the trial? Would there be scientists waiting outside toilets with clipboards and questions? Could he wait them out in here? His reflection stayed silent, looking straight at him with any insight kept to itself. He stared back.

The movement, when it came, was unexpected. Glimpsed at the edges of the mirror, almost lost in the gloom behind him. Slowly, he turned, watching where the shadows darkened to a nigh impossible black. Was there something there? Surely it was his mind again, seeing things, just like the doctors told him. John edged forwards.

'Nothing there, nothing there…' The words drawn out and lacking in conviction.

Fuck.

There, something hidden in the blackness. Wasn't there? The outline of one of *them*.

Them.

He had never given *them* a name. Didn't want to. Didn't dare. That would make them one hundred per cent, rip-your-heart-from-your-chest-while-it-was-still-beating real, rather than just figments. Crouching, he tried to get a better look, shuffling forward an inch, then another, the wall within arm's reach. Was it his imagination or was the air colder here?

The darkness swelled. There was something there. He was certain now. Yet still he crept forward, needing to know, ensnared by curiosity, hand held out, reaching, reaching, reaching…

'What the hell do you think you're doing, John?'

He whipped around, his feet nearly sliding from under him on the slick floor, feeling a burn in his thighs as he stood. There was no one there. Just his reflection in the mirror, the glass cold to the touch as he placed a hand against the tarnished surface, everything behind him forgotten momentarily.

'Was that you?' he asked.

The man in the mirror nodded.

'We're safe here, John. You're not safe.'

'But Dr Fielding promised.'

'She's promised us many things.'

'This time will be different, though.'

'Will it? John, what do you think was about to happen?'

'I don't know.'

'Can't you hear *them*, John? Purring. Purring in the shadows.'

He shook his head. He couldn't. Except…

There it was, a low hum rising around him. Just one at first, purring, followed by a second, then a third, then another from all corners of the room. A familiar throbbing began in his temples almost as if in response to the chorus surrounding him.

'Run, John!'

Angry blasts of hot air shot from the hand driers, adding to the cacophony, a wave of sound building to a crescendo. Swirls of toilet paper and filth flew up into the air, creating flurries of activity; and somewhere in the midst of the storm there was a different kind of movement, more purposeful, dark lithe bodies prowling, as the purrs became growls and the hint of tooth and claw teased forth from the shadows.

'Run!'

And he did, his feet struggling to find grip as if he were running on the spot, arms outstretched in desperation to reach for the door, yanking at the handle, kicking away the creatures swarming around his legs, somehow forcing his way out to the corridor and the illusion of safety as his other self watched impassively from the mirror.

Screams greeted him in the distance. Some young and high-pitched, others older, all filled with pain and surprise, channelled along the narrow corridor like water driven down a gulley. Attacking his senses, attacking him.

He ran. Scrabbling claws on tiles joining the faraway screams at his back. Words formed in his head. A stupid rhyme from his youth.

Run, run, as fast as you can, you can't catch me, I'm the…

Except they might catch him this time.

He burst into the waiting room, the door slamming into the wall, his head throbbing as spiderwebs formed in the plaster. Agitated fingers gripped the door and forced it shut behind him. Body after body slammed into the wood as he turned the lock.

'Do you see them?' he shouted to the cameras. 'Do you?'

Of course not. No one ever did. And even if they did, what then?

Wood splintering could be heard from the other side of the door. He couldn't tell whether it was by tooth or claw. Either way, it didn't matter. Getting out of there was all that did. Grab his stuff from the hooks and go.

The lab coat had gone. Instead, rucksacks hung on the coat hooks, names scrawled in fading black pen along their tops, some of it bleeding into the rough fabric. He knew the names from long ago, ones he had tried to forget. Osgood, Webster, Pasmore, Winkleman, and so many more.

'No, not again,' he whimpered as he grabbed his coat and rucksack, looping the rucksack over his shoulder, the straps tighter than he remembered.

Behind him, the sounds were heightening as more and more of *them* joined the assault. Even now, a small hole was appearing at the foot of the door, thin black tendrils poking through the gap. Broken glass crunched underfoot as he rushed to the exit, the shards sticking to the soles of his shoes. If he could get to the corridor and then the outside world, he could be free. He tugged at the door.

It didn't budge.

Determined, he pulled harder and harder at the door, to the extent he thought the handle would come away in his grasp. He scanned left and right, looking for a button, a lever, anything that would provide some kind of release from what had now become a cell. Ahead, barely visible through the small glass window, he could see the length of the corridor, less than ten metres, a shaft of light at the end illuminating the exit. Freedom. Behind him… he looked back and wished he hadn't.

There were three of them in the room: sitting, watching, purring.

Pain spasmed across his shoulder as he threw himself against the door. Again and again. Battering the window with his fists until his flesh became tender and his skin split. Blood smeared the square of glass in the door.

'Let me out!' he shrieked, 'Let me out! Let me out! Let me out!' As if he believed anyone would truly come to his aid. Calling and calling until his throat was raw.

In the background, the purring stopped.

—

A flurry of activity greeted Dr Fielding as she entered the room; bright lights reflecting against the white walls as a faint smell of urine reached her nose. A porter wrung out a bloodied cloth into a bucket of darkening water before continuing to wipe down the door's glass panel. Two nurses studied charts on a clipboard, discussing just why it had their patient's signature scrawled across the third page and where had he gotten the pen from. Another porter mopped up a pool of piss in the corner mingled with water and broken glass. A mirror stood mounted above a small vanity sink. An outline of a man had been etched across its surface in what might have been lipstick, perhaps, all dried and flaking away. It almost made you believe someone was inside, watching.

John had long since been taken from his room to the infirmary in the east wing of the facility. There, he would receive the care and support he needed until he could be transferred to one of the more secure sections. Then, when all was well, he would be ready to return to the general population.

'Does anyone know why he stopped taking his medication? Wasn't anyone monitoring him?'

Silence greeted Fielding. She was happy to meet it, letting it linger, catching the eyes of her subordinates. Eventually one piped up.

'It's all the cuts. We just can't...' They fell silent and looked to the floor.

Fielding didn't dignify the comment with an answer, merely noted who said it for future reference when the next round of redundancies cropped up.

'We tried to get to him.'

She raised an eyebrow.

'The door, it wouldn't open. No matter what we did. We were calling out to him, hammering on the door. Nothing. Not until…'

'Until?'

'Until he passed out.'

She sighed. Something else to leave out of the report. And there had been so many reports for this resident. Over the years she thought things had been getting better. She had even spoken with him recently about withdrawing from his medication, trialling new options. There was real hope, yet now…

'Out!' she said, no room for argument in her tone.

No one moved.

'Now!'

Then they moved, filing out one by one without a backward glance, glad to be anywhere but there.

'John, what did you do this time?'

She remembered the first time he had been admitted, half-dead and babbling about creatures only he could see. Over time she'd learned about what had happened to him – his trigger point, as she called it – though what he believed to have taken place and the reports she had gleaned from the newspapers never tallied up, almost as if his experience had been unique. There had been times she wondered if she would hear the stories of the other victims – there was no other word for those poor kids – but she had reconciled herself to never knowing. As it was, John was challenging enough on his own.

Her heels clicked on the cold floor as she ventured towards the sink, curiosity getting the better of her. She reached forward and scraped at the outline on the mirror, flecks coming off under her fingernails.

'Not lipstick, then,' she said, sniffing at her fingers, before running them under the tap. It didn't surprise her.

From the corner of her eye, she glimpsed movement deep within the mirror, something lost in the shadows. Probably a trick of the light, except there was a sound now too, almost like humming yet more animalistic, deep and throaty.

That's funny, she thought, *how on earth did a cat get in here?*

Phil Sloman *is a writer of dark psychological fiction. His first story was published in 2014 and he has been writing ever since. In 2017 Phil was shortlisted for British Fantasy Award Best Newcomer for his novella* Becoming David, *and was part of* Imposter Syndrome *from Dark Minds Press, which was shortlisted for British Fantasy Award for Best Anthology in 2018. He also edited the 2020 British Fantasy Award shortlisted anthology* The Woods. *Phil regularly appears on several reviewers' Best of Year lists. Visit his website at www.philsloman.com*

Comments On This Video Have Been Disabled

by

James Everington

Before the 'Borsam House Tape' – before he was a laughing stock – Joseph Brooke's videos of haunted houses and other supposed cursed locations were YouTube sensations. Part of the reason was Brooke's famous, apparent, objectivity: 'This is what I saw,' he'd say, without offering interpretation. 'This is what I saw, this is what I heard,' and the viewer could make of it what they would. Brooke's videos never offered an explanation, not ghosts or psychic residues or group delusion or even outright fakery. His voiceovers were matter-of-fact, deadpan, describing what could already be seen (a blue gaslight glow in an unlit room, ornaments tumbling untouched from an old mantel, the suggestion of a small soot-stained hand vanishing between one shot and the next). When he gave extra information – such as the time, the weather, the sudden rising temperature when the blue light flared – it was always backed up by something he let us see: a glimpse of his phone, a pan towards an outside window, a handy thermometer. Exterior footage of the places he investigated included a postcode or GPS reference in the corner of the shot; digital floorplans identified the location of interior shots within the building. *This Is What I Saw*, he called his channel, with the implicit promise: you will too.

The 'Borsam House Tape' (the only one of his videos to be titled so anachronistically) was not originally posted to *This Is What I Saw* or credited to Brooke, but posted anonymously on an obscure paranormal and cryptid message board. It languished there for over a week before someone tweeted a link with the comment: *but isnt this voiceover @BrookeTIWIS?* Brooke's blue-tick account did not reply; in fact, it hadn't been active for a number of weeks. Yet within twenty-four hours the footage had been removed from the message board and posted to his YouTube channel, albeit without Brooke's usual slick title sequence, appeals for Likes and Subscribes, or links to *TIWIS*-branded merchandise. Within hours of posting it had been watched thousands of times; within days, over fifty thousand.

The first *Has Brooke Lost It? What Is This Shit?* hot take appeared soon after. More followed; Brooke never responded to any of the criticism. In fact, Brooke (if that is his real name) has not been active online since.

The final *This Is What I Saw* video starts like this.

Black screen.

The footage remains black and silent for an uncomfortably long time; just as we might be tempted to move the clip forward we hear a low, ragged

exhalation, the sound of someone too close to a microphone. If we've turned the volume up, we quickly lower it now. The screen stays black as someone starts to speak.

'The irony,' they say, 'the fucking irony. Sat in the dark, for my own good, they say. It's too late for that *now*, isn't it?' It's obvious why people weren't sure if the voice was Brooke. It's softer, more quavering, more uncertain than we are used to.

He pauses; beneath the sound of his laboured breathing we hear the slam of some heavy wooden door – a fire door, maybe – shutting in an empty and echoing space, on the other side of a wall. The screen remains completely black.

'Gary,' Brooke whispers. 'Shoulda listened to Gary.'

Sudden colour; motion blur; noise of footsteps.

In previous *TIWIS* videos, Brooke presented a sequence of events in scrupulously chronological order, the date and time visible in the bottom-right corner of the screen. But the 'Borsam House Tape' plunges straight *in media res*, giving us no clue as to location or time. It is obvious, however, that one of Brooke's trademark investigations into the supposed paranormal is in progress.

The autofocus of a small handheld camera takes a few seconds to adjust and then we see Brooke, walking ahead of us; or rather, ahead of whoever is holding the camera (assumed to be Gary Osgood, Brooke's long-suffering assistant and friend since school). Brooke is walking quickly, purposefully, as if something has just happened or is just about to, positive or negative we don't know. Gary appears to be struggling to both keep pace and keep the shot focused on Brooke (there is a general amateurishness to the 'Borsam House Tape' not found elsewhere in Brooke's work). Brooke is wearing a black T-shirt with the *TIWIS* logo on the back; it has risen up and we can see the small of his back above his jeans. If indeed the man in shot *is* Brooke; we never see his face, only his back. And later on, we can be even less certain, for in most subsequent scenes he is behind the camera, due to Gary's departure.

The surroundings are equally ambiguous, and on first viewing many struggle to make sense of what they are seeing. Brooke is walking alongside what appears to be the interior wall of a house, its surface crumbled so that brick gapes through holes in the plaster. But the light is wrong, both too bright and blurry; when Gary, trying to keep pace, points the camera downwards, we realise the blurriness is not a production fault but strands of mist snaking across a dirty, crumbling parquet floor. Before we can quite make sense of this, the shot levels and we are distracted by an odd movement from the figure we've been following. He stops in his tracks; Gary stops too late, and for a brief second all we can see is a blur as he steps back.

'You okay man?' Gary's voice says. 'Someone step over your grave?' But what we saw wasn't a shiver; it was a jerk, almost a convulsion. We saw Brooke twist his body suddenly, as if to get away from the unexpected touch of something hot or cold or merely unpleasant. There is a feeling of tension or embarrassment from the figure with his back to us.

'What the fuck, Gary?' he snaps. 'Don't do that again.'

But we know – we've *seen* – that Gary didn't touch him.

Cut.

Darkness, the same shallow breathing too close to a microphone.

'I knew, I *knew* it was a bad idea from the start.'

Cut.

A shot of the corner of a room, two exposed brick walls meeting at a right-angle. Again, the contrast ratio appears to be wrong, for everything looks black, white or a muted grey. The shot pulls back; through a hole in the brickwork there's a sudden glimpse of sunlight. Wherever Brooke is investigating, it seems abandoned and partially in ruin. The camera tilts up and there is a dull grey sky where we should see ceiling. A black jackdaw cuts across the sky, cawing, and the camera follows it as if desperate for its movement. The bird lands on the crumbling remains of another part of the house, at a right-angle to this one, with a gabled roof that fades into the mist. Behind the caws of jackdaws there is a persistent and rhythmic background noise that some viewers think is the sea, others merely strong wind or incorrectly set up audio equipment. No one has ever been able to establish exactly where the so-called 'Borsam House' is; indeed what Brooke says next, presumably intended to establish location, has been blanked out in post-production. As if in retrospect he doesn't want anyone to know where the house is, or like he has made the whole thing up, 'Borsam' nomenclature included.

'The [mute] ruins,' Brooke says, his voice trying for drama and authority. 'Where once a grand house stood. And where still, a malignant spirit is said to haunt the old drawing room…'

The footage cuts to a wider shot of the same derelict building, taking in what looks to be the entire remaining structure. Some parts of the building look almost intact, although the fog makes it hard to see for sure; elsewhere the remaining walls jut out in jagged shapes from ground already reclaimed by weeds. The patterns they form do not at first glance give us a sense of an entire house, ruined or not. Brooke gives a little half-laugh.

'Where the fuck *is* the drawing room?'

Cut.

Black screen; haggard breathing.

Cut.

A sequence follows which is closer in production values to the *TIWIS* of old, leading some to speculate that it was shot before Brooke ever saw the ruins. We see a series of external establishing shots of libraries and archives. Then we cut to a shot of a floorplan of a building, presumably Borsam House. Before we can get our bearings, we cut to a different floorplan of the same building, altered. More follow, a structure expanding, shifting and contracting with little rhyme or reason. If indeed it *is* the same building.

Many viewers have cried foul here, as we cut from these plans to Borsam House itself, an implication obvious and unearned. The footage is time-lapsed: early morning fog races eerily round the flat black silhouettes of mouldy walls and collapsed staircases, before being exorcised by the sun cutting through the grey cloud above. The sky's dirty white flares a fiery orange, before a sudden and total nightfall. The blackness is so deep we wonder if we have cut back to the weak-voiced man in the darkness, but then the shot switches to night vision. The ghostly image is still for what seems a long time, with no movement or depth to it, before we *do* cut to that blackness that has punctuated and framed what we've seen so far. 'Nothing,' a voice says at the point of transition, so quickly it isn't clear if they are commenting on the absence of spooks, malignant or otherwise, in what we've just seen, or the darkness we are once again confronted with.

Cut.

Unsteady handheld camera, Brooke's voiceover.

Gary is attaching lengths of fluorescent tape between the crumbling walls of the house and stakes he has wedged into the ground, presumably meant to represent parts of the structure no longer extant. He is guided in this by Brooke, consulting a paper we cannot see. There are several false starts, undoings and re-doings. It is hard not to think the final arrangement represents the point at which they gave up rather than one they think accurate. Some of the tape has red plastic tags snapped across its length; Brooke tells us they represent spaces where the entity has been 'sighted'.

'It was a grand building, once,' Brooke says. 'Now you can almost see it again.' He does not sound convinced.

The shot turns to follow Gary trudging away, towards a trailer parked some distance from the house. The grey of the fog and sky makes it look like he has been shot against one of those blank backgrounds to which you can digitally add anything you want the viewer to see. He doesn't look towards camera when he visibly shivers, looks around quickly as if expecting to see – *what?* – behind him. There is a slight pause in his movements when he realises nothing is there, but he does not look unduly concerned as he continues. Brooke is already turning the camera away, not having noticed anything of significance. We don't get a clear enough look to see if Gary's strange jolt occurred inside the red area or not.

Cut.

Blackness, the sound of a door closing in an echoing corridor.

A soft, almost inaudible whining sound, like someone in continuous pain trying to suppress its effects.

Cut.

Another montage, although one that seems hastily assembled, its governing principle ill-defined. The brown text of aged documents; sepia photographs of buildings and groups of people; stock footage of a candle flickering against the night. A mirror, reflecting nothing. The cuts come too quick, and Brooke's voice speaks too quickly, garbled like he is trying to keep up.

Surprisingly, he is narrating the stories and legends of the ruined house. Brooke had given this approach short shrift before; after all, by definition we can't see stories, can't prove or disprove the anecdotes of the dead. In earlier *TIWIS* videos, Brooke would mention such things briefly, almost dismissively, as if they were merely a prelude to his own investigation. But in this final video we hear him linger in the telling of several such unverifiable tales. He starts with the story of a scullery maid who made allegations that the master of the house had touched her inappropriately despite the fact he was bedridden three storeys up; this is confused in the telling with another servant fleeing the house with her clothes dishevelled, spirits hectic, hands running and running through her hair as if convinced something were tangled in it. Next, a beloved dog that created pandemonium and soiled the floor every time it was forced into a certain, unnamed, room of the building, before it was confined outside and died of exposure one harsh winter. To believe all the tales, the building seemed to have served multiple purposes – domestic, commercial, and even ecclesiastical – in its time, and had its layout continuously altered to match. Its eventual ruin, Brooke tells us, was not caused by the simple ravages of time, but by an elderly and sightless patriarch knocking through successive walls, seeking something his hopeful future heirs couldn't determine, until its structural integrity was compromised too far and one storey collapsed atop another…

Even here at the end, Brooke gets confused, returns to a previous tale about a fearful old miser who banished all his family from the house (and disinherited them from his will) due to the cruel and vexatious practical jokes they tormented him with day and night… and we realise the voice speaking – which has increased in volume, if not coherence, during these tales – is not the Brooke from before, but the hectic and short-of-breath one we know from the darkness. The mishmash of story and conjecture we've listened to isn't someone's preliminary research prior to starting work on a task; it is the sound of someone trying to make sense of something that has happened. The voice of someone *after* the event, looking for sense and antecedent, needing to see an explanation of…

Cut.

A close-up of Gary Osgood's face; before we can register more than his pale skin, the dampness of his brow, he is holding a hand up to the camera, ducking his face away.

'You're filming *this*? What the fuck?'

'Part of your contract,' Brooke's voice says. 'Just because you've broken the terms of it, doesn't mean—'

'Screw your contract!' Osgood shouts. 'There's something here!' His melodramatic words and outstretched arms are somewhat undercut by the fact he and Brooke are having their confrontation inside a large but cramped trailer, filled with monitors, laptops, tripods, and other equipment. But the fear in Gary's face (Brooke has backed away but not stopped filming) seems genuine enough; his eyes are wide and looking around for something he can't see, and he keeps brushing his left forearm with his other hand, as if something unpleasant lingers on him.

'There's nothing here,' Brooke replies bitterly. To prove his point, he turns the shot towards the monitors, zooms in. On them we see the interior and exterior of Borsam House from different angles and elevations; aside from the flicker of the screens themselves, the images are motionless. 'It's a dead end, a dud.'

'Then how do you explain…'

'Nerves,' Brooke says blankly; the shot moves as if with a shrug. 'It's spooky here and I know you've been smoking that—'

'Fuck you, Joseph, I'm not a coward. How many times have we worked together?'

'Twenty-eight. Twenty-nine if you count this time, although apparently you don't.'

'There's something here, Joseph, I *felt* it!'

'Oh come *on*. You know I don't do that crap. Auras, hair standing on end, bad vibes in air, it's too subjective for the viewers to possibly—'

'You're not listening,' Osgood shouts, silencing his soon to be ex-boss. 'I felt it; it *touched* me. It was strong, like something tensed, coiled and… it was sweaty, sticky with it, old sweat…'

'There was nothing there,' Brooke says, briefly turning the camera towards the monitors again. 'I didn't see anything, just you stoned and getting the fear. There's nothing here.'

'Oh yeah?' Osgood says, struggling into a jacket, whether trembling with anger or fear we don't know. 'Then why are you staying?'

Brooke doesn't answer.

'I'll see you, Joseph,' Gary says, walking out of shot. We hear a door open and close, but the camera doesn't turn to show us his exit.

Cut.

Darkness.

'I never answered you.' A long, drawn out exhalation. 'But surely you get it, mate? I had to just *see*. Had to just check it wasn't the same as… as before. As Wellbrook.'

Cut.

We can't immediately decipher what we see next, as if we've zoomed in on something and the resultant image is too grainy to make sense of. It's only when the shot pulls back that we see Brooke has been filming the footage from the monitors in the trailer, which he is fast-forwarding and rewinding. It is unclear why he didn't just include the monitor footage directly into the 'Borsam House Tape'; it is as if he has taken the *This Is What I Saw* ethos too much to heart, and distrusts all he hasn't directly filmed himself.

Each time the monitor footage settles to normal speed, we see a clip of Gary Osgood. We see him pacing the rotten, uneven floors of the old Borsam House, staking out tape, checking lighting levels, rolling a joint. He is framed by morning fog, which jolts to grey cloud, to a golden-hour sunset. Sometimes he is a small figure against dull and crooked walls; only occasionally is the shot close enough to see his face. And in each of these clips edited together (the forwarding and rewinding stops once we get the idea) we see Osgood jerk, flinch, twist from something we can't see, that isn't there. Afterwards, he sometimes rubs his arm, sometimes brushes his shoulder. When the shot is close enough to read his body language, he has the uncomfortable, wanting-to-scratch look of someone in a house with fleas. Cut, cut, cut – close to thirty shots of Osgood consciously or unconsciously reacting to something invisible.

It was this sequence that damned Brooke to mockery as much as anything else. Not just because the result is unintentionally funny (it wasn't long before internet wags were setting Osgood's jerks and lurches to 'Thriller' or the *Benny Hill* music) although it is, at least to start with (most viewers stop smiling as the clips continue and we see the increasingly harried look on Osgood's face). But because something about the sequence seems *manipulative*. Gone is Brooke's previous scrupulousness in making clear the time, the context, the sequence. Many of the shots are poorly framed or out of focus; we can't even see if they all *are* of Osgood or even shot at the house. And once you let doubt in, once you pull that thread, everything can unravel. Just where *is* this decrepit house and why has no one traced it since? Why does the 'Borsam House Tape', for all Brooke's meticulousness, never let us form a coherent picture of the building's layout, its size? Where are its boundaries?

After the succession of clips of Osgood, we jump to a sequence shot on handheld camera, where Brooke is placing plastic markers onto wooden floors or the detritus where they no longer exist; we assume one for each spot where Osgood 'felt' something. A long shot shows the markers forming clusters but no real pattern, especially in relation to the red-taped area of the supposed haunting. A series of shots shows this area being realigned, as if to match variations of the layout of the building. Nothing seems to fit, and Brooke can be heard swearing under his breath.

And if doubts have crept in, if we've pulled at that thread, allowed ourselves a laugh, then the fact that throughout this sequence the camera occasionally judders, jerks as if *Brooke* has shuddered or flinched without conscious realisation, is surely too on the nose to win us over. *This Is What I Saw* – but he doesn't even seem to *notice*.

Cut.

'Did it move on to me after Gary? Or was I just too dumb to notice it before he left? Either way, it was more… confident after that. Its touch surer. And loathsome – god, I can feel it now…'

Cut.

It's unclear if the voice started to sob before we hear the caws of jackdaws, a wind like static, possible waves.

Handheld camera walking through the remains of the house; it is as if it has fallen even further into disrepair and ruin while Brooke has been filming. The remains of old brick walls emerge out of the mist like they weren't there seconds before; when the camera does a one-eighty they've receded into invisibility again.

The same voice but more confident, surer in its telling.

'Maybe it's some phenomenon caused by the house itself, the remaining structure creating channels of chilled air at right-angles to where we walk that feel like, I dunno, a ghostly hand…'

Interior of the trailer, wind and wave replaced by the static hum of a generator. The shot is set up so we can see a blank piece of A3 and a hand holding a pencil. Brooke talks to himself as he draws: squares and oblongs presumably intended to represent the physical remains of the once-solid building, although it is hard to equate this drawing to what we have seen on tape so far. 'The prevailing wind is…' Brooke mutters, and he draws a large arrow in the top-right corner of the page. Then he proceeds to pencil in smaller arrows in the spaces between the ruins; he gets annoyed, rubs them out, tries again.

'Fuck it,' he says, flinging down the pencil.

Cut.

The house, brooding in its shadowy decay, the fog like something rubbing everything from sight.

'Fuck – what was that?'

Blur of the camera being turned rapidly left and right and left. When it slows enough for us to see anything, we see nothing.

Brooke is breathing rapidly, shallowly, raggedly.

Cut.

Blackness. Ragged breath like an echo.

'It was like, I can't… I *felt* it, not some spectral chill but something *physical*, like a hand gripping my shoulder, wiry and knotty with muscle, slicked with sweat. And it *pulled*, but it wasn't like a hand, not fully, I couldn't make sense of it, couldn't *picture* it, even as I knew it was thick and muscled and naked I couldn't make sense of it…

'Shit.

'I pulled away, cried out. Turned to see, half-expecting Gary engaged in some petty revenge. But there was nothing to see; no one there obviously, no footprints in the earth, no fleeing shadow or… But I got the sense something utterly real and solid was just a few feet away from me. Like being in dark room, like being blinded, and… and walking forward and just *knowing* there's a wall in front of you before you walk into it. Senses I couldn't even name shrieking something was there, despite nothing being obviously so. And then, thank god, it moved away. Not faded like a ghost but physically moved away. For whatever reason, it left.

'I wish to god I'd done the same. But instead, I went to check if I could see anything when it was played back.'

Cut.

A blur as the handheld camera is put down, its autofocus struggling to decipher what it sees for an almost comical (or unrealistic) length of time: Brooke rewinding the footage on the trailer monitors. Even seeing little more than his hand (and if the camera was placed down so hastily, why does the resulting image seem composed to exclude anything distinguishable about Brooke, but gives a clear view of the screen he is watching?) we can sense a frantic edge to his actions. When he stops rewinding, and we see a grainy figure silhouetted against equally ill-defined fog, see it flinch and silently call out, it is impossible to see if it is Brooke or not. But what *is* clear, when the figure looks behind, is that there is nothing there.

Brooke starts to swear, but something quavering and new in his voice cuts off the profanity.

The same footage with heat vision on; the same nothing.

The same piece of A3 paper, now with red Xs marked, each with a date and time beneath plus two letters: either 'GO' or 'JB'.

'Next time,' Brooke says quietly.

Cut.

One and a half seconds of a camera panning too quickly, walls shadowy, blurred, and insubstantial in our sight as Brooke turns the camera one-eighty, cries out, is cut short by—

Cut.

Another red X, drawn bigger as if to mask an unsteady hand.

Cut.

Hectic breath in a dark space we can't picture.

Cut.

'Got you now!' Brooke's voice cries out triumphant, the camera turning again in fog so thick it is like something reaching to wipe us out like the rest of the erased world. When the motion stops, all we can see is the fog swirling and shifting in front of us.

'Thought even if it was invisible it would have to make a shape, a *gap*, in fog that thick,' the hoarse, exhausted voice says, dubbed over the top we assume (a trick the Brooke of old would never have stooped to).

The shot lingers on the obscuring fog, switching to slow-mo (another trick) and making its shifting movements more obvious. Of *course* we see shapes, of *course* we can conjure up phantoms. Pareidolia. This short sequence has been subject to endless debate, conjecture and dismissal online. People have produced their own clips, with graphics added to show what they have seen in the grey and unfurling ambiguity of the shot: a young boy with his head in his hands; a woman continually turning to keep her face from being seen; a blue light; a Grey-type alien; Bigfoot; Rick Astley singing *NGTGYU*. And of *course* the debunking that inevitably follows makes no difference, not even the debunking inherent in Brooke's reaction at the time, when he viewed the footage back:

'Fuck. Fuck. But it *was* there, I felt it.' A hollow half-laugh. 'Its touch was so awful, so where the fu—'
Cut.

Blackness, a voice alone.
'Its touch was awful, maybe worse each time; grasping, clutching, *needy*. Something that didn't want to let go. And greasy and clammy and strong, so strong and…
'When I was at school, the cat got fleas,' the voice continues, and we're unsure if there's been another cut or not. 'Back then, when everything was strange. They got into the carpets. Once you knew that, even after they were dead, you felt itchy. Felt them on you, even when they weren't there. This was like that. Once you'd got it into your head, once you became sensitive to every twinge of your own skin, you felt its touch all the—'
Cut.

The piece of paper is filled up with red Xs, overlapping and hinting at a shape beneath, like an uncompleted dot-to-dot puzzle. The lines representing Borsam House are almost completely obscured. A voice cries out in frustration and fear; cut to the same piece of paper with violent red scrawls all over it, someone trying to obliterate both what was there and their attempt to find structure in it.
'I need to *see* it!'
Cut.

Blackness, ragg—
Cut.

Bare floorboards with weeds growing up through them, scattered half-bricks, tendrils of f—
Cut.

Blac—
Cut.

The mocking of jackdaws, a shot straight up into an empty grey sky. Then a mechanical coughing sound, and the camera is picked up, pointed towards the incongruous sight of some machine connected to a generator, pumping artificial smoke across the shot, hiding the shapes of the house. Soon, all is obscure.

Cut.

A heat-vision shot, wide angle, of a person all smudged yellows and greens and a core of red, jerking as if struck, flailing at their body and the cold *empty* blackness surrounding them.

'I *need* to—'

Cut.

A swirling wall of mist? Fog? Dry ice? Presumably meant to show the same event: a shadow jumps and frets inside, alone.

'—*see.*'

Cut.

Darkness. 'Gary. Mate. That's why I did this video; that's why I did *all* these videos. Because of what happened back then. At… that school. You know; you were there too. You *saw*… So I had to; I just *had* to. You know why.'

Cut.

Some kind of white powder spread over the floorboards. The shot turns left and right, showing us two red tags either side, then points downwards. Brooke places his booted foot deliberately into the white powder, and we see the resulting footprint when he steps back.

Cut.

The same powder, but this time its whiteness is disturbed by dozens of the same footprints, most of which are in straight lines marching up and down. But as we follow their path, we see them become askew, the powder scuffed with a panic we never saw. Whoever is holding the camera is breathing heavily, cursing indistinctly. There are no footprints other than Brooke's imprinted in the powder.

The footage of Brooke's attempts to capture an image of the thing he believes haunts him become more confused at this point, lacking coherence or logical order. We see shots of different cameras being attached to tripods; some kind of almost invisible tripwire being stretched across an empty doorframe; footage of some complex image-manipulation software running on a laptop in the trailer; a grainy image of what seems to be a bucket of warm tar or black paint. (Internet wags often insert a clip here of an old cartoon showing a sheeted ghost running through a doorway, covering itself in blue paint from a boobytrapped can above.) We see footage of sodium lights being erected to light up the exterior of the house, then footage of smoke spiralling from a large bonfire. (What was Brooke burning?) A tethered dog, barking and snarling at the corner of an empty, ceiling-less room—

Cut.

Blackness.

'I'm not going to say how I did it. God help you if you work it out.'

Cut.

Camera falling, dropped by whoever was holding it, landing miraculously on something soft enough that it doesn't break, keeps recording. A bright, empty sky occupies two-thirds of the shot: through a hole in the house's roof we can see clear into space.

A voice, off-camera, crying out as if in revelation:

'I, I *saw* it…!'

A pause, during which jackdaws cry and what might be the sea washes invisible around us. The voice, when it returns, is quiet, subdued.

'I can't see. I can't *see*.'

Cut.

Blackness, heavy breathing, a sigh rasping with suppressed pain or emotion.

'The doctors couldn't do anything, couldn't work out what was wrong. Insisted I *could* see; they still do, in this place.' Again, we hear the dulled sound of a heavy door closing in an echoing corridor we can only imagine. 'But I *can't*. Nor do I want to, really. For if I could see again I might see *it* again—'

How can we tell if there's a cut or not in the darkness which is all we see? How are we meant to know?

'It looked as awful as it felt, truly as awful, as awesome as—'
Cut?

'I think it followed me. The doctors say it's all in my mind but—'
It should, of course, be perfectly impossible for completely black footage to appear to jolt, to flinch – and if it did, it could only be digital trickery, especially coming so neatly after Brooke's words. Nonetheless, many people swear this is exactly what they see in this perfect blackness (and frame-by-frame analysis shows it *is* perfectly black). And oddly, even those hot-take merchants who mock Brooke and the 'Borsam House Tape' seem reluctant to challenge or parody this sequence, or even to mention it.

I too have had fleas in my house, much like Brooke, and when I think back on it, when I heard him talk about it, I felt my skin itch and crawl (maybe you did too). In the same way, some people who watch the 'Borsam House Tape' to its conclusion, to this 'flinch-sequence' that is demonstrably nothing of the sort, swear *they* feel something: a clammy and hot and perspiring touch that would be unbearable if it lasted more than a moment. They shiver and jerk and pat themselves—
Cut.

'— *followed* me and oh—'
Cut.

The house, for a split second seeming whole and entire like the building was there all along in the mist and it was just we that we couldn't se—
Cut.

Blackness.
Brooke screams.
By God, how he *screams*.
Cut.

We see the *This Is What I Saw* logo, and a copyright date two years ago.
Cut.

James Everington *mainly writes dark, supernatural fiction, although he occasionally takes a break and writes dark, non-supernatural fiction. His second collection of such tales,* Falling Over, *is out now from Infinity Plus. He's also the author of* The Quarantined City, *an episodic novel mixing Borgesian strangeness with supernatural horror – 'an unsettling voice all of its own' said* The Guardian *– the novellas* Paupers' Graves *and* The Shelter, *and the mini-collection* Trying To Be So Quiet & Other Hauntings. *Alongside Dan Howarth, he has co-edited the anthologies* The Hyde Hotel, Pareidolia *(both Black Shuck Books) and the BFS Award-nominated* Imposter Syndrome *(Dark Minds Press). Oh, and he drinks Guinness, if anyone's asking. You can find out what James is currently up to at his Scattershot Writing site.*

Acknowledgements

So many people have helped with this reconstruction of the Wellbrook yearbook that it's impossible to list them all here.

Thank you, of course, to all the writers who have lent their talents to the preceding pages, picking over the remaining fragments of text to recreate what happened to the survivors of that fateful day in 1993.

As editor, I tried to contact headmaster John Maitland on several occasions to ask for his input and opinions, but he refused to be a part of this project. Eventually he threatened me with legal action and I was forced to leave him to his retirement, and the care home, in peace.

Wellbrook's languages teacher, Mrs Reisland, conceded to a brief interview, and was able to clarify a few points in the preceding stories. We were saddened to hear of her death shortly before this book went to print. I think it's fair to say that the last half of her life was haunted by the tragic events of that day – hopefully she is now at rest.

As for the remaining survivors from the class of '93, none of them responded to my requests and I can only assume they're trying to put the events at Wellbrook behind them. I doubt any of them sleep well at night.

Finally, thank you, as always, to Steve J Shaw – for his faithful recreation of the original yearbook, and his creative approach to filling in the gaps. Thanks to his efforts, Wellbrook High lives again.

__Dan Coxon__ is an award-winning editor and writer based in London. His non-fiction anthology Writing the Uncanny *(co-edited with Richard V. Hirst) won the British Fantasy Award for Best Non-Fiction 2022, while his short story collection* Only the Broken Remain *(Black Shuck Books) was shortlisted for two British Fantasy Awards in 2021 (Best Collection, Best Newcomer). In 2018 his anthology of British folk-horror,* This Dreaming Isle *(Unsung Stories), was shortlisted for a British Fantasy Award and a Shirley Jackson Award. His short stories have appeared in various anthologies, including* Shakespeare Unleashed, Unspeakable Horror 3: Dark Rainbow Rising, Beyond the Veil, Mother: Tales of Love and Terror *and* Great British Horror 7: Major Arcana. *His latest anthology –* Isolation *– was published by Titan Books in September 2022. You can find more of his writing at www.dancoxon.com, or on Twitter at @DanCoxonAuthor.*